THE INN AT OCEAN'S EDGE

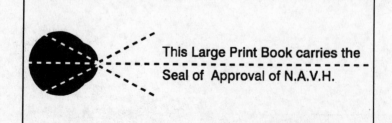

A SUNSET COVE NOVEL

THE INN AT
OCEAN'S EDGE

COLLEEN COBLE

THORNDIKE PRESS
A part of Gale, Cengage Learning

 GALE
CENGAGE Learning·

Farmington Hills, Mich • San Francisco • New York • Waterville, Maine
Meriden, Conn • Mason, Ohio • Chicago

GALE
CENGAGE Learning·

Copyright © 2015 by Colleen Coble.
Scripture from THE HOLY BIBLE, NEW INTERNATIONAL VERSION®, NIV®
Copyright © 1973, 1978, 1984, 2011 by Biblica, Inc.® Used by
permission. All rights reserved worldwide. Scripture also quoted from
The Voice. © 2008 and 2009 Ecclesia Bible Society. Used by permission.
All rights reserved.

Thorndike Press, a part of Gale, Cengage Learning.

Thorndike Press® Large Print Christian Fiction.
The text of this Large Print edition is unabridged.
Other aspects of the book may vary from the original edition.
Set in 16 pt. Plantin.

LIBRARY OF CONGRESS CATALOGING-IN-PUBLICATION DATA

Coble, Colleen.
    The Inn at Ocean's Edge / Colleen Coble.
        pages cm. — (A Sunset Cove novel ; 1) — (Thorndike press large print
    Christian fiction)
        ISBN 978-1-4104-7473-5 (hardback) — ISBN 1-4104-7473-9 (hardcover)
        1. Family secrets—Fiction. 2. Murder—Investigation—Fiction. I. Title.
    PS3553.O2285I56 2015b
    813'.54—dc23   2015004145

Published in 2015 by arrangement with Thomas Nelson, Inc., a division
of HarperCollins Publishing, Inc.

Printed in the United States of America
1 2 3 4 5 6 7 19 18 17 16 15

PROLOGUE

July 4, 1989

The sea was near. Though she couldn't see it, she smelled the salt air and heard its roar as it hit the rocks close by. The branches around her held scary shadows. The forest was thick here, and she put her hand on the rough bark of a tree that smelled like Christmas. Mommy had told her to stay far away from the rocks.

But which way are they?

It was too dark to tell. She was afraid to move for fear she'd tumble off a cliff. All she'd wanted to do was go fishing.

She strained to hear her mother's voice, but only noises like screeches and rustling little things in the grass came to her ears. Tears hovered in her eyes and closed her throat. She swiped the back of her hand across her face. Daddy always said crying wouldn't fix anything. It would just make her head hurt.

Mommy would be so upset when she saw her torn dress. Daddy had bought it for her, and he would be angry when he saw her mud-splattered tights and patent leather shoes. Somewhere she'd lost the bow in her hair, and stringy locks hung in her eyes. There was something on the ground, and she stopped and picked it up. A lady's scarf that smelled of flowers. She bunched it in her hand and stepped over an umbrella in her path.

She stopped and cocked her head. Voices? Even though the angry words were just a mumble, she shivered at how mad he sounded. Then she heard a woman's voice, and she moved toward it. The woman would help her. It might even be Mommy.

Tree needles slapped her in the face and made her want to cry even more. But she was a big girl now. Daddy said only babies cried. She pressed her lips together and planted a muddy shoe atop a small shrub to move closer to the voices.

As she peered through the leaves, she saw two figures struggling in the forest. She couldn't see their faces, but the smaller figure fell to the ground, and the man leaped on top of her with his hands at her throat.

"Stop hurting her!" Her eyes widened as

soon as the cry left her mouth.

The man turned, and she saw a red pelt tied to his belt. The pointy nose hung at his knees, and she felt dizzy when she saw the red fur. She whirled around and ran as fast as she could, but the steps behind her grew closer. Her climbing tree was just ahead. She grabbed for the limb, and her hand went into the hiding place. She wished it was big enough for her to crawl into herself. She left the scarf in the hole, then reached up for the lowest branch. Her fingers missed and she staggered forward.

Then a hand smacked the middle of her back, and she went tumbling into the pine needles.

ONE

Like the masthead of a great ship, the stone walls and mullioned windows of Hotel Tourmaline surveyed its island location of wind-tossed waves and rocks. Off the shore and to the southeast of the Schoodic Peninsula, the hotel dominated the island of Folly Shoals atop its pink-granite cliffs.

It had not been easy getting to this remote location. It had taken Claire five and a half hours plus an hour ferry ride from Summer Harbor to reach this rocky shore. She lifted her foot from the accelerator and let her car slow as she took in the imposing hotel, then pulled into the big circle driveway.

A valet, dressed in black slacks and a white shirt, stepped forward to open Claire's car door after she parked her convertible in front of the grand entrance decked out in gleaming brass and glass. She'd kept the top up since the mid-May wind was cool with the temperatures hovering around fifty-five.

Smiling her thanks at the young man, Claire emerged from her white Mercedes and looked up at the five-story structure. Though she'd never been here before, an uneasy shiver went down her spine. She couldn't take her gaze from the parapets with their insets of watermelon tourmaline in the stone around the entry door.

It was like the sea king's castle in *The Little Mermaid,* only on land instead of at the sea bottom. Which was a weird thought to hit her out of the blue. She hadn't seen that old Disney movie since she was a kid.

She recovered her composure and handed the car keys to the valet. "Claire Dellamare, checking in." Reaching over the door of the Mercedes, she grabbed her oiled leather satchel.

"Of course, Ms. Dellamare. Do you have bags?"

The man's voice faded into the distance. Pressure built in her chest as she continued to stare at the hotel. A flagstone walk wound through manicured lawns and disappeared into the shadow of thick forest. She suppressed a shiver at the gloom there. Through the big glass windows, she saw her father standing at the front desk. Seeing him grounded her, and she exhaled.

He would probably not be happy at her unexpected arrival, but she intended to make sure the merger landed them a bigger piece of the aviation pie.

Squaring her shoulders, she forced herself to smile again at the young man awaiting instructions. "There are three bags in the trunk." Without waiting for a response, she hurried past the doorman holding open the entry.

The pink-granite tile floor was unlike anything she'd ever seen. Black veins ran through various shades of pink granite and gave the floor both depth and light. She homed in on her father standing with his back to her and headed his direction, her heels clacking against the stone tiles as she approached the front desk.

The wood surfaces gleamed with polish, and a gilt ceiling arched over the entry area. She'd been in fine hotels all her life, but this one had something special. Just beyond the registration desk, several overstuffed sofas gathered near the floor-to-ceiling windows that looked out onto the forest behind the hotel. She stopped and peered out the window at the trees arching into the sky.

At the sight of the thick pines, Claire

thought she might vomit right there on the granite floor. Her breath hitched in her chest, and she tried to ignore the rising panic.

She managed to whisper, "Dad," before her throat totally closed.

It's just the woods. Breathe, breathe.

Her father turned at the sound of her voice. A scowl gathered between his eyes. "Claire, what are you doing here?" His voice bounced off the granite floors.

Her mother had always said he had the voice to charm hummingbirds to his hand, and at the sound of his deep voice, a bit of calmness descended. She forced a smile and brushed her lips across his smooth-shaven cheek, inhaling the scent of his cologne, Giorgio Armani. Her fingers sank into the arm of his expensive suit, and she leaned her face against his chest.

He held her a minute, then released her. "Are you ill, Claire?" He looked at the woman standing to one side of the desk. "Please get my key at once."

"Yes, Mr. Dellamare. I have them ready. Yours and your daughter's." The clerk, an attractive blonde in her thirties, handed over two key card sleeves. "You're in a penthouse suite, next to the one by your parents." She smiled at Claire. "I'm Jenny Bennett, Ms.

Dellamare. If there's anything you need, please contact me personally. I'm about to get off work, but my cell number is on my card." She pressed a business card into Claire's hand.

Claire managed a brief nod. "You've been very helpful, Jenny." The woman had quickly arranged a suite this morning when Claire had made the decision to come here.

"You're staying?" Her father's gaze went to the satchel in her hand.

"I came to help you with the merger." The door behind them swooshed open, bringing the scent of pine to her nose. Her chest tightened again.

"I'm perfectly competent to handle it." Her father took Claire's arm and turned her toward the brass doors of the elevator.

As he led her away from the entryway, her lungs compressed and there was no air. She had to get oxygen. She jerked away from him and yanked her blouse away from her neck. Her purse dropped to the floor, scattering pens, art pencils, lipstick, and a compact across the floor. Her face and neck felt on fire as she bent to pick up her things and stuff them back in her purse.

When she stood, the panic swept over her again. "Can't breathe!"

"Claire, lower your voice." Her father

glanced around at the interested guests staring their way.

Her hands and arms tingled, and she couldn't feel her feet. Her father reached toward her, and she batted his hand away. "Don't touch me!" Her scream bounced off the ceiling.

A gray-haired gentleman in a navy suit approached. "Might I offer assistance, miss?"

She backed away, then whirled and rushed toward the entrance. Her feet seemed to be moving in slow motion, and her vision narrowed to a pinpoint centered on the door. Escape. She had to get out of here. Dimly aware of voices calling after her, the door grew closer and closer until she pushed it open and drew in a lungful of salt-laden air.

She leaned her face against the cool stone and prayed for the panic to go away. What was going on? Her left arm hurt.

Her father exited the hotel and hurried to her side. When he started to touch her, Claire flinched. "Don't."

"What is wrong with you? It's not like you to make a scene, to be out of control. This is something your mother would do, not you."

She flinched at the condemnation in his voice. She was *not* like her mother. She

16

inhaled and tried to force her hands not to shake. "My chest is tight and my left arm feels on fire. I'm having trouble breathing. My face is hot. Maybe it's a heart attack."

"You're twenty-nine years old, Claire. It's unlikely it's a heart attack. I think you're having a panic attack. Maybe because this merger is so important. Go for a walk along the beach, and come back inside when you've gotten control of yourself. People will think you're having a nervous breakdown or something."

Though he didn't say it, she heard the implied comparison to her mother again. *Control, I need control.* "You're right. I'll be fine. It was a long drive up from Boston. I just need a walk." The tightness in her chest eased a bit. "Is Ric here yet?"

"Not yet. He's due to arrive tomorrow." His eyes narrowed as he looked her over. "He does like you. Maybe it's a good thing you've shown up."

Her breathing grew easier. "I'm sure of it, Dad. I'll be back in half an hour."

The doorman pulled open the door, and her father disappeared into the bowels of the hotel. The salt-laden air cleared the panic, and she turned to walk down the cliff steps to the waiting sand. The sea would calm her.

17

■ ■ ■ ■

Seagulls squawked overhead in a blue sky dotted with puffs of clouds. The wind tugged Luke Rocco's hair and threatened to rip the ball cap from his head as he guided his boat toward Sunset Cove on the south side of the island. He never tired of this view. Though Folly Shoals was just one of about three thousand islands off the coast of Maine, it was a place apart from any other. The grandeur of the sea cliffs, soaring to just under a hundred feet in all their pink-granite glory, always made him feel small and insignificant. Magnificent pines and slender aspen vied for purchase in the rich soil, and wildflowers bloomed in the thin soil.

The engine belched oil and gas fumes that mingled with the scent of the sea, and his boat rose and fell on the waves. His breath plumed out in the chilly air as the sun began its descent over the peninsula. He should have worn jeans instead of shorts today, but the jacket helped. He squinted at his sister. Dressed in white shorts covered with a red sweatshirt, Megan huddled under the Bimini top, which did little to protect her from the cold wind.

He grinned at her. "Smile. At least we got enough fish for supper."

"It's not that." Her thoughtful gaze met his. "I have something to tell you, and I don't know how."

"You're getting married."

She rolled her eyes. "Get real. You've been home three days and haven't seen a boyfriend hanging around, have you?"

Her tone wiped the grin from his face. "You look scared, Meg. You can tell me anything. I won't bite your head off. Does the farm need money? We're about to go broke?" Part of him almost wanted it to happen. Maybe it would wake up the drunken old man back at the house. He'd never been the same since Mom disappeared.

She shook her head. "I think we're turning a profit this year. The cranberry yield looks to be stellar."

"Then what is it?"

The wind tore a strand of hair loose from her ponytail and whipped it into her face. She pushed it out of her eyes. "I got another job offer. It's in Oregon." She rushed on as if she had to spill it all before he interrupted her. "There's a new research facility that's just opened. They're studying viruses and mutations."

His gut tightened, but he managed to smile and nod. "You loved that in college."

Her dark eyes studied him as if to gauge his reaction. "And I'd finally be using that expensive Vassar education."

"It wasn't expensive. You went on scholarship."

She shrugged as she huddled in her red sweatshirt. "You know what I mean. The diploma is worth a lot, and I haven't used it."

"You've used your study of cranberry farming to help the cranberry bogs. That's why we're turning a profit this year." *Shut up, Luke.* She wasn't fishing for a compliment. She wanted to leave Folly Shoals. And how could he blame her for doing what he'd done three years ago? He'd gone to school in Ellsworth and helped with the cranberries, but when she'd come home from Vassar, he'd been only too ready to let her shoulder the full burden while he joined the Coast Guard.

She fell silent a moment, and he took the opportunity to analyze the objections rising to his lips. Pop's recent stroke would prevent him from helping out much. If Megan left, someone would have to pick up the slack. That someone could only be Luke. The thought of dealing with his father soured his mood. Meg had done it, though. It wasn't fair to expect her to do it forever.

"I see the wheels turning," Megan said. "I know what this means if I leave. I should turn it down."

Her woebegone face made him sit up straighter. "You've buried yourself on this island all your life, Meg. It's your turn to fly. I'm not going to stand in your way. Maybe I can plead hardship to the Coast Guard and get a transfer up here. There's a facility out on Southwest Harbor."

Her brown eyes widened. "But could you do both the bogs and your job? At harvest, it's downright crazy."

"I can try, and maybe we can afford to hire some extra help." He put more confidence into his voice than he felt, but he couldn't let her sacrifice what she really wanted. "If I'd known you weren't happy here, I would have pushed you out of the nest sooner. I thought you loved the bogs and wanted to stay here."

She looked down at her hands, the knuckles reddened from the cold. "I used to. But Pop's gotten even more . . . difficult."

Something in her tone brought him up short. "He hasn't hit you again, has he? I thought he stopped that after I threatened him when I was eighteen."

21

He'd gotten in their father's face and threatened to call the sheriff if he ever lifted a hand to Meg again. Their dad had taken one look at Luke's face and stepped back. As far as Luke knew, he hadn't dared to raise his hand to her since then.

"It's just been since his stroke. He doesn't mean anything by it. The stroke has left him with a short fuse. He's always sorry after. And he's never even left a bruise."

Luke's fingers curled into his palms. If his dad were here, he wasn't sure he could hold himself back. "I'll talk with him."

Pop had always been difficult, especially when he drank too much. Luke had many memories of nights when he and Megan hid in the closet while Pop raged around the house looking for them.

"There's no need." Meg's eyes held an appeal for understanding. "That's not the real reason I want to go. I can handle a grumpy old man. It's just I'm stagnating here. I'm twenty-eight, and I've never been anywhere except to college. If I stay here any longer, I'll never leave."

He nodded and steered the boat toward the slip. "When would you start?"

"In a month. You'll really help me do this?"

"I want you to be happy. I'll figure it out.

That's what big brothers are for."

Her hand swept over the rocky coastline in the direction of their house. "You don't even like cranberries. You were made for the Coast Guard. You thrive on the challenge. And I know perfectly well what's going to happen. You won't reenlist, will you? Even though it's what you've wanted to do your whole life."

"Don't worry about it. I'll do whatever has to be done. I can't let the business just dissolve. It's been in our family for seventy-five years."

She rose on long, tanned legs and leaned against the side of the boat. "And what if he dies? He's been so weak since the stroke. What if you give up your entire life for something that only matters to him?"

His pulse stuttered. "Are you saying you want us to sell the bogs?"

She raked her hand through her short hair, as thick, straight, and black as his. "I want both of us to think long and hard about what's best. Maybe it's time we quit catering to Pop and do what we really want to do."

How had he missed her discontent? And the thought of selling the family cranberry farm didn't settle well with him.

"Let me see what I can do about a transfer, then we'll talk. But no matter what, let them know you're taking the job."

She thrust her hands in the pockets of her sweatshirt. "So now you want to get rid of me and I'm useless, is that it?"

Her voice held no rancor so he just grinned. "Something like that. Your son may love working the land. Or my daughter." Not that he was likely to get married. But the thought of working the bogs unsettled him. He still believed their mom was buried somewhere out there.

Megan reached for the thermos of coffee. "You're thinking about Mom's disappearance, aren't you? Her body's not out there, and believe me, I've looked."

She always could read him. "She has to be somewhere, Meg."

"She's been gone twenty-five years! We'll never find her remains, not up here. It's too remote. Whatever happened to her will remain a mystery."

"Yeah, you're right. But I sure wish we knew what happened." He took a swig of hot coffee. "Ready to head in?"

She nodded.

"Take the helm a minute. I'll get the ropes ready."

She moved to take his place, and he went toward the starboard side. Something floated in the water about eight feet away, and he squinted, trying to make out the markings. "That's a baby orca. Cut the engine."

When Megan complied, he grabbed a paddle and maneuvered closer to the killer whale. The calf lolled listlessly in the water, turning an eye toward him as if asking for help. "It's sick. Skinny too." He scanned the water. "But where's its mother?"

They both studied the horizon and saw nothing. No pod, no mother.

"What if its mother died?" Megan joined him. "We have to help it. We can't just leave it out here to suffer."

"We could put up a sea pen until we can contact an orca rescue organization. I've got some extra netting in the hold."

"But how will you get it to shore? Netting it might kill it."

He shucked off his jacket and shoes. "I'll tow it in."

She grabbed his arm. "Are you kidding? We're five hundred yards from shore, and the water is freezing!"

"I've got this. Just take the boat to our dock. There's already a partial pen along the north and east sides. We'll just have to close the pen on the south."

Megan nodded and went back to the

25

helm. "You sure you'll be okay?"

"Yeah, I'm good." He stepped to the back of the boat and leaped overboard. The cold water took his breath away, and he gasped when his head broke the surface. He waved to show his sister he was fine, then struck off toward the distressed calf. The marine mammal rolled when he touched it, but it was still alive. The skin felt like a warm inner tube, and he caressed it reassuringly. "You're going to be okay, buddy." He hoped it was the truth. This animal was in serious need of attention.

He grasped the orca's dorsal fin and began to tow it toward the sea pen. The calf fluttered its fluke and tried to help, but it was so weak, their progress was slow. His muscles burned, and the cold water quickly fatigued him. By the time he reached the dock, his chest was tight, and he was eager to get out of the water.

Megan had already attached one end of the net and was swimming to meet him. He'd never been so glad to see anyone.

TWO

Pink-granite stones led down a hundred-foot cliff to rocks below, and Claire took them. When she reached the sea, the brisk, fresh air cleared her head. The gulls squawking overhead soothed her. The tightness in her chest was nearly gone, and she felt almost normal. She grimaced as she tossed a pebble into the gentle waves rolling to shore.

It had been a momentary weakness there in the lobby, nothing like her mother's constant histrionics. Claire had just been working too hard, and thoughts of this merger's importance had kept her tossing and turning until after midnight last night. It was nothing.

She leaned down and slipped off her heels, then sank her toes into the sand mixed with small stones. With her shoes dangling from one hand, she wandered down the long strip of rocky coastline. A feeling of contentment surrounded her, like she'd somehow found a piece of herself here. All her life the sea had seemed to fulfill some missing part of her, some innate need she couldn't name.

A shout caught her attention, and she squinted in the strong afternoon sunlight toward a small inlet. A man and a woman seemed to be securing fishing line or rope on a metal ring attached to a small pier where a fishing boat was docked. They were both wet.

Did they need help? Claire started toward them, but she saw a form in the water and stopped. She first thought it was a dolphin, then she recognized the distinctive black-and-white markings.

She pressed her lips together and rushed to intercept them before they could board the boat again, her bare feet slapping the cool, damp wooden pier. "You there! What do you think you're doing with this orca? You can't keep it penned up."

When the man turned to stare at her, her first impression was of impossibly dark eyes that seemed to look right into her soul. He would have been right at home on the cover of a pirate romance. He looked Italian with his thick dark hair and eyes and was probably close to thirty. His white shorts contrasted with his tanned, muscular legs. Water pooled at his bare feet.

His gaze swept over her, and she flushed when she realized how she must look in her slim-fitting blue sheath dress and bare feet. The wind had seriously destroyed her controlled updo.

She pushed an errant lock out of her eyes and scowled at him. "Orcas should never be penned up. This one probably has a matriline and a bigger pod out there missing it."

He raised a black brow. "Not many people have ever even heard the word *matriline*. You some kind of orca activist, or do you just like to show off your education?"

"I volunteer with an orca rescue organization." She tipped her chin up at his derisive tone. "Locking up these beautiful creatures is like imprisoning a baby. I suppose you thought to make a lot of money by selling it to an aquarium."

He tugged on the zipper of his blue sweatshirt. "You don't know me, lady. And this is none of your business."

The woman with him stepped between them. She had the man's dark good looks, but she wore a placating smile. "Hi, I'm Megan Rocco. And my brother, Luke, is not usually this hotheaded. We're not harming the orca. He's injured, and I'm not even

29

sure we can save him. I think his mother must have died. He's starving. We're putting him here for his own good until we can contact an orca rescue organization."

Claire went hot at her assumptions. What had gotten into her today? First experiencing a panic attack and then jumping to unwarranted conclusions. She gulped, then glanced past Megan to Luke as she tried to gather enough courage to apologize. She eyed him and his sister. His sweatshirt had a Coast Guard emblem. His sister's bore a dive shop logo.

Claire looked down at her bare feet and bit her lip before staring back into those dark, dark eyes. "I think I owe you both an apology."

"You think?" He lifted a brow, then turned toward the boat.

A small wave slapped the edge of the pier and dampened her feet. She edged closer to the center. "I'm sorry. Truly. I have a bit of a thing for dolphins and whales, always have. You'd be surprised how many people think there's nothing wrong with captive orcas. They're one of the few mammals who have an actual family unit like ours."

He didn't look at her. "You're preaching to the choir, lady."

"Can I make it up to you and help you

with him? You won't have to call anyone else. I know what to do."

He finally looked her way and seemed to take her measure before he finally nodded. "I'm just going to fatten him up and then let him loose. But you can help before you go back to your froufrou coffee and high-powered dinners."

Her face burned at his accurate assessment of her financial status. "Look, we got off to a bad start. I haven't even introduced myself." She held out her hand. "I'm Claire Dellamare."

His gaze sharpened. "Harry Dellamare's daughter?"

"You know my dad?"

He exchanged a glance with his sister. "I know *of* him. Never met him, though. I was a kid when he was here last. And when you were found."

She rubbed her forehead where it pulsed with pain. "Found? What do you mean?"

"You know, back in '90. After you'd been missing a year out there in the forest." He swept his hand up at the thick forest marching along the top of the cliff. Then a look passed between Luke and his sister before he returned his attention to Claire. "Did you ever remember where you were that year? Did you happen to see a woman the night you wandered off?"

"Luke, enough," Megan said.

The blood drained from Claire's head, and her legs went weak.

"Claire, are you all right?"

She barely heard Megan's anxious voice through the roaring in her ears. Something lingered on the edge of her memory, but she couldn't grasp it. Her vision darkened, and she took a step back. She teetered on the edge of the pier.

"Look out!" Luke's shadowy figure moved toward her.

She reached out for some kind of support but missed her footing. The rough wood cut the side of her foot as she went over the edge. The shock of the cold water cleared her head, and she shot to the surface sputtering. Something bumped into her side, and she saw the orca floating nearby as if to help her. She touched its pectoral flipper, then grabbed hold. There was a splash to her left, then Luke told her to be calm, that he was coming.

But the baby orca was squeaking and nudging her, helping her forget the visions of trees leering at her, of rocks bruising her feet. She ducked her head into the cold water and let it scoop the strands of hair away from her face even as she emptied her mind of the terrifying images.

Luke grasped her arm. "Need some help to shore?"

She shook her head. "I'm okay."

"I'd say. You're a dolphin yourself."

He grinned as she released the calf and struck off toward the pier with a butterfly stroke. She wasn't eager to get out of the water, but she had to talk to her father. No wonder he'd been upset when she arrived.

She'd been here before. Lost. And her parents had never told her.

Why hadn't her parents ever talked about it? 1990. She'd been five when she was found. If she'd been missing a year, that meant she was four when she got lost. And she had no memory of any of it. How was that possible?

Though Luke had draped her with a dry jacket smelling of the sea, Claire shivered in the cool breeze blowing off the water. A gull hopped closer, tipping its head to one side and surveying her with curiosity. The questions hammered in her head, and she knew how Alice felt when she fell into the rabbit hole. Everything was different now, and she didn't know how to process this sudden shift in reality.

Only Father could tell her.

She rose from her seat on the pier. "I have to get back to the hotel. Thanks for everything."

Megan wore a worried expression. "You sure you're okay to go back by yourself? You're still awfully pale."

"I'm fine." Claire needed to hear from her father what had happened in this place. The orca wiggled a fin in the water. "You mind if I come down and check on the orca tomorrow?"

"Come anytime you like." Luke glanced at his sister who gave a slight shake of her head.

Claire saw the questions in his eyes, but she wasn't ready to deal with his curiosity. "Did you see the way the orca wanted to help me?"

He nodded. "They're smart. I'm sure he sensed your distress." His well-shaped lips flattened, and he took a deep breath. "You seemed shocked by what I told you. You don't remember anything about being here when you were a kid?"

Megan's eyes flashed. "Luke, let her be."

"She's fine now. Do you? Remember anything, I mean?"

She thought about not answering at all, but his expression held intense need, not curiosity. "As far as I knew, this was my first

34

visit here. I-I even flipped out a little in the hotel because it felt eerily familiar." She swallowed down a choking lump. "Believe me, I intend to ask a lot of questions."

The glint in his eyes went out. "So you don't remember a woman the night you went missing?"

Megan put her hand on his arm. "Enough, Luke."

He shoved his hands in his pockets. "Just asking."

"It's okay. No, I don't remember a woman. I don't remember anything. Well, other than dark trees. I kind of remember that." She handed him back his jacket. "I'd better go now. Thanks for your help. I'll stop back tomorrow." She gave a slight wave and set off along the beach toward the hotel.

The sun was low in the sky to the west, and the fading light sent shadows looming along the path. If she didn't pick up her speed, she wouldn't make it back to the hotel before dark. But the knowledge didn't cause her to quicken her pace.

What was she even going to say to her father — how did she start that conversation? She'd been lied to her entire life. Keeping something like this from her felt like a betrayal of the worst kind. Her purse felt heavy on her arm, and she wished she hadn't brought it. She'd been gone two hours, and her father was probably worried.

She reached a point where Sunset Cove began to curve back toward the hotel. A crab skittered across the sand by her feet, then darted into a hole when it saw her. Wrinkling her nose at the stench and flies, she waded through a pile of crunchy kelp deposited by the tide and dried by the sun. A gull cried above her, and she looked up the rock face ten feet to her right.

Two figures struggled at the edge of the cliff, ninety feet in the air. The woman wore a pencil skirt and sleeveless blouse that nearly matched the darkening sky. Her silhouette obstructed Claire's view of who struggled with her. Shading her eyes with her hand, Claire watched the woman's slim figure as she tried to prevent the man from pushing her closer to the edge.

"Hey, you! Leave her alone!" Claire looked around for some way to ascend the cliff, but the sheer expanse of jagged pink granite looming above her offered no way to climb it without gear.

She peered up again, this time seeing the form of a man behind the woman. He wore a jacket over tan hunting pants. She got an impression of dark hair and a straight nose, but she was too far to make out his features.

Neither of them seemed to notice her, and she gasped when he shoved the woman even closer to the edge.

"I'm calling the police!" She clawed her cell phone out of her purse and dialed 911. Before the dispatcher picked up, a shriek mingled with the wail of the loons, and Claire whirled to see the young woman plummeting to the ground. She hit the sand with a solid thump, then didn't move.

"No, no!" Claire ran toward the woman who was spread-eagled facedown. She knelt beside her and touched her wrist. No pulse. What should she do? She knew CPR. Get help on the way first, though. She put the phone back to her ear. "Are you there?"

"You need assistance, ma'am?" The dispatcher had a gravelly male voice.

"There's been a murder. Some man just threw a woman over the cliff. I saw the whole thing." She choked out the words.

The woman had landed on her stomach, but her head was turned to one side, and now that she was closer, Claire recognized her as the front desk clerk. "It's Jenny Bennett."

"I'll call the sheriff, and we'll get someone there right away. What's your location?"

"Down the steps from Hotel Tourmaline and about a quarter mile to the north along the beach."

"It's going to take awhile for the sheriff to get out there. Be patient."

Claire ended the call and rolled Jenny onto her back. She knelt and began CPR. It felt hopeless, but she had to try. The back of her neck prickled, but she didn't dare stop CPR to look around. *Lord, help me.*

She leaned forward to administer two breaths, but an explosion of movement from the shrubs in the maritime forest made her heart leap into her throat. Before she could turn to see what was coming at her, a hard blow struck the back of her head. As darkness claimed her, she saw the face of her attacker.

It was the hunter from her nightmares. Only this time there was no fox attached to his belt.

THREE

Leaving his boat docked at the fishing community of Summer Haven behind him, Luke climbed into his old truck and headed toward home on Cliff Road. He navigated the '75 Chevy truck along the muddy road past cranberry bogs on both sides of the unpaved track. Luke's dad had bought this old heap before Luke or his sister had been born, and it held the smell of decades of fish, lobster, and cranberries. The seasons in Maine were summer, fall, winter, spring, and mud. Once the ice and snow melted, any road not paved turned to thick mud that turned slick under bald tires. This time of year he had the four-wheel drive engaged just to navigate the sludge.

Luke couldn't keep his thoughts from straying to Claire Dellamare. Could she know something about his mom's disappearance, or was he assuming too much?

Megan cranked her window down, and

the clean air wafted in the vehicle. "I see the wheels turning in your head. Let it go, Luke."

"You have to admit it seems heaven sent that Claire has shown up right now. She might have the key piece of information we need."

"You saw her reaction. She didn't even know she'd ever been here."

"Maybe."

His sister heaved a sigh. "I recognize that noncommittal tone. You intend to talk to her. You sure it's not just because she's wicked cunning?"

The Maine term that meant *cute* was hardly the word for Claire. Drop-dead gorgeous was more like it. Light-brown hair tipped in honey framed a heart-shaped face and highlighted the biggest blue eyes he'd ever seen. And those dimples? Adorable. She didn't lack self-confidence either. When she'd been outraged about the orca, she confronted them without hesitation. He liked the fire in her.

He grinned. "I only want to find out what she might know about Mom's disappearance."

He rolled down his window. "Seriously, Meg, don't you find it intriguing? Pop has always thought there had to be some connection. He tried to talk to her parents years ago, and they shut him down and wouldn't let him speak to Claire."

"She was *four* when she disappeared. How much do you remember from when you were four?"

He waggled his brows at her. "I remember flushing your Polly Pocket down the toilet."

She punched him in the arm. "And you have never even said you're sorry!"

"Ouch." He rubbed his deltoid. "You had, like, a zillion of them."

"I had three. And that one was my favorite." She fixed a dark scowl on him. "But seriously. Most of us don't remember much from when we were four."

Now he had her. "Except traumatic things. So if you are still mad about a Polly Pocket, shouldn't she remember being lost in the woods for a solid *year*? And I'm not buying the amnesia thing. There has to be more to her forgetting she was ever here. I bet those memories will just take a little probing to come bubbling up."

He rested his arm on the window frame, enjoying the prickle of the wind and the warmth of the sun as he navigated the muddy potholes. He scanned the expansive cranberry fields. The green plants looked healthy and well tended. Meg had done a good job of pruning the vines. In a few months a crimson tide of cranberries would be bobbing on both sides of the road.

He frowned when the family house came into view. The gray car in the driveway wasn't familiar. "Someone's there."

Megan squinted through the windshield. "Looks like Pop's home health-care nurse."

A movement from the corner of his eye made Luke stomp on the brakes. One of their employees, Jimmy Bradley, came tearing from the fields. Though just out of high school, the boy was a good worker. He swiped at the blond hair flopping over his wide eyes, then doubled over, his chest heaving. He straightened, then gripped the top of the truck's door and sucked in air.

Luke got out of the truck in time to grab the kid and keep him from sliding to the ground. "What's wrong?"

His mind ran through the possible problems. Jimmy had been clearing some scrub in a field the farm had acquired a year ago. The next step would be to excavate for a new bog, then lay down sand before planting it. Luke had seen bear scat out there yesterday, and maybe the bruin had come back, though Jimmy didn't seem to be bleeding.

He lowered the boy to the road and

motioned to his sister. "Grab me the bottle of water behind my seat. Hurry!" If the kid got any grayer, his face would match the pavement.

She nodded and slid across the truck to reach behind his seat. "Is Pop okay?"

Luke's pulse kicked. He hadn't even thought of his dad, but knowing the old man, he just might have gone wandering through the fields in his wheelchair to check on them. Cranberries had been his life for sixty years. "Is it Pop?" He uncapped the water bottle and handed it to Jimmy. What if their dad was lying out there dead of another stroke?

Jimmy shook his head, and a hint of color came back into his face. "Not your dad." He took a long swig of water, then wiped his mouth with the back of his shaking hand. "You have to come, Luke. I burned off . . . some cut brush . . . I'd heaped in a ditch." He shuddered and sipped the water.

Megan slid out of the truck. "It spread and you burned down a building?"

"N-No." The boy's eyes were huge as he looked up at them. "I'm not sure, but I think I found a-a dead person." His Adam's apple bobbed. "Bones."

"What makes you think they're human?" Luke had come across plenty of animal

43

bones in his days, and Jimmy was a flat-
lander. He'd moved here from Illinois about
two years ago. He might still be a little
green. *But what if Jimmy has found Mom?*
He didn't dare to hope.

"Hair. There's hair too." The boy's face
was white, and he shook his head. "I don't
want to see it again. I can tell you where to
go."

Luke looked at Megan. "Call the sheriff,
and I'll go see what this is about." He
turned back to the boy. "What's the location?"

Jimmy pointed over the crest of the horizon. "The new field. There's a ditch that
runs through it. Right where it turns and
goes into the woods."

"I know the spot." Luke grabbed Jimmy's
arm and shoved him toward the truck.
"Show me the grave."

Pain. Claire blinked her eyes and tried to
make out where she was. Gritty sand itched
her back and legs. A cool ocean breeze
brushed her legs, and she blinked at the
dusky sky overhead. Her fingers grazed bare
flesh on her thigh, and she tugged her skirt
down.

"Ayuh, easy now." The man leaning over
her was in his fifties with kind hazel eyes in

a sea-weathered face as brown as the bark on a tree. He wore a tan shirt and black slacks. "You've got a lump on the back of your head the size of an albatross egg." He eased her into a sitting position.

Her head spun, and she blinked to clear her vision. The pain in her head throbbed in time with her heartbeat. Only a bit of light came from the western horizon, and that small patch would be gone soon. The surf thundered to her left, and the strong scent of salt and kelp made her stomach turn even more.

She needed to get back to the hotel. "What happened?"

"You tell me, missy. You called the dispatcher and reported a murder. When we got here, we found only you."

The woman. She squinted in the dim light and glanced around, but all she saw was another deputy standing in the shadows. "Could you help me up?" The pain in her head intensified as he got her onto her feet, and she stood swaying until the agony ebbed to a dull roar.

"Her body was right there." She pointed to a depression by a large rock. "I checked her pulse, and I think she was dead, but I tried CPR anyway."

"You're Claire Dellamare? You match the

description."

She nodded. "How did you know my name?"

"Your father called and asked us to look for you. Said you should have been back two hours ago. I'm Sheriff Colton and this is Deputy Waters. Your father said you rushed off all upset after a panic attack, and you'd been gone several hours. You sure you're not imagining it?"

She narrowed her eyes at him, then reached up, wincing as her fingers probed the large goose egg on her head. "Did I imagine this?" His impertinent question was all because of her panic earlier. She'd seen people question her mother all her life, but she was not at all like her mother. Not in any way.

The younger deputy stepped into better view. He was in his thirties with a pencil-thin mustache and pants that hung too low beneath his pendulous belly. "You might have fallen."

Was that a sneer? Claire ignored the avid curiosity in his gaze and tipped her chin up to face down his skepticism. "He hit me on the head from behind."

Colton took her arm and turned her toward the steps up to the hotel. "Ayuh, all I know is some beachcombers from the hotel found you lying here and stayed with you for the hour it took us to get here. Maybe you should get some rest tonight, Ms. Dellamare. Things might be a little clearer tomorrow."

She jerked her arm out of his grip. "I'm perfectly clear now. See that big rocky cliff? They were struggling there. He pushed her toward the edge, and I yelled for him to stop, but I don't think he heard me. The next thing I knew, he tossed her over the edge." The nausea roiled in her stomach again when she remembered the sound the woman's body had made when it hit the sand.

His only reaction was a slow blink of his eyes. She grabbed his arm. "You have to believe me."

"Then where's the body?" The younger cop hiked at his pants.

"Maybe the murderer took it." She rubbed the back of her neck, but the tight knots under the skin didn't ease. "I recognized the woman. It was Jenny Bennett from the hotel." When a slight gasp came from Waters, she glanced over to see all color had washed from his face. "You know her?"

"You sure it was Jenny?" The deputy's voice choked, and his eyes were wide and horrified.

"Positive. I met her when I checked into the hotel. I'd spoken with her on the phone, and she introduced herself."

Colton put his hand on his deputy's shoulder. "Go on home and check." Waters took off for the steps without answering, and the sheriff watched him go. "He and Jenny live together. So I hope you're wrong, Ms. Dellamare. Waters has an engagement ring in his pocket and is planning to ask her to marry him this weekend."

Claire gulped. "And I just blurted it out to him."

He dug a metal tin of Altoids out of his pocket and popped one in his mouth. "You didn't know. And I'm still hoping you're just a little off-kilter and Waters finds her safe and sound at home."

Claire wanted to be wrong. Could she have been wrong about her attacker looking like the man in her nightmares? "I saw him before he hit me." She described him to the sheriff.

"Could be any one of hundreds of hunters in this area."

She was beginning to doubt herself until her head throbbed again. She hadn't imagined someone hitting her. "I'll paint him for you. I remember his face clearly."

"Sounds fine, just fine, Ms. Dellamare."

48

He didn't believe a word she'd said. "I'd better get back to the hotel. My father will be worried."

"Your dad seemed a mite upset."

"I'm their only child. You know how that can be." She glanced at her watch. Three hours. No wonder her father was frantic.

She let him assist her up the step, the pink granite glimmering in the fading light. Muscles she'd forgotten she had began to complain at the long walk up the cliffside. Lights spilled from the hotel windows, and tasteful yard lights illuminated the landscaping along the expansive green lawns.

If only she could crawl into the crisp white sheets waiting in her room. She needed to have all her faculties and strength when she confronted her father about what she'd learned from Luke. But she'd never sleep now if she didn't find out what had happened here all those years ago.

FOUR

Lights blazed from the hotel, and the soft tones of "My Girl" filtered through speakers placed around the manicured lawn. By the time Claire stepped into the lobby, fragrant with watermelon candles, every muscle in her body throbbed, and she limped from the pain in her right hip. She must have gone down hard on that side. Clinking glasses mingled with laughter from the lounge as she walked across the pink-granite tiles toward the elevator.

She waited for the panic to hit her again, but she felt strangely calm and focused. At least now she knew what had caused that uncharacteristic reaction from her. When several people glanced at her out of the corners of their eyes, she looked down. She was still barefoot and had lost her shoes somewhere along the way. Her hair must be filled with debris from the beach as well, and a smear of muddy sand adorned her left leg.

A bellman rushed to intercept her path toward the elevator. "Ms. Dellamare, your parents are in their suite. May I accompany you to that location?"

"My mother is here?"

He nodded. "She arrived moments ago." She would have preferred to have confronted her father alone.

Since she didn't have any idea where the suite was, she let him lead her down a hall painted with murals of singers from the sixties, then on to a private elevator and up to the fifth floor. The thought of telling her parents everything that had happened tonight made her cringe, but she put one foot in front of the other down the hall until the bellman rapped on a door tucked into the end of the hall.

"Mr. Dellamare, I have your daughter with me."

The solid wood door opened, and her mother reached for Claire. Claire's eyes burned as the familiar scent of her mother's Hermès perfume slipped up her nose. Over her mother's shoulder, she caught a glimpse of the room as her mother drew her inside. The suite was white on gray with bold splashes of color and more pictures of

51

famous people from the sixties. A picture of the Fab Four showed The Beatles smiling at the camera with two large striped umbrellas over their heads.

Something about the umbrellas . . .

She slammed her eyes shut, and through a fog she heard her father thank the bellman before the heavy door shut behind her. A crazy swirl of panic rose in her again, and she fought it. She was safe here. There was nothing to fear. She took a few deep breaths, and the pressure eased.

Her mother rushed toward her and drew her close. "I came as soon as I got your message that you were on your way here. You should have told me sooner." Mom took her shoulders and drew her away to give her a tiny shake. "Really, Claire, you frightened me to death! It was almost like —"

"Lisa, can't you see she's exhausted?" Claire's father removed a pillow from an armchair. "Here, sit down, Claire. You look done in. What happened to you? You've been gone for hours."

Almost like . . .

Almost like the other time she'd gotten lost? A time shrouded in mists of forgotten memories? She gripped her mother's wrist. "You came as soon as you heard I was heading to join Dad here, you said. Was it

52

because you were afraid I'd remember the last time I was here? Why didn't you tell me?"

"You remember?" She exchanged a long look with Claire's father. The plea in her mother's eyes made Dad take a step forward.

"Not exactly. But I must remember something, and that's why I had a panic attack." Was that relief in his eyes?

He licked his lips. "I'm not sure it was a panic attack, Claire. You used to have asthma when you were little. Maybe the sea air triggered another one."

"I've never had an asthma attack in my memory. And you're avoiding my question. Why didn't you tell me I'd been here?"

Her father put his hand on her shoulder. "We travel widely, Claire. I couldn't tell you every place you've ever been. And I wasn't expecting you here anyway, remember? You just came of your own volition."

Her gut twisted, and she curled her hands into fists in the lap of her stained and torn dress. The cowardly part of her didn't want to get into it tonight when she was exhausted and shocked, but she'd been drifting too long, asleep in a pleasant dream where nothing bad ever happened. Something terrible had happened here. She could feel it, could sense the way every cell in her body cringed at the sight of this place.

She inhaled, then looked up at her parents. Both strikingly good-looking in their expensive clothing and carefully arranged hair. A perfect couple, everyone said. She'd never heard them fight either. Was her disappearance the reason her mother had always been so fragile?

Her mother twisted the giant diamond on her finger. "You're wearing a peculiar expression, Claire. And look at you. No shoes. You're filthy, and your hair is a wreck. What happened to you this afternoon? Your father even called the sheriff. Are you all right?"

"I'm fine, Mom. Some guy killed the woman at the counter when I checked in, Jenny Bennett. I called the sheriff, but the killer sneaked up on me and hit me over the head." When her mother gasped, Claire shook her head. "I'm okay. The sheriff is looking for him."

"You were attacked? Does he know you saw him?" her father asked.

"I'm sure he does and that's why he hit me." Claire fingered the lump on her head. She badly needed to wash the mud and debris out of her hair.

Her mother put her hand to her mouth. "What if he comes back? You need to leave here. Get to our house where we have security." She looked at Dad. "Harry, you need to hire a bodyguard. If he knows Claire saw him, he might try to harm her again."

Claire leaned forward in the chair. "I'm not going anywhere without some answers. It's time I was told the truth."

Her parents exchanged glances again. Her father turned away to pour himself a drink from the bar. "The truth about what?"

Claire bolted to her feet. "I know, Dad, okay? I know I was lost out there for a year. A *year*! How could you keep something like that from me? And where was I? Surely with all your money you managed to find out who had cared for me all that time. I didn't live with the bears, for heaven's sake!" Her voice shook, and she took a deep breath to calm herself down. She had to stay in control, stay focused.

"How do you know all this if you still can't remember?" Her father turned to face her, his tone cautious.

"Someone heard my name and recognized it."

Her mother kept twisting her ring, around and around. "Who recognized you?"

"Luke Rocco."

Her father snorted. "Rocco. He —" He clamped his mouth shut and took a gulp of his bourbon.

"I want to know everything you know about what happened." She pointed to the chairs on the other side of the fireplace. "I think you'd better sit down. It's going to be a long night."

Smoke choked the air above the charred field. A single white stick protruded out of ground at an awkward angle. Luke stared at what he now knew was a boneyard. LED floodlights threw out as much light as the noonday sun, but they didn't give off enough heat to warm the cold night air. He stood with Beau Callahan, a sheriff's deputy. The scent of fresh, unturned soil mingled with the smell of burned vegetation. The site swarmed with state forensic people combing for clues, though from the state of the skeleton, he doubted they'd find much. The person had been dead a long time, and the elements covered what might have been discovered.

Could it be his mother's body at last? Luke glanced at Beau. When Beau had told him what had happened to Claire after she left him and Megan, Luke wished he'd walked her back to the hotel. "Any word on Jenny?"

Beau shook his head. "We checked the

house, and Jenny is nowhere to be found. I think Ms. Dellamare really saw her murdered. If the tide carried the body out to sea, it may never be found."

"Too bad Claire couldn't identify the attacker." He pressed his lips together. "Um, have you looked at Deputy Waters?"

Beau's brow lifted. "You know something?"

"You and I both know he's a bully, Beau. It wouldn't take much for me to believe Jenny looked at him wrong once too often."

Beau pinched the bridge of his nose. "The sheriff depends on him. I'll poke around, but I have a hard time seeing Danny seriously consider him as a suspect."

"That's all I ask."

"Claire is going to try to paint who she saw so we'll see if it leads anywhere. The sheriff isn't sure she saw anything."

Sheriff Colton turned and waved at the crew. "Over here. We found something."

The search crew scurried to the new find as if it were buried treasure instead of someone's family. Luke craned his neck but saw nothing except the backs of the officials as they bent over their discovery.

Beau took off his hat and ran his hand through his dark hair. "It will be awhile before we know more. You might as well go home, Luke. I can call you if I hear any-thing."

"I'll hang around awhile longer."

Beau squeezed Luke's shoulder. "You think it's your mom, don't you, buddy?"

Luke swallowed hard. "We'd just like answers. That's all we've ever wanted."

"I know." Beau put his hat back on. "You know what folks say around here."

"That she ran off with someone. But none of us ever believed it. Mom wouldn't do that."

But did he believe that? He'd only been seven when she disappeared. He remem-bered warm hugs and a sunny personality. Now that he'd gotten older, he realized she'd been a beauty, too, with the kind of personality that would have attracted any-one. On the other hand, his dad had always been taciturn, almost remote. Maybe a woman like his mother had gotten tired of living with a man who thought laughter was a waste of good work time.

"It happens, Luke."

Luke shrugged. "I know. And to be hon-est, I've done some online searching for her over the years, just in case that's what hap-pened. But if she left Pop, she changed her name and disappeared completely. Who can do that? Not a woman who got married right out of high school and never even set foot in a state other than Maine."

"So what do you think happened to her?"

Luke watched the bustle of activity as a middle-aged man transferred bones, gleaming white in the light, to a box. "She went for a walk every night without fail. Maybe she fell into an old mine. Maybe she ran into a drifter who killed her and buried her. Maybe she drowned in the old gravel pit we use to water the cranberries. Lots of things could have happened."

"True enough."

Luke shuffled and waved away a swarm of small insects. His boots crunched on the blackened vegetation under his feet. This area hadn't been farmed or tended to in any way for more than forty years, and Pop had bought it last year before the drought. The brush had been too thick to walk through, and this ditch where the body had been buried would still be covered with vegetation if Jimmy hadn't burned it off.

A vehicle rattled to a stop behind him, and he turned to see his sister emerge from her Jeep. She'd changed from her wet shorts to a pair of faded jeans and a black Celtics sweatshirt. He waved to her, and she hurried toward him. A frown crouched between her eyes, and she'd wound her dark curls up in a careless knot.

She grasped Luke's arm. "What'd you find out? I had to tell Pop. It was all I could do to keep him away. He's sure it's Mom."

Beau shoved his hands in his pockets. "No news yet, Meggie. Definitely human bones, though."

"Pop was upset?"

She nodded. "You know how he gets. If he'd been able to get out of the wheelchair and into the car by himself, I couldn't have stopped him. The only way I calmed him was to promise to find out what was happening and report back."

The sheriff, Danny Colton, walked briskly toward them. In his fifties, he shaved what little hair he had left, though his handlebar mustache still retained its fiery color. At six foot seven, he towered over most everyone in town. For one brief year, Folly Shoals residents had watched breathlessly when he'd played for the Celtics until an injury swept him off the court. But the brief stint of stardom had won him the hearts of everyone in the county, and he'd been the sheriff for over twenty years.

He tipped his hat at Megan. "Sorry to keep you all out here in the cold." His hazel eyes were shadowed, but he held Luke's gaze. "Got something to show you two. This

60

might be hard. Come with me, please."

Luke exchanged a glance with his sister, and they followed Danny to the back of the forensics van. His pulse throbbed in his neck, and he glanced around the area. Several boxes held soil and rocks, but a bright splash of color in the third box caught his eye. He stepped closer and bent down, catching a pungent whiff of soil. "Meg, look here."

Something red peeked out through the soil. His fire truck lay partly uncovered in the box. He curled his fingers into his palms.

"I take it you recognize this item?" Danny's voice was soft.

"It's my fire truck." His tongue felt thick. "It disappeared the night Mom did."

"Thank you. I thought it might be." .

"So it's probably Mom?" Meg's voice was barely above a whisper.

"We won't know for sure until we get the bones identified. But it might be."

FIVE

Claire threw open the balcony windows and inhaled the scent of the sea. From her vantage point, she could see the waves expending themselves on the rocky crags before foaming back with the ebb of the ocean's tide. She felt just as battered as those rocks out there. She'd barely slept, and at the first rays of the sunrise, she'd slipped out of the sweet-smelling linens on her king-size bed.

She turned at the tap on her door and a call of "room service." Tightening her robe's sash, she unlocked the door and opened it to allow the woman to wheel in the cart with breakfast. The server wore a perky smile that extended to the lines around her eyes. Her short salt-and-pepper hair curled around her face. She looked familiar in some way. Maybe it was the turquoise suit worn by all the hotel staff.

Claire glanced at her name tag as she

tipped her. The food and beverage manager was delivering food? "Um, Priscilla, have you worked here long?"

The woman accepted the tip. "Thank you. Yes, I've worked here thirty-five years." Her broad Maine accent didn't hit the *R*s in her words. "I started out in the kitchen and worked my way up." She touched her name tag. "We were shorthanded today, so I'm pitching in. I don't mind. I don't often get a chance to mingle with the guests anymore." The light in her eyes dimmed a bit. "I hope you're feeling better, Ms. Dellamare. We prayed for you in the staff meeting."

Claire finally placed her as the woman standing by the pillars when she'd had her meltdown yesterday afternoon. "Much better, thank you." *Thirty-five years.* It was worth asking. "I don't suppose you remember me, do you?"

Priscilla's expression sharpened, and she tucked a salt-and-pepper curl behind her ear. "From yesterday, you mean?"

Claire shook her head. "My parents were here when I was a child, and we had a birthday in the garden. I was four."

The woman took a step toward the door. "I was here then, yes. I really should be getting back to work. As I mentioned, we're shorthanded."

63

Claire reached a hand toward her. "Please, just a few questions. I didn't know I'd ever been here before until I had that panic attack yesterday."

Priscilla took another step toward the door. "Well, no wonder you were fearful. It was a terrible thing."

"Can you tell me what happened? I don't remember it at all, and some details might help."

Priscilla sighed. "It was a long time ago, Ms. Dellamare. Maybe it's best if you don't remember. It had to have been traumatic. We searched for days for you."

We? "Did you search too?"

"Oh yes, nearly all the employees and guests took part." She clucked her tongue. "A thing like that — a child lost in the woods — is every parent's nightmare. The entire region was in an uproar over it."

Just thinking about it made Claire's gut clench, and she didn't even have children. "How did it happen?"

"Your parents had invited the children from Folly Shoals to your birthday party as well as close friends, and the garden was overrun with children. There had to have been over a hundred youngsters playing and shrieking, frightening the ducks and the gulls. Your mom was running around trying to keep everyone happy and fed. I brought out your cake, and she called for you to blow out the candles, but you didn't answer. No one had seen you, and the entire scene turned to bedlam when you were nowhere to be found."

Not a shred of memory tried to surface. And Priscilla's description of Mom trying to care for everyone wasn't like the woman Claire had grown up with. "No one saw me leave?"

Priscilla shook her head. "There were lots of theories. Some kids said you'd left with the boogeyman, and a few others said a witch had snatched you away, but we had no credible leads. The children were hysterical as it became clear something had happened to you. Some of the local youngsters had nightmares for weeks."

"And how was I found?"

"To be honest, it was another puzzle. I found you crying under the hedge in the back."

"*You* found me?" Maybe that was the real reason Claire had felt so comfortable in the woman's presence.

"I had stepped outside for a smoke." She wrinkled her nose. "Back in the days when I smoked. I recognized you instantly. Those big blue eyes, you know. They're pretty remarkable. Your hair was a little darker and you were taller, of course. But I knew it was you even before I read the note pinned to your top that gave your name. I took you inside and called the sheriff." Her green eyes misted. "When your father arrived to get you, he just sobbed. I would have too."

Claire could almost feel her father's fierce hug. The memory was nearly there. Why couldn't she retrieve it? "Where was I all that time?"

"No one knew. You kept asking for your mother, but when your father came, you hid your face and cried." Priscilla wrinkled her forehead. "But it had been a year, after all."

Claire felt the need to pace, to throw something, any kind of action that would relieve the ache she felt inside. "How had I found my way to the hotel by myself?"

"Another enigma. The entire situation has so many unanswered questions." Priscilla edged toward the door again. "I'm so sorry, Ms. Dellamare, but I really have to go. If I remember anything else, I'll let you know. I hope you come to grips with all of it. I'll pray for you."

"Thank you, Priscilla. I appreciate your help and especially the prayers. It's been very challenging." She shut and latched the door behind the woman before going back to the balcony.

The dark woods looming over the sea drew her gaze and she shuddered.

Silverware tinkled against plates in the outdoor dining space. Claire skirted the line at the buffet table and exited the back doors onto the dining patio. The scent of fresh flowers from the outdoor tables hung heavy in the air. She spied her mother seated near an arbor and paused to take in her pale skin and shadowed eyes. Any stress usually took its toll on Mom, and Claire had expected her mother to be in bed most of the day.

Claire pulled out a chair opposite her mother. "Good morning, Mom. I'm surprised you're up this early."

"I couldn't sleep." Her mother went quiet when the server, a college-aged blonde, stepped to the table to refill her coffee. The server poured Claire's coffee too.

Claire ordered quiche. "Where's Dad?"

"He went to the airport in Bangor to pick up Ric." A thread of stress ran through her mother's tone. "He'll be gone until dinnertime."

Claire poured cream into her coffee and took a sip. "I would have gone with him. I'm eager to talk to Ric."

"I've never liked that man, Claire. He has

a terrible reputation with women."

"I'm just going to close the merger, not date him."

Her mother pressed her lips together and moved her scrambled eggs around on her plate with her fork. "Did you hear from the sheriff this morning?"

"No, but I thought I might call him and see if they found Jenny." At her mother's blank expression, she explained the name. "The murdered woman."

Her mother shuddered. "I'd rather not think about it."

"Why did we have my birthday party here when I was four? I want to know more about what happened."

Her mother picked at her plate again. "My family often vacationed here when I was growing up. My parents had a vacation home in Bar Harbor. I met your father that summer. He was caddying for my dad. And we were married here and had our reception at this hotel. It seemed so romantic to be married in the area where we'd met and fallen in love. And we came back here every year for your birthday. At least until you went missing. Then I never wanted to see the place again."

At least her mother had faced her distaste and come rushing here to make sure Claire was all right. "Are you going home today?"

Her mother's lashes swept up, then back down. "I think I might stay, at least until you're ready to leave."

What was her mother afraid of? Memories?

Gulls, drawn by the pungent odor of the fish in Luke's pail, swooped low and squawked overhead. One particularly bold one landed and tried to peer into the bucket.

"Oh no you don't." Luke swatted it away, and it flew off with an indignant squawk.

The day glowered with gray skies and the promise of a storm. Luke's mood matched the dark clouds overhead. Night had brought little rest as he'd tossed and turned in bed all night. Had his mother finally been found, or would a final resolution be snatched away?

The baby orca swam close when he dangled a fish over the water from his perch on the pier. When the little guy was close enough, he dropped the food into the calf's mouth. "You look better today, fella."

Megan dropped onto her belly and dangled her arms over the edge of the pier. "He does, doesn't he? His eyes are brighter, and he's swimming much more strongly. I think he's going to live." She inclined her head toward the shore. "It's a good thing, or you might have to answer to her."

He glanced up and saw Claire Dellamare picking her way along the rocky shoreline. Sturdy water shoes replaced the heels she'd carried yesterday, and she wore sensible jeans today. A bright-pink blouse peeked over the top of her yellow rain slicker. Her golden-tipped curls were up on top of her head, more neatly this time.

The pier shuddered a bit under her footsteps. "He's swimming better." Her dimples flashed when she smiled at the little orca.

The sweet scent of her perfume wafted toward him, pulling him toward her. "He's hungry too. Want to feed him?" He suppressed a grin. No way would a woman like her touch smelly fish.

"Sure." Claire lowered herself onto the pier on the other side of the bucket and reached in. She must have noticed his shock because one perfect brow arched up. "I can bait my own hook with a worm too, just in case you're wondering."

Meg burst into laughter. "She got you there, big brother."

An answering grin tugged at Luke's mouth. "Appearances don't tell the whole story, huh? I would have guessed you hadn't set foot in a fishing boat, in spite of knowing about orcas."

Claire tossed the killer whale another fish. "There's something about the sea and its creatures that call to me. I could sit for hours and just watch the waves." She watched the orca swim away, then back for another snack. "If he keeps eating, we might be able to release him in a week. I might stay to make sure he's okay."

"It's not that easy. I need to see if I can find his pod. He'll have the best chance of survival if he's with his family."

"They're probably close by."

He shook his head. "There are at least three pods out here."

Those gorgeous blue eyes turned his way. "How do you know that?"

Meg rubbed her hand over the orca's head. "Luke is an orca geek. He's in the Coast Guard and has studied them for years. He cares more about this little guy than you can imagine."

Luke stifled a grin at his sister's defensive tone. While she felt free to correct him, no one else had better try. "You probably know every pod has its own dialect of vocalization. I've been listening to him." He pointed out his hydrophone strapped to one of the pilings. "I'm recording him, and when he's ready, I'll go out searching for his family.

I'll play the recordings and see if I can attract the right pod."

"It's all gone, little one." Claire rinsed the scales from her fingers. "Exactly what I would have done. You really *do* know orcas."

They watched the antics of the little orca for a few minutes in silence. The little guy vaulted into the air and emitted small chirps and clicks. Even though Claire laughed at the right times, Luke sensed a sorrow in her, some kind of distress that made her gaze off into the foaming waves.

She finally blinked and sighed before turning to look at Megan and him. "Have they found the body yet?"

How had she heard about the find already? "I was there when they found the bones."

Her blue eyes darkened. "Bones? How could there be only bones so quickly?"

Of course, she was talking about what she saw last night, not about the grisly discovery in the cranberry field. "One of the deputies told us you thought you saw a murder."

"I didn't *think so.* I actually saw it. Here, feel this."

She took his hand, and the shock of her touch sent a current through him. She tugged his hand to the back of her soft hair and pressed his fingers against a bump.

"The guy hit me on the head." She released his hand, then turned and pointed at Old Man Ledge. "I saw a man shove a woman off right there. I rushed to help her, but she was already dead. Then he clobbered me from behind. When I woke up, the sheriff was there, but the body I'd seen was gone."

"That's crazy. Are you okay?"

"I'm fine, but I'm eager to learn what happened to Jenny. It was pretty awful what that man did to her. And the police didn't seem to believe me —"

"Wait, how do you know the victim's name?"

"I met Jenny when I checked in to the hotel yesterday, and I'd spoken to her on the phone before my arrival."

"We had an eventful night too," Meg put in. "One of our workers discovered some human bones on our property. We think we might have finally found our mother. She went missing the same night you did."

The bracelet on her slender wrist clinked when Claire gasped and put her hand to her mouth. "I'm so sorry. So that's why you asked if I saw a woman."

Meg nodded.

"With Mom found, maybe we can all get on with life again. She's been gone from our lives for years, but our dad hasn't been

73

able to let her go."

"I can't imagine how painful that must've been. Our identities are so tied up in our families, don't you think? I'm still reeling from what you told me yesterday. I need to find out more about that missing year. Is there a newspaper in the area that might have an account of what happened?"

He nodded. "*Folly Shoals Soundings.* The library might have old copies on microfilm, but there's no telling." The forlorn expression in her eyes stirred his heart. "I can go with you and show you if you like. I know the librarian."

Her eyes brightened. "Oh, would you, Luke? My parents told me to leave it alone, but I can't. I have to know even if it upsets them. I have to be careful, though. Mom is kind of delicate."

He understood her urgency all too well and stood. "I've got time right now."

The lightening of his spirit had nothing to do with the thought of spending some time in her presence. A woman with Claire's background wouldn't look twice at a sea dog like him, even if he was interested.

Six

Folly Shoals was a fishing village straight out of a Norman Rockwell painting. Shingle and clapboard cottages in pastels of blue, yellow, and white stair-stepped the hillside, and lobster traps lay heaped in the yards. Boats of all sizes and conditions, from pleasure boats to fishing boats, bobbed in the waves at their moorings in Sunset Cove. Bigger, nicer homes with manicured lawns sandwiched the older homes occupied by fishermen. People with coolers awaited the fishing and lobster boats chugging toward the pier.

Claire clung to the armrest in Luke's old truck as he drove the narrow and winding streets to the library. She was only too glad to get out of the cab, rank with the odor of fish and bait. She stood on the brick sidewalk and looked up and down the street. The aroma of fudge mingled with the scents rolling out of the candle shop next door.

She would have to stroll through the shops when she had time.

She'd tried to find out about her missing year online, but Folly Shoals was still stuck in the last century and only the last few years of articles were online. She hoped Luke was right and they'd find stashes of microfilm or even the physical papers themselves in some dusty room inside. Though, surveying the small, sea-weathered building, she had her doubts. And what if she found something that rocked her world even more?

"Wait here first. I'll check and see if they have any old papers." Luke touched her shoulder, then bounced up the steps to the library.

While he was gone, Claire observed the town. Had she lived in one of those houses when she was four? Doubtful. Not with so many people searching for her. Whoever had kept her likely lived out in the forest somewhere, miles from here. How did she go about finding out the truth when it happened twenty-five years ago? Could her nightmare about the man with the fox be something she actually experienced during that missing year?

Luke came back down the steps shaking his head. "No papers, but the librarian was sure the newspaper would have them." He pointed to a building two doors down.

The acrid odor of ink assaulted her when she stepped inside, but the young man named Victor was pleasant enough, and minutes later she and Luke were in the archive room. Wooden tables nearly groaned under the weight of stacks of newspapers.

The old floorboards creaked under him as Luke approached a stack in the back-left corner. "He suggested we start here."

She joined him, leaning in close enough to feel the warmth emanating off his skin. Moving away a few inches, she took a stack of newspapers from his hands and carried them to the old wooden table in the center of the room. Half an hour later, black ink covered her hands, but they were getting close. The last paper she'd looked at was only a week away from her disappearance.

Luke held up a paper. "Got it! Front page news." He moved beside her and smoothed open the newspaper.

TINY HEIRESS LOST IN THE NORTH WOODS
  Searchers fanned out Saturday over the island of Folly Shoals and into all of Hancock and Washington Counties in a quest to find the only child of millionaire Harry

Dellamare and his wife, Lisa. Claire Dellamare, four years old, wandered off during a birthday party at Hotel Tourmaline. The blond, blue-eyed girl was last seen wearing a pink lace party dress, white tights, and patent leather shoes.

A K-9 search-and-rescue team showed up to assist in the search, but so far, no trace of the child has been found. The child's mother, Lisa Dellamare, has been hospitalized for hysteria and remains under sedation. Anyone with information leading to the child's whereabouts is instructed to call the sheriff's office. A reward of a hundred thousand dollars has been offered for information leading to the child's discovery.

Claire's chest felt tight, and her eyes prickled. She would *not* cry. All this happened years ago. It had no power to affect her life now. She only wanted to know what happened. Sniffling, she reached for a wet wipe and washed her hands, then handed him one. She didn't look at him as they cleaned off the ink in silence.

Luke's hand, warm and strong, came to rest on her left shoulder. The press of his fingers conveyed reassurance, support, and comfort. "You okay?"

"Fine." Her voice came out hoarse and choked. "It's just all so shocking to find out something this dramatic happened to me and I don't remember anything about it." Her gaze fell farther down the front page. "There's no mention of your mother's disappearance."

He leaned down, his breath stirring her hair. "My father couldn't do anything for twenty-four hours since she was an adult. It should be in the next week's paper. Let me see if I can find it." He shuffled through the papers and retrieved one. "Here it is."

SEARCH CALLED OFF FOR CLAIRE DELLAMARE

After a week of unseasonably cool night temperatures, four-year-old Claire Dellamare remains missing. Searchers from the island and all of Hancock and Washington Counties have been unable to locate the child. Her shoes were found in a small islet north of Sunset Cove, and the sheriff's department has surmised she went swimming and drowned. Her father, millionaire Harry Dellamare, checked his grieving wife out of the hospital and took her back to Boston yesterday, where she was admitted to a local psychiatric hospital. The community offers its prayers and condolences to the Dellamares.

And underneath that article, she saw the one about his mother. Judging from her picture, she'd been very beautiful, with long dark hair and eyes that seemed to take in the world with a hint of humor. Megan looked a lot like her.

CO-OWNER OF ROCCO CRANBERRIES MISSING

Victoria Rocco went on her customary evening walk and never returned. Available searchers were thin because of Claire Dellamare's disappearance, but friends and neighbors fanned out over her known path. Victoria's husband, Walker Rocco, asks anyone with information to call him personally.

Claire glanced up to find his gaze on her. "That's all? It almost sounds like no one expected to find her."

"I don't think the town did. Most folks thought she left of her own accord, but we never believed she'd do that." His lips flattened, and so did his voice. "And now it appears we were right."

"There isn't much to go on for either of us."

His brow furrowed. "I was a kid myself,

80

so I don't have any clear memories of it other than searching for her and crying myself to sleep every night."

She winced. "Whom can we talk to about it? Your dad?"

"He had a stroke and isn't making a whole lot of sense these days. Let's start with Mom's sister, my aunt Nancy. She runs a day care here in town." A dimple appeared in his right cheek, then he reached over and rubbed his thumb, still damp from the hand wipe, over her cheek.

He was a man who worked hard with his hands. His thumb was rough against her skin. "Got it. I should probably wash my face too."

Her face heated when she rose and followed him after such a curiously intimate exchange. She never let people close this fast. Never.

It took five minutes for Luke to drive Claire to where his mother's sister lived. Nancy Prescott kept an immaculate yard around her shingled house. Her roses were impressive. She'd already cut the shoots back and had prepped the beds lining the front of her gingerbread house. He eyed Claire to see what she thought of the blue house with its crisp white shutters.

Claire's eyes widened. "How cute."

He parked at the curb. "When we were kids, Megan thought Snow White's dwarves used to live here. It looked like the picture in her book. The house has all these great nooks and crannies too. Perfect for hide-and-seek."

"Will she mind us dropping by without calling first?"

He shook his head. "I'll get what-for since this is the first I've stopped by since I got back to town, but it'll be worth it for her peanut butter cookies and coffee." He got out and shut his door.

They strolled up the brick walk lined with freshly upturned dirt. His aunt would be dying to get her annuals planted along the sidewalk. She took pride in trying new varieties every year. He mounted the steps and pressed the doorbell. The windows along the front of the house stood open, and he caught the faint scent of lemon polish.

The door opened, and she beamed up at him. "I wondered when you'd find time for your old aunt." In bare feet and cropped pants, she grabbed him in a fierce hug, then stepped back to survey him. "You're too thin."

"I haven't had your cookies in six months." He followed her into the sunny living room with its warm wood floors and bright rug. "Aunt Nan, this is Claire —"

Claire interrupted him, holding out her hand. "So nice to meet you."

He shot a glance her way, and she smiled back blandly. Maybe she didn't want his aunt to know her last name yet.

The dimple in his aunt's cheek was like his and his mother's. About fifty-five, she had bright-pink polish on her toenails and her dark hair up in a ponytail. "I do believe this is the first time Luke has ever brought a girl to meet me, Claire. You must be very special to him. Have a seat, you two."

Pink ran up Claire's face. "Actually, we just met yesterday." She settled on the over-stuffed beige sofa.

"Oh well, that doesn't mean you're not special. I have fresh coffee, and I made cookies last night. I'll be right back." She vanished through the kitchen door.

"Whew, she's a whirlwind," Claire whispered. "Where does she get all her energy? I like her already."

"She's always been that way. She's been more like a mom than an aunt to me and Meg."

Nancy returned, a Nemo tray topped with cups and cookies in her hands. "The coffee is strong so I brought lots of cream and sugar."

Claire accepted a cup. "I like it strong. Are you a Disney fan?"

Nancy laughed. "Sorry, the only tray I have is one I use for the day care kids. They're crazy about Nemo."

"Are there kids here now? I don't hear anything."

Nancy shook her head. "My helper took them to the library for story hour. Believe me, you'd know if they were here. I'm ready for the weekend to start after they all leave tonight. I'm not sure how much longer I can keep up with them."

Luke took a cup of coffee and cookie, then settled on the sofa beside Claire. It did his heart good to see her warming up to his aunt so quickly. What would Aunt Nan think when she found out Claire's last name?

His aunt took a cup of coffee and dropped into the upholstered rocker by the stone fireplace. "I have a feeling you're here for more than a casual visit. What's up, nephew?"

He realized he hadn't even told her about finding the bones. "I have some news, Aunt Nan. Um, you know that field Pop bought last year? I had Jimmy burning it off to get

84

it ready to excavate and plant cranberries. He found some bones buried in a ditch. The heavy spring rains uncovered them enough that the fire exposed them."

The color drained from his aunt's face, and coffee sloshed over the side of her cup onto her white pants. "Vicky." Her voice was barely a whisper.

"I think it might be. My fire engine was there too." Nancy's coffee cup wobbled, and he reached over to take it from her. "We won't know for a while. Danny said it'll take awhile to get a positive ID."

His aunt's throat made a clicking sound. "Finally, after all these years. I knew she didn't just run off. Oh, Luke, what happened to her?"

"We don't know, not yet. The place was crawling with forensics people last night, so I'm praying we have some answers soon."

"Oh my." She fanned herself and inhaled a gasp of air. "I never expected to hear this." She looked hard at Claire. "And are you a forensics investigator? Is that why you're here too?"

Claire bit her lip. "Maybe now is not the time to discuss my questions."

His aunt's lips trembled, but she tipped up her chin. "I'm fine. It was just a bit of a shock, after all these years. Vicky was my baby sister, a year younger than I am. I always blamed myself, you know."

Luke frowned. "Why would you blame yourself? That makes no sense."

She wrung her hands. "I tried to tell them, but no one would listen to me. I know her disappearance had something to do with that little girl who went missing at the same time."

Claire made a tiny gasp, but he kept his eyes on his aunt. "Why are you so sure of that?"

"She called me, Vicky did. Before she disappeared. She said she'd heard a child crying out in the woods. She told Walker, but he insisted it was an owl."

"Did he hear it too?" Claire's voice was strangled.

His aunt nodded. "He told her he'd check it out, but when she looked, she found him sleeping on the porch. I know my sister. She couldn't ignore a crying child."

"Pop never said anything about it."

Aunt Nan looked down at her lap. "What does this all mean?"

"We don't know yet. The victim hasn't been identified." If his aunt went any paler, she was apt to keel over right here on the floor.

Her slim fingers pleated the paper napkin

on her lap. "I told the sheriff." Her voice was stronger now, more confident. "But your dad and the sheriff were good friends, so who do you think he listened to?" She looked over at Claire as a tear rolled down her cheek. "My dear, why are you crying?"

Luke glanced at Claire. "Aunt Nan, I didn't mention Claire's last name. It's Dellamare."

His aunt's eyes widened, and she looked from him to Claire. "You're the Dellamare child?"

Claire nodded. "I'm sorry if I was the cause of your sister's death."

"Oh, honey, it wasn't your fault! No, no, I didn't mean that." Aunt Nan leaned forward, her hands clasped in front of her. "But this has to be God's providence that you're here now when Vicky has finally been found. You can tell us what happened. Did she help you in some way?"

Claire's hand went to her mouth, and she smothered a sob. "I don't remember. Oh, dear Lord, why can't I remember?"

He reached over to take her hand, but she wrenched it away and bolted for the door.

SEVEN

Claire stumbled along the tree line through the debris left by a long, hard winter. Bits of twigs, leaves, and small pebbles slid into her water shoes and bit into the soles of her feet. She found a path into the dimly lit forest and took it.

She wanted to slap her skull and force herself to remember. Something important had happened that night, something that took the life of Luke's sweet mother. Guilt twisted itself around her gut. She leaned over and retched. Though nothing came up, the nausea subsided, and she wiped a shaky hand across her damp brow.

Luke would be worried, and she ought to go back, but she wasn't ready to face the man. His childhood had been ruined because of her. She tried to remind herself she'd been a child, but she still felt responsible.

The path wound past a small waterfall,

and she stopped and absorbed the landscape. Was it somehow familiar? Her imagination, surely. The path beckoned on, and
she followed the call. Fifteen minutes later
she smelled the salty tang of the ocean
before she saw it. Her steps quickened.

Stepping from the dappled shadows of the
forest, she stood on a high cliff overlooking
the Atlantic. Powerful waves battered themselves against the foot of the great rock.
From here, she could see the distant shoreline of the Schoodic Peninsula. The storm
clouds glowered and spat rain her way, but
she lifted her face into the moisture and
closed her eyes.

She stood there inhaling the scent of the
sea and listening to the squawk of the gulls
overhead. The tension had begun to leave
her shoulders when she heard a footfall
crunch on dead leaves. Smiling, she started
to turn to greet Luke, but a hard shove on
her back pushed her close to the edge of
the precipice.

Her arms cartwheeled, and she tried to
regain her balance. A gust of wind aided
her, and she dropped to her stomach and
grabbed an outcropping of root for all she
was worth. The pungent scent of mud and
moss filled her head as she pressed her face
to the earth to try to thwart her attacker's

intent to throw her off the cliff. Her shoes had come off, and she dug her toes into the ground as well.

A hard boot hit her ribs, and the explosion of pain through her midsection loosened her grip on the ground. One leg went over the edge, dangling in the air. *No!* She tightened her leg until her toes found purchase on the side of the rock. She dug her fingers in harder, barely feeling the way her thumbnail tore loose. She wanted to scream, but it took all her energy just to hang on.

He is going to kill me.

She barely had the sense left to pray for help.

Through the roaring in her head, she heard Luke shout from the forest, then the sound of someone running away. Daring to raise her head, she peered up and saw a bulky form dressed in camouflage rushing into the forest. Struggling to breathe, she got to her hands and knees. It hurt to try to pull in oxygen.

She sat back on her haunches and drew in a shallow breath, then another. Luke rushed toward her from the tree line. His eyes widened as he approached, and she raised a shaking hand to her hair. Her hair was no longer safely held atop her head and lay in disarray on her shoulders.

When he reached her he dropped to her knees. "Claire, are you all right? What happened?"

"H-He tried to push me off the cliff, just like Jenny Bennett." Sobs bubbled up, but she forced them down. A Dellamare didn't lose control. It had happened once, but never again.

His rough fingers caressed her cheek. "You're having trouble breathing. I need to get you to the hospital. Can you walk?"

"I think so." She let him help her to her feet, but every breath caused a red-hot shaft of agony through her midsection. She took two steps, then sagged against him. "I-I can't breathe."

She expected him to say he'd call for help, but instead he swung her into his arms and plunged into the woods with her.

"You can't carry me that far." It was getting harder to breathe, and spots of color danced in her vision.

She didn't hear his answer as roaring filled her head and the world went dark.

Folly Shoals Hospital, barely bigger than a clinic, squatted between two giant maple trees. Several old-timers lounged on the benches in the shade and looked up curiously as Luke burst from his truck, then went around and lifted Claire from the passenger seat.

He'd broken all speed records getting here in the driving rain. At least it had stopped, but the muddy road had slowed him down. Claire was too weak to cling to him as he carried her through the glass entry door. "She can't breathe!"

The receptionist looked up at his shout, and her gaze went to Claire's pale face. "This way, last room on the right." She hit a button, and the doors to the emergency area opened.

The muscles in Luke's arms and back finally began to complain as he made it the last few feet to the examining room. The sting of antiseptic stung his eyes. He laid her gently on the table, then stepped back as a nurse and doctor rushed in. "She was attacked up on Sweet Gum Ridge. Some guy kicked her in the ribs and tried to throw her off the ridge."

"Can't breathe right," Claire gasped. Her color was gray, and her eyes fluttered closed.

"Probably a rib poking your lungs." The young doctor looked about seventeen, but his manner was brisk and professional as he bent to listen to her chest. "You her husband?"

"No, just a friend." He curled his fingers into his palms. They weren't going to throw him out if he had his way. "I interrupted the attack." He stared at her dark lashes resting on her cheeks and willed her to open her eyes again.

"Did you call the police?"

"Not yet."

"You can't use your cell phone in here. Step out into the lobby, and we'll let you know when you can come back. We'll get the portable X-ray machine down here."

Luke pressed his lips together, but he knew the doctor was right. He would just be in the way here. At least he'd be allowed back in later.

He squeezed Claire's fingers. "I'll be right outside."

He stepped into the hall and found a waiting room that smelled of new carpet, then pulled out his cell phone. He settled in a brown upholstered chair and called his friend.

In five minutes, Beau strode into the waiting room wearing his uniform and a somber expression. "You okay?"

Luke rose and shook hands with Beau. "Just wish I had a chance to land a punch. I saw the attack from the edge of the woods and yelled. He ran off when he saw me coming. Big guy dressed in camouflage, like he'd been out hunting." Luke closed his eyes briefly at the thought of Claire hurtling to her death. "I was barely in time."

"Have you spent much time with her?"

Luke eyed his friend. The question held a double edge to it, and Beau's reserve was new. "What aren't you telling me?"

"The sheriff would shoot me if he knew I was talking about this, but as an investigator with the Coast Guard, you can help us figure it out." Beau stuffed his hands in his pockets. "We got an anonymous letter in today's mail. The writer said the sheriff should investigate Claire Dellamare, that she isn't who she says she is. It was postmarked on Wednesday before the Dellamares arrived, and though the letter wasn't signed, the postmark was local. We swept it for prints and found some."

"And?"

"We found Jenny Bennett's prints on the envelope. Her prints were in the computer from the investigation into her disappearance, and they popped up as a match this morning."

Luke took a step back and absorbed the implications. "So you suspect Claire may have killed Jenny and faked the attack?" He shook his head. "I don't buy it."

"The sheriff does, though."

"And you? What do you think?"

"She doesn't seem the murderous type. But the sheriff is up for reelection, and this case is high profile."

"The new attack might make him doubt his assumptions about her guilt." Luke knew Danny well, and once the sheriff got something in his head, he didn't often change his mind.

"What were you two doing up there anyway?"

Luke told him about what went down at his aunt's. "You ever read the accounts from my mom's disappearance? The part about hearing a child crying?"

Beau's mouth flattened. "As a matter of fact, I pulled out those old accounts this morning. I ran across her comments, but family members find clues where none exist."

"And it explains why my fire truck was with her. If we find out the body is her, anyway."

Beau's green eyes softened. "I left a message on your voice mail earlier because I wanted to talk to you. We got some dental records back." His hand came down on Luke's shoulder and squeezed. "We have a positive ID, Luke. We found your mom.

95

Don't tell your dad yet. Danny wants to do it."

Though he'd been expecting the news, Luke closed his eyes shut and inhaled. He'd never dreamed they'd really find her. What had happened twenty-five years ago and how was Claire involved? He exhaled and opened his eyes, staring at Beau, who wore an expression of concern.

Beau removed his hand. "We're going to find who killed her. I'll go talk to Nancy and see if she remembers anything else."

"And talk to Pop. See why he dismissed Aunt Nancy's concern." Bile rose in Luke's throat. Why had his father ignored his mom? She might still be alive if Pop had taken her seriously.

"Your dad up to it?"

"He slurs his words a little, and he can't get of the wheelchair without help, but his mind is still sharp. When do you think Danny will tell us the news officially?"

"Probably Monday. He's in Bangor for the weekend."

The door to the waiting room opened, and the doctor entered with a file in his hand. He looped his stethoscope around his neck and smiled at Luke. "Just got the results back, and your girlfriend doesn't have a punctured lung, which is what I feared. But she's got a cracked rib. Whoever did this put some heavy force behind those kicks."

Luke didn't correct the doctor's assumption about Claire being his girlfriend. "Will she be all right? Do you have to keep her?"

The doctor shook his head. "She'll be in some pain for a couple of days, but she can go home. I want her to keep ice on the injury and take ibuprofen." He reached into the file and withdrew a sheet of paper. "Here are the care instructions. I'll call in a stronger pain med just in case she needs it."

"When can I see her?"

"In a few minutes. The nurse is removing the IV and giving her a shot to help her relax. She should lie on the side that hurts the most. It will let her breathe more deeply so she doesn't get pneumonia. And encourage her to walk so she keeps using those lungs. Inactivity is the worst thing for her right now. Her inclination will be to avoid anything that hurts, but it's the wrong prescription for getting better."

"I'll make sure she does that." Luke shook the doctor's hand and thanked him.

"The poor woman is going to be a mass of bruises from her neck to her knees."

His gut clenched hard. What kind of man would do that to a woman? The same man who killed his mother?

EIGHT

The small clapboard cottage where Kate Mason grew up sat squarely in the middle of their blueberry barrens just off Highway 1, about fifteen miles north of Summer Harbor. Seeing the cottage always made her happy. The placement of its windows and shutters made the house, painted two shades of blue, seem to smile a welcome. The wild blueberries in this area weren't planted. They'd sprung up where God intended them.

She parked her yellow Volkswagen in front of the house. "So far so good. No sign of Mom's car."

Her friend Shelley McDonald twisted a red lock of hair around her finger, a sure sign she was nervous. "What if she comes back early?"

"You've been a teacher too long. I hear the stress in your voice at the thought of breaking any rules. It's not like you're about to get caught cutting class. It shouldn't take us more than two hours to install the new closet, and I don't expect her back until dinnertime. Uncle Paul promised to keep her gone at least until then."

Shelley opened her door. "It feels like we're breaking and entering."

"A surprise isn't a crime. Surprises are good."

"This sounds like a big job. Are you sure you're up to it? You look a little pale today."

"I'm fine. You worry too much." Kate stepped out of the car and inhaled the sweet aroma of blueberry blossoms. The tiny white flowers covered the wild bushes as far as the eye could see. She opened the trunk and retrieved the tools she'd need. She'd built the same closet in her own cottage on the other side of the barrens, and her mother had mentioned she'd love one in her room. It was going to make the perfect birthday present. She'd rest later tonight from the exertion.

Shelley joined her at the rear of the car. "Need me to carry anything?"

"I've got it." If only people would quit asking her how she felt. She'd gotten used to those anxious gazes from everyone who knew about her condition, but it got wearing at times. She was fine for now. She hadn't even had an incidence of fainting or rapid heartbeat in a while.

Kate handed her a ring of keys and several boxes of screws and nails. "You can get the door. It's the key with a dot of blue nail polish on it." She latched the tool belt around her waist, then picked up a box of closet racks and shelves. "We'll get these in and come back for the rest."

Shelley laughed. "You look like you could be on a home improvement show." She turned and surveyed the house. "Looks like it's just been painted. I bet you did that too, didn't you?" She mounted the steps to the low-slung porch, decorated with white spindles and corbels.

Kate followed her. "Actually, Uncle Paul did it, and I supervised."

Shelley unlocked the door and shoved it open. "You ever regret dropping out of college to help out with the blueberry farm? You'd have made a terrific designer. You have such a great eye."

"Sometimes. But I still get to decorate for fun." They both knew the blueberry farm wasn't the real reason she had dropped out of college. Her diagnosis had changed everything.

Kate stepped inside and glanced around. The wood floors gleamed, and she smelled the lemony scent of furniture polish.

Shelley dropped the keys on the entry table, a walnut antique with a marble top. "Wicked cunning. I love blue and yellow decor. Where you want these screws?"

Kate pointed. "Mom's room." She led the way down the hall to the last room on the left. Her arms were about to break by the time she reached the bedroom. She stacked the closet items on the area rug so they wouldn't scratch the wood floor.

Her mother's room was the most recently redecorated. Kate had chosen crisp white and tan bedding that complimented blue-gray walls. The picture of the barrens in their full autumn glory added a bright splash of red to the elegant room with its white beachy furniture.

Kate opened the door to the walk-in closet. "Let's get started hauling stuff out of here."

The aroma of cedar and perfume wafted over her. If she closed her eyes, she could remember hiding here with her imaginary friend, Rachel. They'd stifle their giggles as Mom called for them. Mom had worn White Linen for as long as Kate could remember. She ran her fingertips over the smooth surface of her mother's silk blouses. Maybe it was time to get rid of some things too. Mom hadn't worn anything this glamorous in ages.

In a few minutes, clothing lay in mounds on the bed, and the women had moved on to carrying out shoes and miscellaneous boxes. Reaching on her tiptoes, Kate tugged at one last box nestled in the back corner. She finally managed to nudge it to where she could grab it better, but as she pulled it down, she lost her grip and the box fell on its top, spilling the contents onto the oak floor. It was a mishmash of pictures and mementos. And her favorite doll when she was a kid, Miss Edith.

"Fudge!" Kate knelt to put everything back. She laid her doll aside. "I'm taking her home. I forgot she was here." Her fingers paused over a familiar face.

She studied the old picture. Her father had been so handsome. His blond hair and striking blue eyes made him look like a surfer. She must have been around four here, and he was in his twenties. The adoration on her face as she'd looked up at him made her heart clench.

Shelley peered over her shoulder. "Is that you with your dad?"

"Yes."

"You never talk about him. Did he die?"

The pain in Kate's chest intensified as she

shook her head. "He and my mom were never married. He did have a wife, though. I was about twelve the last time I saw him. I have this crazy collection of pictures of him in my closet at home. Once I called his office, but I got chicken and hung up. Which I guess is good because Mom would've been furious. She forbade me to contact him."

Shelley put her hand on Kate's shoulder. "I'm sorry, Katie. That has to really hurt. Why didn't your mom want you to contact him? You're still his daughter. He owes you something."

"He bought Mom the blueberry barrens. I guess it was his payoff to get rid of us. Mom has this fear that if we ever break his edict about no contact, he will take it all away."

"I guess you wait until he contacts you, then. I bet he will."

Kate put the picture in the box and closed the lid. "Maybe someday."

The way her heart tried to beat out of her chest was from this reminder and not a symptom of her disease. But when her head spun, she stayed seated and pretended to look at other things in the closet. She'd be fine.

Claire shifted in the chair in her sitting

room at the hotel while her mother hovered nearby with a plate of fresh veggies, warm bread, and hummus. The aroma of fresh sourdough bread filled the room. Her stomach revolted at the thought of food. With the pain med humming through her veins, Claire forced herself to take a deep breath, then another. She shook her head when her mother tried to set the plate on her lap.

"You haven't eaten since breakfast, Claire Nicole, and it's after five."

Claire forced herself to accept the small plate, though she couldn't bring herself to take a bite yet. "I'm fine, Mom. I just need to rest. And, Dad, could you open the door? I need some fresh air." She'd never sleep with them fussing over her. There had to be some way to get them out of her room.

Her dad pulled open the drapes and opened the French doors to the balcony. The sea breeze rushed in and cleared Claire's head. When he turned, his expression was grim. "Someone tried to kill you today, Claire. And someone hit you over the head yesterday. You have to have some idea of why. What have you gotten yourself into? Have you offended anyone at work?"

The condemnation in his voice tightened her gut, but she lifted her chin and glared at him. "I hardly think it's my fault, Dad. I never even got a good look at him, though Luke says he was wearing camo. I wondered if he was poaching and thought I'd seen him and would turn him in."

She knew she was grasping at straws. Why commit murder over a little thing like poaching? "I have to wonder if it's the same guy who pushed Jenny off the cliff. He was wearing camo hunting clothes too."

Her father frowned and dropped into one of the chairs by the balcony door. "And what were you doing with that Luke Rocco? A man with his background is just interested in your money."

Her father's favorite tactic was misdirection. He didn't have any idea of the kind man Luke really was. "You're only upset because he told me something you'd hoped I'd never find out. You should have told me yourself." When her father's lids flickered, she knew her barb had struck home. "When do we meet with Ric to talk about the merger?"

Ric Castillo had arrived, but Claire hadn't seen him yet. She winced as she reached for her case. "I have the balance sheet and our income and expenses for the past ten years. Even I was surprised at how much our bottom line has improved. With the Castillo name and fortune behind us, we'll be in a position to rival Cessna."

The hard line of her dad's jaw eased, and he smiled. "I like the way you think. Our first meeting is tomorrow. With the time change from Madrid, Ric wanted to rest up and be fresh for our discussion."

She glanced at the door. "I'm really tired. I think I'll go to bed early. The meds are making me sleepy."

Her mother rose. "I'll check in on you before I go to bed."

"Don't bother. I'll be sleeping. If I need you, I'll call your cell phone." Claire tried to ignore the hurt in her mother's eyes, but a prickle of guilt made her reach out and grasp her mother's hand as she turned toward the door. "I'm sorry, Mom. I'm just a little grouchy."

Her mother's eyelids flickered, but she reached down and brushed a kiss across Claire's cheek. Her Hermès perfume made Claire's eyes water, and she pulled away as soon as she could. When the door shut behind them, she heaved herself up, ignoring the tightness in her back and chest. She'd be lucky if she could move tomorrow.

Opening the closet, she lifted out the satchel containing her paint supplies. Even the slight weight made her wince, but she pulled out the small canvas and propped it on the table against the vase. With her brush in hand, she closed her eyes and tried to remember the man's face she'd seen so briefly before he struck her yesterday. She'd been sure it was the same man she painted over and over again, but what if her terror had clouded her thoughts?

Dipping her brush in the green watercolor, she began to paint. An hour later she studied the image. The man's blue eyes had cruel lines around them, and his mouth held tight-lipped anger. Was this Jenny's killer or some remnant of her constant nightmares?

NINE

A light kiss brushed over Claire's forehead, and she opened her eyes to see her grandmother hovering over her with a gentle smile. "Grandma." She sat up and brushed her hair out of her face. "Where did you come from?"

"Your mother called us and told us what happened. I couldn't stay home."

Nearly eighty, her grandmother was still beautiful to Claire in spite of her wrinkles. Her dark hair and hazel eyes glowed in her olive skin. In her day, she'd been drop-dead gorgeous, and Grandpa had swooped her up when she was nineteen and he was twenty-two. Claire nestled into her grandmother's embrace and soaked in the unconditional love. Tabu, the perfume her grandmother had worn as long as Claire could remember, was just a faint scent this late in the day.

Her grandmother smoothed Claire's hair.

"Are you okay? You're very pale."

"I'm fine, Grandma."

"I am going to see the sheriff tomorrow. He must find that man at once."

No one was ever able to resist Emily Cramer's determination. Claire pitied the sheriff for a brief moment. Her grandmother would roll into that office like an implacable machine and demand results. She was richer than Croesus, but her main power over people was the way she loved them. No one wanted to see the light in her hazel eyes dim.

Claire pulled away from the embrace and swung her legs off the bed. "The sheriff will find him. In the meantime, I'll stay close to other people."

Her grandmother rose and smoothed her blue dress. She'd taught Claire the art of a perfect French roll, and not a hair on her head was out of place. She'd never adopted the bare-leg rage and always wore hosiery and pumps. But in spite of her care about her appearance, she was the most genuine person Claire had ever met.

Claire rose and began to roll up her hair. "What time is it?"

"After nine. I intended to come up the moment I heard what happened to you, but your grandfather insisted I finish dinner. You know how he can be. And your mother said you were resting. Neither of them would give me a key to your room, so I had to cajole one of the hotel employees." Her grandmother caught her hand. "Leave your hair down, honey. Get your pajamas on and climb right back into bed. If your mother comes in and finds I've disturbed your rest, I'll be in hot water."

Claire smiled. "You wouldn't be there for long. No one can stay mad at you."

She did as her grandmother suggested and let go of her hair, then raked her fingers through it. Her slacks and top were wrinkled from sleeping in them, and she went to the dresser and pulled out pink silk pajamas, wincing at the movement.

"It hurts to move?" At Claire's nod, her grandmother came to help her.

Claire let her grandma assist her in the dim light, and two minutes later she climbed under the sweet-smelling sheets. Her grandmother always made her feel treasured. Being with her was like catching a whiff of heaven.

Grandma pulled up a chair beside the bed and plumped the pillows before having Claire lean back. "I know everything that's been happening, Claire. I told Lisa all along she should have been honest with you about what happened here, but your father was adamant about keeping it mum. Your mother is entirely too easygoing with him."

Her mother had always been content to let her husband handle the messy details of life while she put her hands over her eyes. For a strong woman like Claire's grandmother, having such a weak daughter was probably a trial.

"What can you tell me, Grandma? Did I say anything after I was found that might tell you where I had been all that time?"

Her grandmother blinked and looked away. "Some of this needs to come from your father, child. One thing I can tell you is that I've loved you from the first moment I laid eyes on you."

A strange response. Claire stared into that beloved older face with its wise eyes and loving mouth. "I know that, Grandma. I've never doubted how much you love me. But about that missing year . . ."

Her grandmother leaned forward to brush another kiss across Claire's cheek. "Rest now, honey. I told Harry this day would come, but he didn't believe me." Her lips trembled. "I fear the repercussions now." She took hold of Claire's shoulders and looked into her face. "Promise me you won't ever forget how much you're loved."

Though she didn't understand her grand-

mother's intensity, Claire nodded. "I promise."

Claire watched in puzzlement as her
grandmother rose and rushed for the door.
What kind of repercussions?

Kate smiled as she watched her mother take
in the closet transformation in the light of
the overhead lamp. Dressed in jeans and a
flannel shirt with her light-brown hair
caught back in a ponytail, Mary Mason
looked closer to forty-five than her fifty-five
years old. Her flawless skin needed no
makeup, and as far as Kate knew, she'd
never even dyed her hair. She had that
elusiveness so many men found attractive,
but that standoffishness sometimes made
Kate feel as if she were an afterthought. Or
a duty, like a dog needing to be fed twice a
day.

Maybe that was why Kate tried so hard.
Just like this closet redo. Someday she
would do something that would make her
mom rush to embrace her and tell her she
loved her. Those three words had seldom
come out of her mother's mouth.

Her mother's smile was radiant. "Kate,
it's just beautiful."

"I'm glad you like it, Mom." No hug. Kate
had been silly to hope for one.

Her mother turned to her brother, Paul, who looked on with an indulgent smile. "And you were in on this?"

Kate had always adored Uncle Paul. Ten years younger than Mom, he'd been like an older brother or a young father to her. He was her island to stand on in the middle of a raging ocean. When Mom got the blueberry barrens, he'd sold most of his lobster pots and taken the reins of the business. He learned everything there was to know about the wild bushes, and Mason Blueberries flourished. He'd never married, though his dark good looks attracted plenty of female attention. Kate had seldom seen him without a girlfriend, though he changed them nearly every season.

He straightened his tall, rangy form and grinned at his sister. "Now you know why I didn't hurry you in the yarn store. I wanted to give Katie time to work her magic."

"Well, it's a lovely surprise for my birthday. And do I smell German chocolate cake?"

Kate nodded. "Yep, Shelley made it. She had papers to grade tonight but said to give you her best wishes."

Her uncle turned toward the door. "And I have several pounds of fresh lobster all ready to go. I'll get them started in the kitchen."

Her mother smiled at him. "No wonder you turned down my offer to buy dinner."

Kate waited until her uncle's heavy footsteps faded and she heard the squeak of the aging refrigerator door. "Mom, I need to talk to you about something."

Her mother closed the door to the closet. "Yes?"

Kate refused to let her cool tone put her off. "I've been thinking about Dad. Have you heard anything from him at all?"

Her mother's eyes widened before they shuttered back to their usual placid green. "No, and I don't expect to. He is out of our lives, Katie. You know that."

"D-Does he even know I've been sick?"

Her mother narrowed her eyes. "He doesn't need to know. He made it quite clear he wants nothing to with either of us."

"He's my father. What if he's a good donor match?"

Her mother moved toward the door, her movements brisk, as if she could erase their entire conversation. "You're doing fine. Just look at all you've done today — all this work! You're in perfect health."

The fatigue that hovered close seemed to settle in a heavy weight on Kate's shoulders. She wasn't about to show it to her mother,

114

though. The lobster waiting in the kitchen would help. She hadn't eaten since breakfast.

Her mother paused in the doorway and looked back at her. "Besides, haven't we been getting along just great without him all these years?"

Kate gave a jerky nod. "I was just thinking about him. He was always so much fun."

Her mother whirled to face her. Bright spots of hectic color spotted her cheeks, and her eyes burned. "And was it fun when we saw him in town that day?"

Kate's eyes filled. "No."

She'd been twelve, and it was the last time she'd seen her father. They'd gone to a blueberry festival in Bar Harbor. She spotted him across the street and shouted, "Dad!" before starting to run to him. He took one look in her direction before all the color drained from his face and then he dashed into a liquor store. Her mother had caught her arm or she might have followed him inside.

The humiliation still made her face burn.

"I didn't think so either. That's when I knew we couldn't go on the way we had. None of us."

"Why did you do it, Mom? Why did you let him treat us like that? You deserved better. So did I."

Her mother's hands curled into fists. "I loved him. I thought someday he'd change. That someday he'd leave his wife for me. But that never happened."

This was the most honest conversation she'd had with her mother in her entire life. Most of the time Mom brushed off questions like an annoying bee. Kate craved more.

"Maybe he has changed. I can find out where he lives."

Her mother's eyes went wide, and she reached out a hand toward Kate. "You can't contact him! Promise me, Katie. Never, *never* go near him."

Kate backed away. "I don't think I can make that promise, Mom. I want to at least see him. Even if it's from a distance."

Her mother shook her head with so much vehemence that her ponytail loosened. "I forbid it!"

"I'm twenty-nine years old. I'm not a child."

Her mother grabbed her arm. "Then stop acting like one! That man doesn't want anything to do with you. What happens if you waltz in and introduce yourself? You think he will welcome you with open arms? His wife will take one look at you and call security."

Kate winced when her mother's nails bit into her skin. "I don't want to hurt you, Mom, but all I can promise is I'll think about it." She gently disengaged her mother's grip. "Let's go eat dinner."

"I'm not hungry." Her mother shoved her through the doorway, then slammed the door shut behind her. The lock clicked.

Sobbing came from the other side of the closed door. Kate rapped on it. "Mom?"

A distant slam told her that Mom had gone into her bathroom and shut the door. There would be no talking to her tonight.

Her uncle appeared in the hall. "What's going on? I heard yelling."

"I messed up, Uncle Paul."

He draped his arm over her shoulders. "Your mom will get over it. The lobster's ready. You need to eat something."

She let him guide her toward the delicious aroma of butter and lobster, but she wasn't hungry any longer.

TEN

Claire touched her bruises as she twisted and turned in the mirror. No wonder she felt like she'd been hit by a speeding boat and left for dead. Lurid black-and-yellow marks covered her from her breastbone to her hips. The guy meant business. Why had he tried to kill her? Was it because she'd seen him when he killed Jenny, or did it have something to do with her missing year?

The meds made her head too fuzzy to think it through. Turning away, she pulled on a flirty red dress, then slipped her feet into strappy sandals. Ric had made no pretense about his attraction to her, and she intended to use every weapon in her arsenal to land that merger.

A tap on the door signaled room service with her breakfast, and she hurried to open the door. The broccoli-and-cheese omelet on the room service tray should have smelled delicious, but Claire's stomach still churned from the pain meds. The man carrying the tray propped the door open, then carried the tray into the room and set it on the table by the fireplace.

"Knock, knock," called a female voice from the doorway.

Claire turned to see Megan Rocco at the door with a vase of flowers in her hand.

"Mind if I come in?" Her dark hair was in a ponytail, and she wore faded jeans and a yellow long-sleeve T-shirt. The brightness of the shirt matched her smile.

"Megan, how great to see you. You're just in time for breakfast." Her gaze went over Megan's shoulder, but she didn't see Luke with her. *Fudge.* She tipped the server, then shut the door behind him and turned to gesture for her visitor to have a seat.

Megan handed her the flowers. "I wanted to see how you were feeling. Luke stopped by this morning and told me what happened yesterday. He's livid."

"I'm better. Still sore but I'll live. These are beautiful. I love lilies of the valley." Claire plunged her nose into the intoxicatingly sweet scent of the flowers, then set the vase on the fireplace mantel.

"Luke said to tell you he was meeting Beau Callahan, a sheriff's deputy friend, for breakfast to see what he'd found when he went up to the ridge yesterday. Luke will be down at the orca pen this afternoon, then he'll pop by to check on you when he's done."

"What time is he going to see the orca? I should get out and move around a bit. I could meet him before my dinner business meeting."

Megan settled in the seat by the fireplace. "About one, I think."

Claire handed her a cup of coffee. "Would you like some breakfast? This omelet is big enough to share, and I don't have much of an appetite anyway."

Megan poured cream in her coffee and took a sip. "I already ate, but thanks."

Claire smiled at Megan over the rim of her coffee cup. She needed a friend in this place. Even with her parents and grandparents here, she felt alone. Mostly because she still had no idea who she was. An entire year of her life was missing. Had it shaped her in ways she didn't even understand?

She needed to eat before she could take more pain meds, so Claire lifted the metal lid over the plate and tasted the cheesy omelet. It was as good as it smelled, but her stomach only handled a few bites. "Any idea who might have attacked me, or is the sheriff totally stumped?"

120

"The woods are full of men in camo, including my dad and brother, so that's not much of a clue. And Jenny still hasn't been found. I'm not sure Sheriff Colton knows what to believe about you seeing her falling from the cliff."

"The fact she's missing should be enough. Plus, the knot on my head and the attack that happened yesterday."

"You'd think, especially with his deputy pushing him. Andy Waters is sure she would never just leave. All their things are still at his house, and her car was in the employee lot at the inn. So something happened."

"Have they checked security cameras here at the hotel? Maybe they would show her going off with that guy."

"I'll have to ask Beau." Megan's gaze went over Claire's shoulder. "You paint?"

Claire glanced at her easel by the sliding glass door. "I just dabble. It relaxes me." She rose, wincing at the movement. "I painted the guy I saw. Maybe his face will be familiar to you. Take a look."

Megan followed her to the easel. "You're really good." She stared at the picture, then shivered. "I wouldn't want to run into him myself. He looks mean. I don't recognize him either." She frowned and pointed to the splash of red at the man's waist. "Had

121

he taken a fox? It's not hunting season for them."

Claire inhaled and studied the telltale slashes of red in the corner. She swallowed down the nausea churning in her stomach. "I did it again."

Megan took her arm. "You just went white. Here, sit down." She guided her to a chair by the door. "Should I call the doctor?"

"No, no. It's that fox. I never intend to paint one, but every now and again, after I've finished a painting, I find I've painted one into the picture somewhere. I must do it when I sleepwalk, though I never remember."

Megan's dark eyes widened. "Maybe you saw a fox hunter sometime when you were small and it scared you?"

"I've never even seen a fox, living or dead. So it's weird that I paint it in periods of high stress." She rose and went to the painting. "I wonder if I saw something like this the night I disappeared."

She studied the fox's lifeless eyes as it hung limply from the hunter's belt. It was always the same. She never painted a living fox, only dead ones. It always gave her the creeps, but today it held a special significance. It might be a clue to her past.

Megan touched her arm. "Have you re-membered anything at all of that night? Do you remember playing with a fire truck?"

Claire called a red fire truck to mind. Did it evoke any kind of emotion? "I wish it did. I don't remember anything. It's just a big blank." She rubbed her head. "I want to remember so much." She stared at Megan. "Would you take a walk with me? I'd like to wander in the woods around the inn and see if it refreshes my memory."

"I'd be glad to. There's some connection between you and my mom. I just hope we can find it." She glanced at Claire's shoes. "You might want to change those."

Claire smiled. "And this dress. I'll have to be back by three, but we've got time to try to find that missing piece of my life."

Summer Harbor Public Library was small, consisting mostly of donated books. The winters, long and hard here, were the perfect time for curling up under an afghan with a book. And the library had Wi-Fi, something Kate didn't have at home.

Libraries had been her haven since she'd discovered this one when she was eleven and could talk her mother into bringing her. The scent of decaying paper and old carpet took her to faraway lands. Between the pages of books like *Moby Dick* and *Treasure Island,* she'd gone on adventures that made her forget her small, cramped room. It was the perfect place to feel safe while she embarked on an adventure. The librarian always had a new suggestion for the gangly, awkward child she'd been.

"Let's find a quiet corner." Her pulse throbbed in her neck. It wasn't like what she was doing was wrong. She just wanted to know about a part of her family that had been hidden for far too long.

"We're really going to do this?" Shelley pulled her computer from its backpack.

They were secluded in this northwest corner near the section of genealogy books. An appropriate spot for what Kate had planned.

Kate unpacked her computer from her satchel and pulled out a chair across from her friend. "Mom clearly isn't going to tell me anything. I should have tracked him down long ago."

"But what if your mother is right, and you lose everything by contacting him? You love the blueberry barrens. What if you have to leave? Sometimes it's better to let things be, Kate."

Kate chewed her lip. "Right now let's just see what we can find out. Before I contact him I'll check with the attorney about our ownership of the barrens. I won't reach out unless we're safe. Will that satisfy you?"

"A good plan. Where do we look first?"

"Let's just Google him." Kate called up a web browser and typed in her father's name. Many articles about him appeared, but nothing that indicated his current address. She went back to the original search and opened an interview in *Fortune* magazine. "Look at that car in the background. I think it's a Jaguar."

Shelley leaned in closer. "You come from money, girlfriend."

Kate straightened. "I don't care about that."

Shelley's green eyes held compassion. "I know feeling like your dad didn't want you has been hard. Maybe there's more to it than you know and he's wanted more contact with you."

Kate blinked at the sting in her eyes. "I wish that were so, but it's not." She told her about the incident where he'd avoided her. It wasn't something she liked to think about, and she'd kept the humiliation of that incident to herself.

"There might have been a good reason. Maybe his wife has all the money, and he didn't want to run the risk of tipping her off."

"I never saw him after that. If he cared about me at all, he'd have made sure I had the money to go to college, that I had enough food and clothing. He has never so much as called Mom to check on me."

"Are you sure?" Shelley said the words carefully as if she were picking her way through a field of briars.

"What do you mean?"

"It's not unheard of for moms or dads who split from each other to be jealous and try to turn their kid against the other parent."

Kate considered that for a moment. Mom made no bones about her dislike of her dad. Was it possible? Though her mom wasn't the warm, affectionate type, Kate didn't want to believe she'd be so vindictive.

She shook her head. "I don't think so, but I guess if I contact the family, I'll find out for sure."

Shelley began to click away on her computer. After a few minutes she sat back with an irritated grunt. "I couldn't get his cell, but you said you have his address and home phone number in Boston."

"I want to contact him, but let me check something." Kate pulled out her cell phone.

"I'm going to call our attorney and make sure he can't hurt Mom."

She spoke to him for a few minutes, then laid her phone back on the table. "He says the property belongs to Mom, and there's no way my father can get it back."

"Do you think your mother just told you that to keep you from contacting him?"

"Maybe." Kate rubbed her eyes, then glanced up at the clock on the wall. Her afternoon nap seemed very far away. Thankfully, Shelley had driven them. "I think I should go see him in person."

"Boston is close enough for a weekend. We could leave after school on Friday."

Kate's mood lightened. "You'd go with me?"

"I wouldn't let you do it alone."

"You're the best!" She opened the calendar on her iPad and looked at her schedule. "The blueberry plants have all been pruned so I can get away next weekend."

"Road trip!"

Kate smiled at Shelley's enthusiasm. They'd need all the energy they could get to do this.

ELEVEN

The evergreen needles littering the path released their piney scent underfoot as Claire wandered the pink-granite walkway with Megan. In the shade of the spruce, red oak, and white pine, the foggy breeze rolled down her neck. Her heart rate was running as fast as the bunny that dashed away when they approached. Her throat felt tight, as though she would burst into tears at any moment.

She took several deep breaths to calm herself. She'd like to rush from the forest and find her way to the ocean's edge where she'd find a soothing rhythm in the tide, but she forced herself to stand her ground. Running wouldn't fix anything, and it certainly wouldn't allow her to discover the truth.

Moving hurt, but she continued anyway, and the activity eased some of the pain. Something about the carpet of white flowers to her right triggered a shudder that ran clear through her. She stopped so quickly that Megan nearly bumped into her.

"What's wrong?"

"I'm not quite sure." Claire stared at the wildflowers. "That's spurge, isn't it?"

"I'm not a botanist, but that's what my dad always called it."

Claire leaned down, but the flowers held no fragrance. She touched a soft petal. "I'm a city girl, and the thought of hiking or the wilderness gives me hives. It's normally all I can do to tell the difference between a dahlia and an iris. But I know the wildflower's name and that it's poisonous." She straightened and examined the vegetation in the dappled clearing. "It's all I can do to stand here and not run away. What is this place? I-I think I've been here before."

"We call it Hunter's Circle. I'm not sure why, but my dad might know. I think it's from an old Indian legend. On the other side of the clearing the forest gets really thick and deep. Any manmade path ends, and you'll find only deer trails. It stays that way clear up to Canada." She looked back at Claire. "There are supposed to be a lot of fox in this area."

"Maybe this is where I saw the hunter with the fox on his belt. The more I think about it, the more I believe it's a real memory, not just a nightmare."

Megan touched her shoulder. "You are breathing pretty fast. You want to get out of here?"

Claire shook her head. "I want to go as far as the trail end and see if I remember anything." Ignoring the sour taste in her mouth, she set off on the granite path again. "I have to find that missing year. I have to know what happened to me."

"You've got grit, girl." Megan fell into step beside her. "But you were just a kid. Why does it matter so much?"

"I didn't live on my own in the woods for a solid year when I was only four. Someone had me while the entire state was searching for me. Why did they keep me? I have to wonder if there's something bigger going on. Maybe the attacks on me have to do with what happened so many years ago and have nothing to do with Jenny's disappearance."

Her words rang true. Her entire world had been turned on its head. She wasn't even sure she could trust her parents anymore. What had been their motive in hiding all this? Nothing made sense.

The leaves rustled under Megan's feet as she stepped forward. "The path goes this way. We might as well get this over with."

Claire followed her, but with every forward motion, her breathing grew more labored. At first she thought it was just her injury, but the fluttery sensation along her spine told her it had nothing to do with her broken ribs. Terror, pure and simple, swelled with every step.

This direction led to something that heightened every sense and narrowed her vision to a pinprick. Her legs felt weighted down as she moved along the path. The trees grew thicker and denser here, blotting out the sunlight.

Her gaze fell on a gnarled and aged tree, and she went toward it as if in a trance. She'd seen this tree in her nightmares. She touched her fingertips to the bark. The shock of the rough texture rooted her to the moment. She knew this tree.

"There's a hole in this tree. Back here." Claire stepped around the tree. "There."

The hole was about chest level. Off to one side, the initials *C.D.* were carved into the bark. Claire Dellamare. Standing on her toes, she reached up and plunged her hand into the hole. Her fingers closed around something soft, and she pulled it down. "It's a scarf."

The scarf was riddled with holes from

animals, but the silk had once been beautifully patterned with rose flowers. She closed her eyes and could almost see the woman wearing this scarf, but the memory flitted by as fast as a hummingbird.

Megan inhaled sharply. She took the scarf, then lifted it to her cheek. "Claire, this belonged to my mother. She's wearing it in the pictures taken the day she disappeared. How did you know it was there?"

"I don't know." Claire's gut clenched when Megan's face fell. "I want to remember, but I just can't."

The silk scarf seemed to burn a hole in Luke's pocket as he opened the door to his dad's farmhouse with Claire and Megan on his heels. "He's probably napping." He shut the door behind the women.

Knowing Claire was seeing the space for the first time, he looked at the house through new eyes. The old floorboards had seen better days. His boots had left his fair share of chips in the old oak over the years, and the railing and baluster could use refinishing. He'd rolled his toy cars and trucks down the battered steps many a time. The wallpaper hadn't been updated, though the dainty blue flowers were still in good condition and clung tightly to the plaster walls.

The living room was just off the entry, and he peeked inside to find his father, clad in his customary overalls, snoring in the recliner. The stale scent of sweat hung in the air. Since his stroke, his father had resisted showers and only recently allowed Luke to help him. The wheelchair was beside the recliner, and Pop's head tilted to one side in an awkward angle. What did Claire think of the threadbare orange-and-brown plaid sofa and chairs and the battered end tables? Though clean, nothing had been replaced in all the time his mother had been gone.

How would Pop react when he saw the scarf? Luke prayed it wouldn't trigger another stroke. He cleared his throat. "Pop?"

His dad's eyes fluttered, then opened. He fixed his pale-blue eyes on Luke for a moment before straightening. His gaze went to Claire and lingered. He swiped at his sparse white hair. "I'm all stoved up. Who've you brought in, Luke?" His slurred words were soft.

"This is Claire Dellamare."

His rheumy eyes sharpened, and he looked her over. "Dellamare. The little girl who

133

went missing?"

"Yes."

"You don't say! After all these years!"

Luke motioned for Claire to have a seat. "We found something today. I'm pretty sure I know what it is. Beau is on his way here to retrieve it, but I wanted to show it to you first."

He reached into his pocket and entangled his fingers in the soft material. When he pulled it out, he wasn't sure at first his dad recognized it. He stared blankly at the scarf. Then his father's face sagged, and he blinked rapidly. "The body was hers. The one in the bog."

Luke had to evade the question since Beau had asked him to let the sheriff tell his dad about the dental records ID. "This was hidden in a tree trunk." Luke turned his head to stare at Claire. "Claire found it." He inhaled. "Pop, I don't want to upset you or make you feel I blame you for anything, but I have to bring up something Aunt Nancy said."

His father blinked and frowned. "I suppose she brought up that wicked-crazy idea she had about that missing kid." He pronounced *kid* like *shid* with his speech difficulty. "Don't think I haven't wished a thousand times I'd listened to her and gone out myself that night." He sagged back in his chair like a deflated ball. "She might still be alive if I'd paid attention." His rheumy eyes glimmered with moisture.

Her expression intent, Claire leaned forward. "So you *do* remember she'd mentioned the child? That little girl who was missing was me, Mr. Rocco. I don't know how I knew where to find the scarf, but I did. What did she say about me?"

His dad reached up with a trembling hand to rub his liver-spotted forehead. "Lordy, I can't remember exactly, girlie. It was more than twenty-five years ago. I thought it foolishness at the time. We can pull-haul all afternoon about it, but it won't change nothing. She's still dead and has been all these years. Some people thought she left me, but I always knew better."

Luke studied his father's face and found the guilt and remorse in his teary eyes a bit too pat. If he'd been regretful all these years, why hadn't he ever mentioned it to his children? For the first time, he looked at his father with a critical eye. There'd been whispers growing up. Some adults suggested Walker Rocco had killed his wife and buried her body in the cranberry bogs. Luke never believed it, but what if all his father's determination to find his wife was to quiet those rumors?

He glanced at Megan and saw his own doubts reflected in her dark-brown eyes. Their father was a taciturn man, and for the first time in his life, Luke wondered what dark events fueled those secrets.

TWELVE

Claire leaned against the warm hood of Deputy Callahan's car and listened to Megan tell the officer how they'd found the scarf. The cranberries covered the bogs in the fields across the road, and two workers walked between the low bushes.

She couldn't quite decipher the expression on Luke's face since they'd talked with Mr. Rocco. Luke seemed quiet and reflective, though as far as she could tell, his father had been honest with them.

Callahan lifted a brow. "So you just knew it was there and you have no real memory of the night Victoria Rocco put it there?"

"That's right. I recognized the tree, and I knew there was a hiding place. I didn't know what was in there until I put my hand in the hole." She curled her fingers into her palms at the memory of first touching that silky material. There had been just a flash of . . . something, but she hadn't been able to grasp it before it blew off like a dandelion puffball.

"I see."

Was that skepticism in the deputy's eyes? She desperately wanted to be back at the hotel while she lost herself in painting. Her chest hurt, and so did other muscles. But Luke had brought her here, and she didn't have a way back to town until he was ready to take her. Which needed to be soon. She had to be back by three to get ready for her business dinner with Ric and his family.

Callahan straightened. "How well did you know Jenny Bennett?"

"Not well at all. We spoke once on the phone, but we never talked of anything personal."

"You're sure?"

"Of course. I met her for the first time on Thursday when I arrived."

"Then why would she send a letter advising the sheriff that you're not who you say you are?"

A wave of dizziness washed over her, and she reached out to find something solid to hang on to. Strong, warm fingers grasped hers, and Luke's arm came around her waist.

She opened her eyes and looked into the deputy's shuttered expression. "I-I don't understand. How could she say something like that when she didn't even know me?"

"You tell me." He pulled a paper from his pocket and unfolded it. "The sheriff will have a fit if he knows I'm showing this to you, but I think there is more to this than we know. Here, take a look."

The paper was a photocopy of a typed letter. She skimmed it with Luke reading over her shoulder.

Dear Sheriff Colton,

Harry Dellamare is coming to Folly Shoals this weekend, and I've recently learned some disturbing information about Claire Dellamare. She's not who she says she is. There is a huge conspiracy swirling around her, and if you get to the bottom of it, I think you'll discover a murderer. Look back about twenty-five years.

A Concerned Citizen

It was all she could do not to ball up the letter and toss it in the deputy's face. She glared at him as she handed back the letter. "You think this letter implicates me in her murder, don't you? I certainly didn't hurt Jenny. I was only four."

Callahan refolded the letter and put it in

139

his shirt pocket. "Do you have any idea what it means?"

"No." Her hands curled into fists. "You think I killed her to cover up whatever she thought she knew."

The deputy hesitated, then shook his head. "If I thought that, I wouldn't have shown you the note. But it's pretty clear that whatever Jenny knew got her killed."

Luke's breath whispered past her ear. "So we need to retrace Jenny's steps and see if we can find out what she meant."

Callahan glanced from Claire to Luke. "We won't have long. Danny is ready to hang her."

Claire inhaled and pressed her hand to the sharp pain in her chest. She hated feeling weak and out of control. "Should I contact my attorney?"

Luke's grip around her waist tightened. "You want to sit down? There's a swing on the porch. I should take you back."

"It's time for more pain meds," she admitted. "I'm pretty done in, and really, there's nothing more I can tell you, not even about that night, let alone about what this letter means. I must have seen your mother, but remember, I was only four. I can't recall the dress I was wearing, what kind of cake we had, or the toys I received. It's all a blank."

But was it? When she said the word *dress,* she had a flash of an image. She closed her eyes and pursued the memory. "I-I think I remember my dress. It might have had ruffles, like a princess dress." She opened her eyes. "I have to ask my mom!" She pulled her cell phone from her purse. "I'll call her." Her gut clenched as her mother picked up on the other end.

"Claire, where are you? I've been looking everywhere for you. Ric wanted to meet you for coffee before dinner."

"I'll be back by three." Focus, she had to focus. She couldn't let her missing year derail this merger. "Mom, what did my dress look like at my fourth birthday party?"

"Let's not worry about something that happened over twenty-five years ago, Claire."

She turned her back to the rest of the group. "This is important, Mom. What color was my dress?"

Her mother heaved a sigh. "It was pink with lots of ruffles. I had it designed especially for the party, and you twirled around like you were a princess in it."

Ruffles. "That's what I thought. Listen, I have to go. I'll talk to you later." She hung up over her mother's objections. She turned back around to face the deputy and the

141

Roccos. "It was pink. With ruffles."

Callahan's expression sharpened. "So you are beginning to remember. Have you ever thought about being hypnotized to see if you can uncover more?"

She shuddered. "I'm not about to let someone take control of me when I'm sleeping. I can't fathom anything more repugnant. Since I'm starting to remember, I'm hopeful more will come." She turned toward Luke's truck. "I need to get back to the hotel, Luke. Would you run me there?"

"Of course." He took her arm.

The strength of his fingers wrapping her forearm made her want to move closer. Why did he draw her so? Could they have known each other when she was small?

Callahan glanced at Megan. "Can you take me to the site? I want to search in that tree cavity a little more in case there's something else in there."

"Sure, but I shone my flashlight in it before we left and didn't see anything."

"I still want to check." The deputy opened his car door. "I'll just follow you."

"Sorry if this set you back some. I wasn't thinking,"

"It's perfectly all right." She slid into the cab of his truck after he opened the door for her. All she had to do was compartmentalize this, tuck it away until she could take it all out and examine it. Tonight she had to close that merger and prove to her father that she could handle anything.

Kate and Shelley left the library and went down a street and over two blocks, guided by the Presbyterian church spire, its white steeple vivid against the blue sky. She wanted to mull over what she'd found at the library, and wandering the market would give her a chance to think.

The Farmer's Market took up a full city block. It started in the church parking lot and spread west. Tables displaying everything from flowers to candy and trinkets intermingled with preserves and canned goods. Come summer, there would be baskets overflowing with local produce.

Shelley zipped her jacket to her chin. "Looking for anything special?"

"Maybe some dried herbs. I thought I'd try a new chili recipe for supper."

The May wind raced down Kate's back. Maybe this hadn't been such a good idea when she could go home and curl up with her knitting. She'd been so cold today, another bad sign. She stopped to finger some local wool in a brilliant blue hue, then bought four skeins, though the price made her wince.

She stuffed them in her oversized bag. "This will make a gorgeous throw for the foot of my bed."

Shelley wandered over to a table with dried herbs. "Is this what you're looking for?" She pointed out hanging bunches of herbs.

"Sure is." Kate purchased some baggies of oregano, cumin, and chili powder. "I'm ready to get out of this wind. I say we head back to my place and have some coffee."

She hefted her bag to her shoulder, then froze when she saw a familiar span of shoulders. Her lungs didn't want to work, and she stood gaping at the man until she could draw in some oxygen. There were wings of white at his temples, and he'd shaved his mustache, but she'd recognize her father anywhere.

"What's wrong?"

"I-It's him." Kate could barely manage a whisper.

Shelley craned her neck. "Who?"

Kate's heart tried to pound its way out of her chest. How long had he been here? More importantly, was he here to see them?

She gave a quick nod his direction. "My father. He's *here.*"

"You're kidding." Shelley turned to study

the couple standing in front of a display of quilts. "Is that his wife?"

Kate tore her gaze from her father's handsome face and looked over the woman with him. "I think so. I've never met her, but I saw a picture of the two of them together."

Her attention went back to her father. He wore white slacks pressed to a crisp line. His navy jacket over a white collared shirt was casual and elegant at the same time. A gold watch gleamed at his wrist. And those shoes looked like Italian leather. Even on vacation, he made sure his attire proclaimed his wealth.

Kate's eyes blurred, and she blinked back the moisture. So many years without a word, then he showed up here in the middle of town.

"You think he called your mother?"

"No. He wouldn't have called Mom with his wife here. He probably thought he could bring his trophy wife here without running into Mom." She didn't look like a trophy wife, though. Yes, she was well dressed with perfect hair and makeup, but there were fine lines around her eyes. This was the same woman he'd been married to when he'd been sleeping with Kate's mother.

Jealousy snaked through her stomach. If not for this woman, she and Mom might have had a perfect life. She might not have had to wear the label of illegitimate. Dad had loved this woman more than Mom. More than his own daughter. Her jaw ached from clenching her teeth. She took a step toward them.

Shelley's fingers landed on her arm. "This isn't the time or place, Kate. Think this thing through."

Kate stopped and tried to swallow, but her mouth was too dry. "He's walked in the shadows for too long. It's time he was exposed for who he is."

"If you do this, you'll never have a relationship with him. You have to approach it gently, humbly. Without making demands on him or throwing blame in his face." Shelley's voice was low and passionate. "Don't let your emotions ruin what might be if you do this differently."

Breathe. In and out. In and out. Kate let Shelley's persuasive words sink in. "You're right. But what if he leaves before I get a chance to talk to him? He might just be passing through."

"I don't think so. Look." Shelley nodded at them as they walked toward the pier. "They came on the Hotel Tourmaline ferry. They just handed their shopping bags to my cousin who works there. They're staying in the area, at least for tonight. Most people who go out to Folly Shoals stay several days at least. You can think about it and maybe approach him when he's alone. Let me ask my cousin how long he's staying and that will tell us how quickly you need to act."

They were leaving anyway. Kate nodded and watched her father hold his wife's elbow. He assisted her into the shuttle, and she turned a loving smile his direction. A smile that should have belonged to her and her mother.

The Oyster Bistro hummed with low voices and the clink of silverware. The scent of seafood made Claire's mouth water since she hadn't eaten since breakfast. Once her eyes adjusted to the dim light of the dining room, she spied her parents and the Castillos seated in a large back table by a big window overlooking the patio, gaily lit with string lights. Her father had probably demanded the best spot in the house.

Her gut tightened when she saw Ric's dark head bent attentively to her mother, and she stood for a moment to steel herself for the coming skirmish. They hadn't been served yet, so the evening stretched much too long in front of her. Ric's sister would make the evening fun, but his father and stepmother's bickering would make navigating the merger talk very treacherous. The older Castillos opposed the merger, but Ric and his sister held the majority vote since his father's semiretirement.

Her father, dressed in crisp slacks and a collared blue-striped shirt, stood. He smiled and motioned for her to join them. Her legs felt heavy as she wove through the restaurant to the table.

Ric stood and took her hand when she arrived. His eyes caressed her. "There you are, my dear. I've been waiting breathlessly all day to see you." His Spanish accent added to the charm of his words.

She wanted to snatch her hand away when he rubbed his thumb sensuously over her palm, but she forced herself to smile up at him. This merger was more important than his flirtation.

Claire smiled across the table at Francisca, Ric's sister. "Sorry I'm late."

Francisca was Claire's age, and since their families ran in the same circles, the two of them had been casual friends since childhood, coming in contact once or twice a year. Like Ric, Francisca had dark-brown hair and eyes. On Ric, that darkness simmered in a brooding countenance, but his sister's frank, open smile welcomed everyone into an inner circle.

Francisca's eyes held worry. "I heard what happened to you. How are you feeling, my friend?"

"It still hurts to breathe, but I'm doing all right. It was good for me to be out and about today."

Ric directed an intense stare her way. "You look beautiful tonight, Claire. I've missed you. I thought we might go out on my boat one day this week if you like. We can discuss the merger at length."

Her smile felt brittle and forced. "You sailed it up the coast?"

"Not me, but my captain. I thought you might like to see the new clipper. She is most spectacular. He tells me he saw some humpbacks breaching all along here as he came in. I am quite sure we can see some when we go out. I shall captain it myself on our trip, of course."

Ric knew her love of all things to do with the sea, and it might be the best opportunity to get him to agree to the merger. "I'd like that."

He leaned back in his chair with a confident smile. "I look forward to it."

Ric's stepmother, Bridget, smiled in Claire's direction. "Francisca cut her hair since you saw her last. It's very chic, though

I'd look terrible bald like that."

Claire exchanged a commiserative glance with Francisca. Her friend's hair still covered her ears so it wasn't that short, but Francisca was used to dealing with Bridget's constant sense of competition. Bridget had been a model when Alberto met her at a society function. He promptly divorced Ric and Francisca's mother and married Bridget five years ago, though he was twenty years older.

Francisca reached for her water. "You should try this style, Bridget. Everyone says it makes me look five years younger."

Bridget's eyes narrowed, and her mouth grew pinched. She didn't respond to Francisca's barb, probably because she didn't want to discuss age. The trauma of turning forty had sent her to bed for a week. Claire suspected the "trauma" had actually been a facelift and, judging from Bridget's still-reddened skin, had been harsher than necessary.

Claire took out the file folder in her satchel. "I have some figures for you to look at, Ric. As you will see, the merger will be hugely profitable for you. We have several small jet models that are filling a much-needed niche in the market. It's an area that Castillo Aviation hasn't ventured into yet."

Ric took the folder and slid it under his chair. "I'll take a look at this later. Let's talk more about this when we're alone, Claire."

His glance at his father told her the older Castillo still opposed the merger. She reached for her water. "Of course."

THIRTEEN

The setting sun threw rays of gold and red over the roof of Hotel Tourmaline. The backdrop of color against the stone added to its charm. Kate had never taken the ferry out here before, and she gawked at the grand yet welcoming hotel. She imagined her father sipping wine as he smiled and chatted with his wife. What would he think if he knew she was out here? How would his wife react?

Shelley touched her arm. "I just talked to my cousin. He said your dad has reservations at the Sea Room, a really nice restaurant in the hotel, for tomorrow night so he'll be there at least a couple more nights. He also has a tee time at the golf course at seven thirty tomorrow morning. I'd bet he'll be here all week. You have time to figure out what to do."

Kate took a step toward the front of the hotel where light gleamed out of floor-to-ceiling windows. "I know exactly what I want to do. I want to go in there and ask the front desk to call him."

Shelley's red hair swayed with the shake of her head. "I think you should talk to him alone. If you get his wife mad too, you'll get nowhere. What if you approach him after his round of golf? He and his father-in-law are playing eighteen holes, so they should be done around twelve thirty. You could come a little earlier than that." She turned and pointed to the south side of the building. "That path leads from the clubhouse to the inn. There's a nice grove of oaks with some benches along the walk. You could wait there."

The thought of all that family she didn't know clogged her heart with regret. "I probably have cousins. Maybe even another aunt or uncle. And grandparents." Her mother's parents lived on the West Coast, and she'd only seen them twice in her life. She had her uncle Paul and he was great, but even cousins might have supplied the closer sibling-like connection she longed for.

Shelley rubbed her forehead. "Don't get your hopes too high, Kate. Your mom has already warned you he doesn't want to have anything to do with you. Be prepared for him to turn you away."

The thought of that rejection made Kate's stomach clench. Could she handle it? She straightened and stared at the inn. "I won't let him." She glanced down at her jeans and sweater. "How about we have dinner in the Oyster Bistro tonight?"

"It's more casual than the Sea Room so we're probably dressed appropriately. You want to see if he's hanging around, don't you?"

"I just want to observe him a little. I've only seen him at my house. Seeing how he acts in other settings might tell me more about his character."

Shelley pursed her lips and frowned. "We already know his character leaves a lot to be desired. He had a long-term affair and abandoned his daughter. Not a good guy in my book."

Kate held back a wince. Shelley was just speaking the truth. "I still want to see what I can find out. You game?"

"I'm always game." Shelley started up the walk toward the massive glass entry doors.

Kate fell into step beside her, though her heart hammered in her chest. What if her dad recognized her? But no, he hadn't seen her in seventeen years. She was an adult now, and she looked very different than she did when she was twelve. Back then, she'd been all arms and legs and no shape. Her hair had been wild too.

The blond doorman, handsome in his dark-blue jacket, opened the door with a welcoming smile. "Welcome to Hotel Tourmaline, ladies. Anything I can do to help you?"

"Which way to the bistro?"

His blue eyes held appreciation as he looked Kate over. "Down the hallway to the right of the front desk. You can't miss it. The chef's special tonight is oyster po'boys. I had one for lunch, and it was delicious. Enjoy your evening."

His enthusiasm was so infectious, Kate had to smile back. "Thanks." She stopped and eyed him a moment. Did she dare ask him about her father?

Shelley frowned and gave a slight shake of her head. Fudge. Her bestie always knew what she was thinking.

Shelley grabbed her arm and propelled her across the gleaming hardwood floor. "He might have told your dad. Just play it cool, Kate."

She allowed Shelley to tug her past the front desk and the comfortable seating area in front of the fireplace that practically called to her. But once they reached the hall by the elevator bank, the aroma wafting from the bistro made her mouth water. They hadn't even eaten lunch.

Though they didn't have a reservation, it was early enough that they were seated right away. They'd scored a back corner table where she'd be able to see nearly every table and even out the door of the restaurant. They both ordered the special, and Kate surveyed the restaurant over the rim of her sweet tea. She didn't recognize anyone in the place, but the bistro's clientele was mostly tourists staying at the hotel. Locals tended to congregate at Downeast Roadhouse, a bar and grill just south of Summer Harbor.

Her po'boy was nearly gone when a group moved past her table. She instantly recognized her father. She barely glanced at the other people. "Shelley, look! Wait, don't turn. I don't want to cause a scene." Her gaze ranged over her father's face. She watched hungrily as the group walked out of the restaurant.

Kate paid the bill and rose. "Let's get out of here. I don't think I can take any more."

The moon glimmered on the whitecaps rolling into the rocky shore, limning the sea with ghostly light, and the scent of kelp and salt hung in the air. Feet dangling off the edge, Luke sat with Meg on the edge of the Folly Shoals pier.

Claire was in the hotel, a mile away, yet much further in reality. And why did he care? He'd only known her a few days, yet his thoughts turned to her constantly. Something about her vulnerability and determination drew him. He reached into the bucket and threw a fish to the orca. The little mammal caught it in midair, then almost seemed to smile at him and beg for another. He obliged and tossed him another fish.

Meg leaned back on her hands, and the moon illuminated her face. "You're awfully quiet. I think we're both worrying about the same thing. We might as well talk about it."

Luke glanced at her. "Pop's reaction this afternoon was peculiar. He never mentioned that crying child before today. Tell me I'm wrong for being suspicious."

"You aren't wrong. I feel awful for even thinking it, but what if he had something to do with Mom's death?"

With her bald statement, the fear lay bare and stark. And somehow ridiculous. "It's not possible, is it?"

She sighed and crossed her ankles. "I wish I could say it wasn't, but you're older than I am. I'm sure you remember how they

157

fought even more than I do. And he hit her a couple of times, I think."

"He did. I heard him apologize once, but he's always been a hard man."

"I'm sure they investigated him when Mom disappeared and didn't have any evidence."

Luke had been holding on to that hope, but it was a flimsy thread to cling to. "There's no telling what other evidence they found in the makeshift grave. What if they uncover something that implicates Pop? What if he really did it?"

Did he just say that? He rubbed at the sting in his eyes. What kind of son suspected his own father of something so heinous?

He tossed the orca the last of the fish. "My life was a whole lot less complicated a month ago. I'm beginning to wish I'd never come home."

Meg lay back on the pier, her face up to the sky. "You would have had to now anyway. This is something we have to face together. I'm going to believe in Pop's innocence until there's no other option."

"I don't want us to be blindsided, Megan. I have to know the truth."

"And how are you going to find it out? The sheriff's department will tell us if there is anything to worry about."

The orca leaped into the air and splashed down. The cold spray striking Luke's legs sharpened his thoughts. He didn't have the greatest confidence in the easygoing sheriff and his limited resources. Their father had been part of the community all his life. There had been a Rocco family living in that old house for five generations. Sheriff Colton had been their father's friend for thirty years. The sheriff was apt to give the family a pass unless the evidence was over-whelming.

"I'm not so sure, sis. Colton would do just about anything for Pop. There have been a lot of rumors over the years. Maybe we've been wrong about what we believed. I just know I have to find out the truth. Even if I don't really want to know it."

Meg fell silent, but her gaze never left his face. She finally cleared her throat. "Okay, I'm with you. Knowing the truth is better than pretending there are no monsters among us when we know there are. I just don't want to think our dad could be one of them."

"I don't either." He heaved another sigh. "There's more, Meg." He told her about the letter Jenny sent to the sheriff.

Meg's eyes grew wide. "What could Jenny have meant?"

"I don't know, but I think we need to see if we can retrace Jenny's movements and find out who told her what."

A frown hovered between her dark eyes. "Claire's totally gotten past your defenses, hasn't she?"

"I like her, if that's what you mean. I think Jenny was given false information."

"I don't think she's to blame for anything, but she's connected to Mom's death in some way. That should be enough to make you guard your heart. This whole ordeal may turn so ugly that she has to escape all thoughts of it. Where will that leave you if you fall for her?"

He considered the question. Meg knew him too well, and trying to lie to her would be futile, even if he were so inclined. "I'm not falling for her. I just want to find out what happened."

She laughed and shook her head. "I like her too. She's not running from this but is facing it head-on, even if it brings her discord with her family. I admire that. But she runs in very different circles. She's been used to the best of everything. I suspect she'll take over the family business soon. I'm not sure I'd like to see you married to an executive who has to fly all over the country every week."

He got up and grabbed the empty bucket. "Whoa, no one said anything about marriage! I just met the woman. Yes, I like her, but you're making some pretty huge assumptions."

Meg hopped up too and slipped her feet into her flip-flops. "I might be your baby sister, but I've got eyes in my head. I've never seen you look at any woman like you look at her."

He set off toward the shore, his bare feet slapping the weathered boards of the pier. "Let's worry about what happened to Mom and forget my love life."

She fell into step beside him. "I will if you will."

"Deal."

FOURTEEN

On the balcony of her suite, Claire lifted her face to the sea breeze and inhaled the night scent of sea, dew, and newly mown grass. Moths, drawn by the light flooding from the French doors, fluttered against the glass in an eerie staccato that set her nerves on edge.

Francisca kicked off her heels and sank onto the lounge chair beside her. "I was so ready to get away from Bridget."

"She seemed very curious about me missing for a year. I was uncomfortable."

Francisca lay back on the lounge. "What do you remember?"

"Nothing really. I feel like that entire year I was missing has been hidden from me on purpose and I don't know why."

"Wait, you mean your *padre* did not discover your whereabouts during that time?"

Claire leaned on the railing and lifted her

face into the breeze, smelling of kelp. "Dad claims he doesn't know. I mean, I was *somewhere* for that year. I think he knows but doesn't want to tell me. What could be so terrible that he has to keep it from me?" She turned to face Francisca.

Francisca wrapped a lock of dark hair around her finger. "What did your parents say when you asked for specifics?"

"Nothing. I have to wonder how hard he looked, though, because if he'd really looked, surely he would have found something. He's a very determined man."

Francisca adjusted the pillow at the top of the lounge and eased back. "Downeast Maine is such a remote area. Maybe some family out in the mountains had you. If they didn't have any close neighbors, no one would have reported anything."

Claire bit her lip. "But wouldn't they have reported a child they'd found? And then how did I get back to my parents? I have even begun to wonder if I'd been kidnapped and held for ransom, but my parents don't want to tell me."

Francisca gasped and put her hand to her chest. "Kidnapped! That's pretty farfetched."

"It happens all the time, and it would explain a lot of things. Like my grandmother's reaction." Claire hunched her shoulders and turned to look out at the sea. She probably shouldn't have brought it up. "Like why no one wants to admit where I was."

"But why would kidnappers hold you for an entire year?"

Claire thought about it. "Maybe the money drop went wrong, and they were trying to teach my dad a lesson. Maybe it took him awhile to get the money they wanted." Weak excuses. Francisca was right. There was more to it than a simple kidnapping. She rubbed her chest. "I'd better take some more pain meds. This is all so confusing." She retrieved her purse from beside her and shook out a pill, then swallowed it with a sip from her water bottle.

"Maybe you should rest. You could have died out there, Claire. What is the sheriff doing to find who did this to you?"

"I don't know. He hasn't shared any details with me."

"Wait here. I have an idea." Francisca rose and shooed away the moths before she opened the French doors and stepped inside. She returned a few moments later with Claire's sketchpad and a pencil. She handed them to Claire. "Draw what you remember."

Claire's fingers closed around the pencil. The familiar feel of it gave her comfort. "I told you I didn't see him clearly."

"No, but you saw his feet and his pants leg as he was kicking you. You heard something. Write it all down."

The pain in Claire's chest was easing with the medication. She flipped open the cover of the pad and ran her hand over the thick, heavy paper. The touch of her favorite medium opened her imagination. Images began to flood her mind. "You're right. His boots were heavy and just over the ankle. His pants were khaki, and he had them tucked into his boots."

The pencil scratched over the thick paper almost of its own volition as the images flowed from her fingertips. By the time she was finished, she knew the sole was loose on the man's boots, and he probably wore about a size twelve. There was a tear on the left hem of the hunting pants too. It wasn't much, but it was more than she'd had this morning.

Ankles crossed, Kate sat with Shelley on a bench along the green belt between the hotel and the golf course. A fog mull had moved in from the ocean during the night and hovered about three feet above the ground in a chilling mist that abruptly gave way to clear blue skies overhead. A few flags on the greens flapped in the brisk wind at the top of the hill.

Weariness dogged her as she jiggled her foot and watched the path. Her fatigue wasn't a good sign. "You'd think they'd be done by now." Glancing down at her attire, she hoped she'd dressed up enough with the skirt and pumps. She'd nearly pulled on her usual jeans, then decided to take it up a notch. He wasn't apt to welcome her with open arms if she dressed like a yard keeper. She picked at a piece of lint that didn't want to come off.

"It's Sunday, so the course is packed." Shelley tucked a strand of red hair behind her ear. "It should be soon. My cousin said the new group teed off at ten so they'll have to be done and out of the way soon. Do you know what you're going to say?"

"I thought I'd wing it, maybe strike up a conversation about the weather. I want to see if he recognizes me."

Shelley frowned. "Kate, you shouldn't get your hopes up."

Kate opened her mouth, then closed it again. What rebuttal could she have? Shelley was right. What would she gain from this exchange today? He wasn't suddenly going to welcome her into his life with open arms. Though he'd done just that once upon a time when she was small.

The realization made her sag against the park bench until Shelley tugged her arm and hissed, "There he is! His father-in-law is with him."

Her pulse hammered as she watched him stroll along the path beside the older man. Neither of them had their clubs, so she assumed they were being handled by an employee. Her father wore khaki slacks and a red shirt that made his graying hair gleam. He had an easy stride that proclaimed his status and confidence. He no longer looked like a surfer as he had in the old picture she'd found in her mother's closet.

When the men were five feet away, she casually rose and stepped toward the edge of the green space. Her gaze met her father's and she smiled. "Hi, you must be Harry Dellamare. I recognized you from a-a newspaper article."

The relaxed smile moved to an alert one. "That's right. And you are?"

She reached for some kind of answer that wouldn't get his guard up. "Um, Katherine, my name's Katherine." She waved vaguely. "I live in the village, and I'm a big fan of airplanes. I've always wanted to learn to fly, and your planes are beautiful. I've read everything I can about how you make them. I don't suppose you flew here in one, did you?"

"I brought the jet. Glad you're such a fan. The local newspaper will have pictures in next week's edition."

"I'll check it out."

She recognized the telltale way he glanced past her at the hotel. He was about to walk away. A confession hovered on the tip of her tongue. She couldn't let him go. This was her one opportunity to speak to him without his wife. Would his father-in-law have heard about her?

He started to step past her, but she put her hand on his arm. "I can't lie to you anymore. My name is Kate. Kate Mason." She watched for the flicker of his lids as he recognized her, and she felt a tingle when it came.

His polite smile didn't reach his eyes. "Ah yes, you e-mailed me about an interview. I'll answer your questions later. I really must go now."

Her mouth dangled open and she closed it. Of course. He didn't want his father-in-law to know. His manipulation took her breath away.

Shelley sprang to her feet and stood in his

path. "Um, I'm Shelley. I teach school, and I was wondering if I could talk you into speaking to my kids about setting goals to achieve their dreams. I'm sure there had to be some goal setting in your life."

He frowned. "I'm here on vacation, and I'm afraid I can't take the time."

So like Shelley to try to help her, but this time Kate needed to step up, to make him acknowledge her existence. To stop his pretense. "I'm Kate. Your daughter Kate." Her voice got smaller with each word.

He looked at his watch again. "I know you young people like to pull pranks, and I admit it's funny." His smile didn't reach his eyes. "But we need to be going."

He tried to shake her hand off, but she tightened her fingers, bolstered by his bald-faced denial. "Yes, let's call the sheriff, and he can fetch my mom. Will you look past her too? How about we do a DNA test if you're of a mind to reject me? That would be easy enough to prove, wouldn't it?"

The color drained from his face, and he looked away from her.

The other man smiled at her with a thoughtful line on his forehead. "I think she's got your eyes, Harry. It's not going to take a DNA test to prove." He put his hand on Kate's shoulder. "There's a coffee shop down the street. Why don't we all go there and talk this out a bit?"

Her father's lips flattened. "This isn't the time or place for any discussion. How about you give me your number, Kate, and I'll call you later?"

His lids flickered, and she knew he was lying. He planned to brush her off, then dodge any discussion. "Let's do that, and I'll be sure to call the newspapers and magazines. I'm sure they'll be interested in how you maintained a secret family for years. I can tell them all about how I wasn't supposed to acknowledge you if I saw you around town. And they'd be very interested in the property you bought Mom." She pulled out her phone. "Who do you want me to call first?"

His smile seemed fixed. "Honey, this isn't the time or place."

The glib endearment rattled her. Of course, that was his intention too. He was used to getting his own way with his charm. She marshaled her determination and tipped up her chin. "I simply want to know why you abandoned me, your own daughter. What happened that made you leave and never come back? I thought you loved me. You used to be so glad to see me when you'd come. Then it all changed. You may have fallen out of love with Mom, but did you have to turn your back on me too?" She choked back a humiliating sob. "And I've been *sick,* and you never even called to see how I was doing."

His eyes widened, and his gaze swept over her. "You don't look sick. I'm sorry you were hurt, honey. Like I said, I'll call you later."

The second endearment made her snatch her hand away. Through blurry eyes, she watched him hurry off with his father-in-law. Even if he was a good match for her, she didn't want his bone marrow. But he wasn't getting rid of her that easily.

FIFTEEN

The small church had drawn Claire from the moment she first laid eyes on it. Atop a small knoll, the white chapel seemed to exude welcome and acceptance. She had hurried to make the nine o'clock service with her grandmother by her side.

They entered the large oak entry and slipped into the back pew. The pain in her chest was some better today. Stained glass windows reflected colored light around the room, and the scent of decades of worshipping history hung in the air. She hadn't seen a hymnal at the back of a pew in her life, and she lifted it from its slot and turned the yellowed pages. Her church threw the worship song lyrics onto a large overhead screen.

"I like this church," her grandmother whispered. "It's been a long time since I was in a church this old and quaint."

The choir leader directed the worshippers

to turn to page 432, and she joined the chorus of "How Great Thou Art" with some awkwardness. The tune sounded vaguely familiar, but even though the song wasn't one she knew, the sense of holiness in the place reached her where she needed it. Her grandma sang with gusto as though the words resided deep inside her in some half-forgotten place.

A rich baritone voice joined in the chorus beside her, and she turned her head to see Luke and Megan had slipped into the pew with her. Luke's shoulder brushed hers, and she resisted the urge to lean into his warmth. She drank in the pastor's message about the importance of family bonds.

Maybe she'd been a little harsh judging the way her parents had kept the incident from her. Their motives had been to save her heartache.

At the final prayer, she rose with Luke and Megan. "This must be your church. It was nice."

Luke's red shirt flattered his dark hair and eyes. "We've come here since we were babies." His gaze went past her to her grandmother. "I'm Claire's friend, Luke Rocco. This is my sister, Megan."

Her grandmother extended her hand. "Emily Cramer, Claire's grandmother.

You're a handsome fellow, Luke Rocco."

Megan snickered and picked up her Bible. "Luke has never figured out that he's a chick magnet, Mrs. Cramer. He's not the heartbreaker he appears."

"I'm glad to hear it." Claire's grandmother adjusted her spring-green jacket and picked up her cream purse. "Claire, I'm going back to the hotel to rest a bit. I'll call for room service for lunch. Have fun with your friends." She pointed a pink-tipped nail at Luke. "Don't keep her long."

Claire bit her lip as her grandmother walked toward the door. Why was Grandma evading her? Did she fear Claire's questions that much?

"You look troubled," Luke said.

"Grandma knows more about my missing year than she's telling."

Megan grabbed her hand and nodded over Claire's shoulder. "There's Jenny's best friend. Let's see if she has any idea why Jenny sent that letter."

Claire turned to see a woman in her thirties heading down the church aisle. She wore jeans and heels with a white ruffled top. Her brown hair was cut in a short, sleek bob.

Luke moved to block her path. "Isabelle, you got a minute?"

"Sure, Luke. I have tuna salad waiting for me at home and an impatient cat." Her eyes flooded. "I was supposed to be in the Outer Banks with Jenny this weekend."

He put his hand on her shoulder. "I'm so sorry about Jenny."

Isabelle looked down. "Thank you."

Megan touched her arm. "Let's move to the corner so we have some privacy."

Claire glanced at the time on her iPhone. She'd need to leave in the next half hour. The group moved to the west corner under a stained glass mirror depicting a shepherd holding a lamb.

"This is about Jenny," Luke said. "We heard she sent a letter to the sheriff's office anonymously. Did you know about that?"

Isabelle's mouth gaped, and she swiped at her cheeks. "How did you know about that? She didn't sign it."

"Fingerprints. Do you know what she heard or why she felt compelled to warn the sheriff?"

Isabelle's blue-eyed gaze fell on Claire. "You're Claire Dellamare, aren't you? I recognized you from your picture in the newspaper."

Claire's chest tightened at the condemnation in Isabelle's voice. "Yes."

Isabelle turned away from Claire as if to

shut her out. "I'm not sure she should be here."

"I don't believe Claire has done anything wrong. Whatever Jenny heard probably led to her death. If you want to help us, you'll tell us what she was talking about and who told her."

"I tried to get her to tell me the man's name and she wouldn't."

"Who was this man she was talking about? Did you tell Andy anything about this? I know he's devastated."

Isabelle shrugged. "I didn't want to break Andy's heart. He doesn't know it, but he dodged a bullet."

Luke frowned. "What kind of bullet?"

"She was cheating on Andy with this older guy. She was really into him, at least at first. I found out about it and got so mad at her. She was going to break it off with Andy, but then something happened and she ended it with the other guy. She seemed afraid of him and said he had to be stopped."

"She gave you no clue as to who he was?"

"All I know is that he lives near Summer Harbor."

"Maybe he killed her," Claire put in.

Isabelle hit her with a sharp glance. "Or you did."

"I liked Jenny. I wouldn't have hurt her. I

wouldn't hurt anyone." She should stop her prattling. Isabelle wasn't buying any of it.

Kate sat on the porch of her small bungalow looking out at the sun blazing over the blueberry barrens. The stiff breeze in her face carried the sweet scent of blueberry blossoms. Her father's rejection had reverberated through her heart, and she felt numb. Alone and unloved. Why had she ever gone to see him? She should have listened to her mother's warnings. She knew just how powerless the young bird struggling to fly in the breeze felt.

How did she tell her mother what she'd done? She *thought* he wouldn't go through with his threat, but what if an attorney showed up tomorrow and pulled everything away from her mother?

She stiffened and exhaled. If he dared to do that, she'd follow through on her threat to call the newspaper. What did she have to lose by exposing him at this point? He was not a nice man. That was the hardest thing she had to admit to herself. She'd had him on a pedestal and had been sure if she could talk to him, he'd welcome her with open arms. How foolish and naive she'd been.

Tires crunched on gravel, and her uncle's old Jeep grumbled to a halt in the drive.

177

The door slammed, and his rangy form loped toward the porch. "Hey, sweet pea, what are you doing sitting out here by yourself?" Uncle Paul mounted the steps and dropped into a chair beside her.

"Just licking my wounds."

He frowned. "Wounds? What's happened?"

"I talked to Harry Dellamare today." She would stop calling him Dad. The sooner she realized there was no real fatherly love there, the better. She'd been living in a dream, but not anymore. It was time to wake up to reality.

He sat forward in his chair. "Claire, you didn't."

"Yep. And it didn't go well." The boulder in her throat grew as she relived the humiliation and rejection. "He made it sound like I was playing a joke on him, but his father-in-law realized who I was. Harry said he'd call." Her laugh was hollow. "He won't, though. He couldn't get away from me fast enough."

Paul pulled out his pipe and lit it. The pungent aroma of pipe tobacco curled along the porch. "What about Mary? Did he threaten to take her settlement?"

"No." Kate glanced at her uncle, haloed in a white fog of smoke. "He was scared. I don't think his wife has any idea that he had another family hidden away."

"Did you expect he had told her? I knew he never would. His wife was the one with all the money. If she left him, she'd take his cushy life with her. I've always suspected his in-laws heard about Mary and insisted he break it off."

"Have you ever seen his wife?" Kate couldn't explain her hunger to know more of her father's life. His other world had no relevance to hers, so where did this insatiable curiosity come from?

Uncle Paul puffed on his pipe. "I saw her with him at a restaurant once. Pretty woman, fragile, with chin-length blond hair and green eyes. A real looker. She seemed to hang on his every word." His tone held derision. "I wanted to march in there and tell her what her precious husband had been up to on his business trips here."

"But you didn't."

"Mary wouldn't let me. She still loved him back then."

"Do you know what changed? I mean, I remember how he was when I was small. He seemed to, well, to care about Mom and me. Then one day he just quit coming. I think I was about ten the last time he came here. Then I saw him that last time at the

179

festival when I was twelve."

Uncle Paul rose and tapped the remnants of the pipe tobacco out over the side of the porch into the shrubs. "It was the near exposure at the blueberry festival over in Bar Harbor that did it. I think it shook him up when he saw you both. He realized if he kept it up, sooner or later his wife would find out."

"How did he ever meet Mom? I mean, how did their relationship happen?" She'd daydreamed about it a thousand times. The course of true love often didn't run smoothly, but when she was younger, she'd believed her parents would eventually be together.

"I think you'd better talk to her about that."

"What did he do when she told him she was pregnant?" Kate had asked her mother these same questions several times, but Mom had stonewalled her and changed the subject. There was so much she didn't know.

"Again, talk to your mom."

"She won't talk about it! I can't believe she stuck with him all those years."

"She wanted to believe he loved her."

"Just like I wanted to believe he loved me. He's nothing but a manipulator. Who knows, maybe he has another family tucked away somewhere else in the country."

Her uncle gripped her shoulder, then his heavy footsteps went toward the house. When the screen door banged, Kate picked up her cell phone. "Shelley, how about we do a little surveillance?"

SIXTEEN

The hotel lobby hummed with activity as guests arrived for check-in. Claire sat with her grandmother on the sofa in front of the soaring stone fireplace while her father went to have the hotel car take them to the ferry. They were meeting Ric and his family at a restaurant in Winter Harbor for more merger discussions. Her mother and grandfather stood beside her father in front of the big glass doors, and Claire could speak without fear.

She put her hand over her grandmother's age-spotted one. "Grandma, you've been avoiding me. Why won't you talk to me?"

Her grandmother's hand twitched. "Your father is the one who has to explain it all to you. It's none of my business."

"Are you saying he knows where I was during that year?"

The older woman placed her other hand atop Claire's. "You're not going to pressure me, child. I love you dearly, but this isn't something I can get involved in. Your grandfather would be very upset if I did."

Claire glanced at her grandfather, who had turned the other way to speak with her father. "He's not listening. Where was I for that year, Grandma? And what repercussions do you fear?"

Her grandmother's hazel eyes filled with tears. "I fear this family is about to reap the whirlwind, Claire. The whirlwind." Her voice was low and choked.

The phrase sounded biblical. "What does that mean?"

"Sometimes we dabble in sin and think it will never come back to haunt us, but it does. It comes back so much worse than if we'd just been honest from the beginning. I've told your father this, but he doesn't listen. From the moment I met him, I knew he was hardheaded, intent on having his own way." Her grandmother pulled away her trembling hand. "We must all be strong enough to weather what's coming. Especially you, Claire. Reach deep to find the bedrock of your faith as the winds begin to blow."

"Grandma, you are making no sense at all. Don't talk in riddles. Tell me plainly what's wrong."

Her grandmother's gaze searched hers. "Always remember who you are, Claire. You belong to your heavenly Father and no one else. All that you are is found in him. Don't let anything shake that knowledge."

"You're scaring me, Grandma. What could be so terrible that you won't tell me?"

She looked over Claire's shoulder, and a fixed smile appeared. "They're ready for us, honey."

Claire followed her to the door, held open by the valet. She couldn't even begin to figure this out on her own. Maybe it was time to press the matter with Mom. Her dad always knew how to sidestep every issue, but her mother was bound to cave if she pushed hard enough.

With her newly dyed red hair, Kate hardly recognized herself in the mirror of The Fisherman's Inn bathroom so she doubted her father would give her a second glance. She'd be able to observe him and his precious family.

"I can't believe I let you talk me into following them." Shelley's eyes were anxious in the mirror.

"We won't get caught." After a final glance, Kate crossed to the door and marched toward the dining room with her head high. Shelley followed her.

The Fisherman's Inn in Winter Harbor was practically an institution on the Schoodic Peninsula and had been in business since 1947. Though housed in a white wooden building with plain furnishings, the food was the real star, especially the smoked salmon spread served as a free appetizer. The restaurant looked out on the harbor at Winter Harbor. The windows were set high at the booths. The scents of seafood and smoked meats teased her nose, and Kate's stomach rumbled. She spotted her target in the back dining room. There were nine people at the far table, and her father, his expressive hands moving as much as his mouth, sat in the center.

She smiled at the hostess, Kathy Johnson, who ran the restaurant with her husband, Carl, who cooked up the fare in the kitchen. "Could I get that booth there, the one overlooking the harbor?" It was the first dining room, but she'd be able to get a clear view of her father since he was just through the opening into the second dining room. She planned to sit with her back to his table. Close enough to eavesdrop, but with her face obscured.

Kathy, an attractive middle-aged redhead, picked up two menus. "Of course. This way please." She led them to the booth and placed the menus down. "Vivian will be your server tonight. Enjoy your dinner."

Kate slipped into her booth before her father looked her way. "He might recognize you. Sit here beside me so he doesn't see your face."

Mumbling under her breath, Shelley slid into the booth beside Kate. "This is crazy, Kate. What do you hope to find out?"

"I just want to know more about all of them."

Harry's father-in-law picked up his wine glass. "I told Harry that company was ripe for the plucking, and it was. It was really what launched our business into the stratosphere."

Kate wrinkled her nose. She had no real interest in hearing of her father's wealth and power. That wasn't anything new. She wanted to know what made the man tick, why he would abandon his own daughter and treat her so coldly.

Footsteps came her way, and she looked up, expecting to see the server. She gasped. "Mom, what are you doing here?"

Her mother's hair was disheveled and out of its usual ponytail, her face furious. Mud stained her pink T-shirt, as though she'd heard what Kate planned and immediately dropped what she was doing. "Keeping you from destroying our lives. Come with me right now," she hissed.

"I'm not going to talk to anyone. I just want to see what his family is like."

Her mother's face crumpled, and tears slipped down her cheeks. Kate nudged Shelley out of the booth. "We'd better step outside before he notices us." The women quickly went out the front door and stood in the salty breeze off the water.

Her mother stepped to her car. "Your father is not someone to mess with. He can destroy our lives. You don't know what he's capable of doing. You have no idea how he's hurt all of us."

Something in her mother's tone caught at Kate's heart. "All of us?"

Her mother hesitated. "Us — you and me. Harry Dellamare holds what's his with an iron fist. He's ruthless, and he doesn't care who he hurts." She hugged herself. "I'm afraid he might take you away from me."

"How did you even get mixed up with him, Mom? Didn't you know he was married?" Kate didn't mean the words to sound so accusatory, and her mother winced. Kate reached to take her mom's hand. "I'm sorry, that came out wrong."

"Of course I knew he was married, but I

thought . . ." She bit her lip and looked down. "Men will tell you whatever they think will get them what they want. I was starry-eyed."

Kate calculated her mother's age at the time. Twenty-five wasn't all that young. Maybe *desperate* would be a better word. "Did you get pregnant on purpose?" She whispered the question before she stopped to think.

Her mother's green eyes widened, and she wrung her hands. "Did he tell you that?"

Kate read the naked truth in her mother's face. "You really thought he'd leave his wife if you were pregnant? Mom, that's so . . . naive. What did he say when you told him you were pregnant?"

Her mother lifted her chin. "He laughed, thinking it was a joke. It was terrible timing. He'd just found out that *she* was expecting — his wife. I knew then he'd never leave her."

Kate filed that information away. She had a sibling. "What did you do?"

"He offered to provide for me. What else could I do? I had no other job, no way of providing for a baby. I had to accept his terms. And I still held out hope that he'd realize he loved me, not her."

"But he never did. He'd never intended to

leave his wife for one minute."

The entire situation sickened her. Kate's head was pounding, and her limbs felt heavy and weak. A trip to see the doctor was long overdue with the way she'd been feeling. She dug into her purse for her keys. "Let's go, Shelley. This was a stupid idea."

SEVENTEEN

Luke's dad looked a little brighter on Monday morning. His mouth didn't sag much at all, and his pale-blue eyes were clear and alert. Color bloomed in his face, and he didn't list to the side in his chair.

Claire sat on the sofa beside Luke. She'd said she was tired, but she didn't look it. Her hair was up in its usual French twist, and her blue silk top made her eyes sparkle. "You look well, Mr. Rocco. Thanks for seeing me today." A small painting leaned at her feet against the sofa.

"That physical therapist won't let me be, but her torture appears to be helping." Pop's hand shook a little as he lifted a cup of coffee to his lips. "I'm planning on ditching this wheelchair as soon as possible. She let me use a walker around the house today."

Luke leaned forward. "I didn't know that. Be careful you're not moving too fast, Pop."

"I've got to get well before you take it into

your head to go back to your post. When's your leave over?"

Luke saw the calculating glint in his dad's eye. He'd dodged that manipulation too many times over his life to fall for it now. "I'm due back in another three weeks." His dad didn't need to know he was considering his options or he'd push even more. "Claire, tell my dad what's happened to you so far." He leaned against the back of the old plaid sofa, smelling of years of pipe smoke and cranberry candles.

He didn't want to eye his father with suspicion, but he'd agreed to Claire's request because he wondered if his dad might know this guy. What if he'd hired the hunter to kill Mom all those years ago? It felt wrong to worry about something so horrific, but Luke couldn't get it out of his head.

"Someone has attacked me twice." Claire leaned forward. "You've lived in this area all your life. I wondered if you might recognize this man." Reaching down, she seized the canvas and turned the painting around so his father could study it. "This man is a frequent visitor in my nightmares." She pointed out the bright-red figure in the corner. "And I sleepwalk and paint this dead fox into every painting. It's very bizarre."

He reached out a shaky hand. "Hand it here, missy." When she put it in his hands, he held it up to the light streaming through the window behind him. "Never seen him before, but he looks like a hunter."

"He's been in hunting clothes every time I've seen him."

"This isn't trapping season for fox, though. That's not until fall. He had a fox when you saw him? There're a lot of fox down the road apiece just outside Summer Harbor."

"He didn't have a fox when I saw him. But I think I might have seen him when I was four. My birthday is October 30, so that would make sense."

Pop handed the painting back to her. "There's a place in Bar Harbor that buys pelts. You might show the painting there. Trappers can make a decent living. This here fellow looks like a serious trapper or hunter. He's even got a knife attached to his belt."

Luke hadn't noticed that detail, but he looked closer when Claire sat back down with the painting in her hands. "It looks like his vest is fur lined too. And those boots look like Rocky Max. See the design of the camo mixed with tan? So this is a serious hunter."

"I remembered details about the incident at the top of the cliff in the woods," Claire said. "The boots looked like these, and the sole was loose."

Claire put the painting back down by her feet. "We could check outfitters in the area."

"Good idea. And gun sellers." Relief settled over him like a warm blanket. Pop hadn't seemed taken aback by the picture in any way, and he hadn't tried to evade the questions.

Maybe Luke had it all wrong. He rose, and Claire took his cue that it was time to leave. She grabbed her purse and thanked his father. Her heels clattered on the wood floor as she followed him onto the porch.

She slung her purse strap over her shoulder. "Are you okay? You seemed tense and worried in there."

He hadn't told her his fears. "I have to admit I was wondering if my dad might have been responsible for everything that happened twenty-five years ago, even your disappearance. I'd hoped having you in there talking to him might tell me for sure about his guilt."

She followed him to his truck. "And what did you decide?"

"I don't think he's guilty." His heart felt lighter with the words. "Now we just have to figure out who did have a hand in all this." He opened the truck door for her. "Now where to?"

She glanced at her watch. "I have to meet the Castillos for merger discussions at seven, but I think we have time to run to the mainland. It's only one."

"Who are the Castillos?"

"Business friends." She slid onto the cracked and worn seat, then pressed her lips together. "We both own small aviation firms. A merger would make us one of the bigger players. Ric's father is opposed to losing autonomy, and I think he's not too sure a woman at the helm of Cramer Aviation is a smart idea."

"He doesn't know you."

The warmth in her eyes ratcheted up a notch at his words. "It will take some work to convince him."

He leaned against the open door. "So no boyfriend in the wings?"

Her lips tipped up, and she shook her head. "I don't trust men easily. You never know what they're after."

Those direct blue eyes seemed to see his thoughts, and it was all he could do to keep from blurting out that he hadn't thought of her money even once in the few days he'd known her. If other men saw her bank account first, they were blind.

Claire blinked in the brilliant sunshine bouncing off the harbor dotted with white boats. The strong scent of the sea mingled with the stench of car exhaust and the perfume of passersby on the crowded sidewalk. "Now what?"

They'd struck out in the outfitters they'd hit in Ellsworth. No one recognized the man in her painting.

He pointed out a Victorian building across the street. "Let's get a coffee. I need to think. There are half a dozen outfitters sprinkled around the area."

She followed him across to the Rooster Brother coffee shop. Luke opened the door for her. The rich aroma of espresso teased her nose and made her mouth water. The wood floors gleamed with welcome, and the cheery turquoise color lifted her spirits. She ordered a mocha with whip, and Luke got straight black coffee from the dispenser by the door.

She closed her eyes at the first rich sip. "Coffee solves every problem."

He grinned and took a sip of his coffee. "We have enough of them at the moment,

195

so we'd better have seconds."

She followed him to the stoop outside looking onto the busy Ellsworth Street. They leaned against the railing and sipped their coffee. When she turned her head, she found him staring at her. "What?" It was impossible for her to look away from those dark, dark eyes and that devil-may-care grin.

Smiling, he leaned over and ran his thumb over the corner of her mouth. "Whipped cream."

He licked it off his thumb, and something stirred in her chest, a wanting for more of that intimacy. "Thanks."

"Anytime." The moment wiped away his smile and left an expression of tenderness on his face.

She looked down at her coffee, twirling it in her hands. "I don't think I have the time to stop at any other outfitters."

"I'll run you to the ferry, then check the rest of them out myself. We'll get a copy made of your painting and I can show it around." He took a gulp of his coffee. "I took a picture with my phone, but it's not big enough to see well."

The silence stretched between them, but it wasn't uncomfortable. It was as if they'd known one another forever and were content to just stand and look at each other.

She broke the silence first. "You told your dad your leave is over in three weeks. It sounded like he was hoping you'd say you weren't going back."

"He wants me to stay here and work the cranberry farm. I don't want to see it pass from our family. It's been part of our heritage for generations. I love the history of that, but it would mean giving up my job in the Coast Guard. I think I'm going to have to, though. My sister has a job opportunity she wants to take, and it's her turn to get out into the world. I can't deny her that."

"You're one of a kind, Luke. I don't know many men who would sacrifice their careers for their sister."

"Meg has given up a lot to stay here. She wouldn't brag, but she has a Vassar degree. She's overqualified for running a cranberry farm."

She took a sip of the deliciously strong coffee. "I don't know much about the Coast Guard. Tell me what you love about it."

"Everything. The open sea, the camaraderie with other Coasties. I've investigated countless drug runs and other maritime crimes. Every night when I go home, I know I've done something that mattered."

The passion in his voice stirred her. "I

wish my job was that glamorous."

"You're a bigwig in a huge corporation. A dream come true for so many."

Then why did she still feel like she was drifting? She shrugged and stirred her coffee. "It's because of my name and family. I never would have gotten there by sheer work alone. Those kinds of openings don't just happen. They are manipulated."

"You sound pensive and sad. If you could do anything you wanted, what would it be?"

She stirred the whipped cream into her coffee to avoid looking at him. "You'll laugh."

"I won't."

The humor in his voice caused her to look up. "I'd work for a nonprofit out on a research boat. Maybe studying orcas or whales. Or maybe I'd fish for a living. I love the sea." She looked out the window at the boats bobbing in the waves, then turned back to him.

"That sounds doable. You wouldn't make much money, but some things are more important than money."

She smiled back at him. Fudge! He had no idea how attractive he was with those killer dark eyes that looked into her soul. A straight black lock of hair had fallen across his forehead, and her fingers itched to reach over and touch its soft texture, to smooth it back into place. "My dad would have a fit. If only I had a brother or sister to follow in his footsteps. That would take the pressure off me."

"So you never had any siblings?"

"I used to dream about having a sister. We could share clothes and makeup, and I could run into her room when I was scared at night."

"Do you get scared in the night often?"

"I have nightmares sometimes. I think it's all related to what happened here." She moved restlessly. "I don't like to think about it."

"Maybe there is truth in your nightmares somewhere." He took her hand and turned it over to run his thumb over her palm.

She shivered at his touch. "They're just nightmares with no sense to them. I'm running in a forest and there's always a red fox chasing me. Its tongue is hanging out, and it keeps making little sounds like barking noises. I know if I can find my way through the trees that I'll be safe. My mother's arms are waiting in the shadows, but I can't find her. I open my mouth to scream for her. I know if I start screaming I won't stop, but I can't help it. That's when I wake up."

His thumb was still tracing circles on her

palm. "Maybe someone really was chasing you. You said you wondered if you'd been kidnapped. Maybe that's what happened."

"Maybe." She pulled her hand away while she still could.

EIGHTEEN

Luke had come back to the house too late for dinner after a fruitless search of the outfitters all day on Monday. The scent of coffee mingled with the aroma of the lasagna Luke had stuck in the oven to reheat. He heard tires crunch on gravel through the open window, and he turned to look. When he saw the sheriff's car in his dad's driveway, his gut did a somersault.

He exchanged a glance with Meg. "It's Danny." He opened the screened back door and waited for the sheriff to enter.

Danny Colton's expression was somber as he hiked up his pants and lumbered toward the back porch. Luke had no doubt the body was that of his mother, but now that the moment of truth had arrived, he wasn't all that eager to hear it.

Danny nodded at him and his sister. "Luke, Megan. Your daddy around?"

"He's in his chair in the living room."

Luke let the screen door slam behind the sheriff and turned to lead the way. "I take it you have news?"

"I do. I'd rather tell you all together."

His tone told Luke the story. Would the sheriff know more than just the fact that the bones were Victoria Rocco's? Luke watched Colton approach his father.

The sheriff stopped at the foot of the recliner. "Walker?"

Pop's eyes blinked, then popped open. He struggled into a straighter position. "Danny," he slurred. His gaze sharpened and went past the sheriff to focus on Luke. "What's this all about?"

Megan motioned to the chair. "Have a seat, Sheriff. Want some apple pie? It's warm out of the oven."

"Don't mind if I do." Danny folded his long legs to sit on the old brown sofa.

Luke glanced at his sister. "Need help?"

She shook her head. "I'll get it in a minute. Say what you came to tell us, Danny."

The sheriff's lips twitched and he nodded. "Sure thing, honey." He looked at their dad. "You probably were already pretty sure the bones were Victoria's, Walker. We got a match on the dental records. No doubt it's Victoria." Danny cleared his throat. "I also have a cause of death. Her neck was broken."

Luke's fingers twitched against his sister, and he felt her flinch too. A broken neck sounded deliberate, but then, hadn't they suspected murder?

Luke's dad plucked at his flannel shirt. "An accident?"

"I don't see how. The body was concealed pretty well. If she'd fallen in a hole or something, the body would have been exposed and easy to find. She was partially covered with rocks, and it appeared she likely had been fully buried with stones until that last storm washed so many away. Someone murdered her, Walker."

Luke watched his father to gauge his reaction. It felt terrible to be so suspicious of his own father, but he knew Meg was paying attention too. They had to know the truth.

Pop's mouth went slack, and his gaze went to his hands. He said nothing for a long moment, then he exhaled. "I always knew she'd never leave me."

Was that all he cared about — his ego? The sadness Luke had been trying to keep at bay washed over him. His thoughts went to Claire. She'd want to know this news, and he found he wanted to be with her. He shoved his hands in his pockets. As soon as Danny left, he'd call her.

"Any clues to her murderer?" Meg's voice was low.

Danny hesitated, then shook his head. "Nothing I can talk about yet. There are a couple of leads we are tracking down. Peculiar thing was how her neck was broken. Cleanly, like a man used to killing. Or dressing out game." He didn't look at Luke's dad.

Luke suppressed a shudder. He'd seen his dad break a deer's neck with one precise blow. Barely daring to breathe in case he betrayed his suspicion to Danny, he turned his back and went to stand by the window. His eyes burned, and he imagined what it would look like if Danny showed up to haul his dad off to jail. Pop would never survive in prison, not in his current condition.

He turned back around. "What's next?"

"We'll release her remains sometime next week."

Luke glanced at his sister who was as pale as the light-gray walls. "We can plan a memorial service."

"No service," their dad barked. "Let's just get her in the ground. Her burial is long overdue. And it's pointless this long after her death." His agitation made the slurred words harder to make out.

Meg fixed her dad with a fierce glare. "We're having a memorial service, Pop. You will *not* deprive us of paying our last respects. Aunt Nancy will want to do the same, and Mom had plenty of friends in town."

Their father glowered back. "I said no."

Luke clenched his hands into fists. "And we're both saying yes. You don't have to come if you don't want to, but we *will* have a service, Pop." He sent his father a challenging look.

Pop's face twisted in a snarl, and he snatched a wedding picture off the table next to him and flung it to the floor. He froze when the frame broke, his face flushing. Then he leaned down and grabbed the picture off the wood planks. He smoothed the old picture, exposed through the broken glass, and wheeled himself out of the room.

Luke turned to Danny, who wore a furrowed brow. Did he find Pop's reaction odd? "Thanks for all you've done. After all this time, I didn't think this moment would ever come."

"I didn't either." The sheriff held Luke's gaze. "I intend to find her killer next."

Was there an undercurrent to Danny's words? Did he suspect his longtime friend too?

■ ■ ■ ■

She'd expected fewer people in the hotel lobby on a Tuesday afternoon. Kate could hardly hear over the pounding of her blood in her ears as she tried to look like any other guest. The polyester gray skirt felt alien against legs used to the cool brush of denim, and her jacket constricted her movements, but she'd wanted to fit in with the hotel's elite clientele. A night in this place was easily five hundred dollars.

The two-story windows filled the space with light that gleamed off the oak floors. Guests spoke in hushed tones except for a toddler who giggled as she ran from her mother. Kate glanced at the cream leather furniture by the fireplace. It might be a good place to park herself and watch who came and went.

"May I help you?" a perky female voice asked.

Kate looked to her left into the inquisitive face of a woman about her own age. Dressed in a navy pencil skirt and a white blouse, the woman's stylish ballet flats probably cost more than Kate's last paycheck.

Kate gulped and shook her head. "I-I was looking for the ladies' room." She wanted to slap her hand to her forehead. What a stupid thing to say.

The woman's face cleared. "It's past the elevators in the hallway to the left. You can't miss it. Is there anything else I can assist you with?"

"No, you've been very helpful." Kate fled the woman's questioning eyes and rushed into the bathroom, tiled in travertine and filled with gleaming granite counters. The gold-and-black light fixtures added even more elegance.

She stepped into a stall and leaned her hot forehead against the door's cool metal. What had given her away? She'd dressed in her nicest clothes and had even put her hair up. She bit her lip, then flushed the toilet so being in here didn't appear odd. Holding her head high, she unlocked the door and stepped toward the bank of sinks with confidence.

But the woman standing at one of the sinks held Kate transfixed. Her light-brown hair, in a stylish updo, was a shade lighter than Kate's natural color, but her blue eyes were like looking into a mirror. They had similar noses and mouths, full with a defined bow in the upper lip. The woman wore designer jeans with rhinestones on the pockets and heels high enough to cause a nosebleed. The glittering rocks in her ears had to be real diamonds, at least two carats each. She oozed money and confidence.

Their gazes met in the mirror, and the young woman turned around. "Is something wrong?" Her voice was a little husky, and her smile seemed genuine. Those blue eyes held concern and caring.

Kate wetted her lips. "You remind me of someone, and I was trying to place you."

"What's your name?" she wanted to scream, but people like this elegant lady didn't usually have to field questions from strangers. Kate tried a tremulous smile, and the woman smiled back.

"You look a little familiar too. Have we met? I'm Claire Dellamare."

Dellamare. The name pierced Kate's heart. Her sister. What would Claire say if Kate told her they shared the same father? That Harry Dellamare had once bounced Kate on his knee and brought her expensive dolls? She licked her lips again and searched for the right words, but they weren't to be found.

It was no wonder Claire didn't see the resemblance with this crazy red hair Kate now sported. "I'm Kate Mason. I have never been out of the state of Maine, so unless you've been here before, I guess we've never met."

Kate turned, and the unfamiliarity of the heels made her stumble. She reached out to catch herself on the counter but missed. Her ankle turned, and the sharp pain radiated up her leg as she went down. The tile bit into her knee, and as she struggled to her feet, she realized the warmth trickling down her leg was blood.

Claire sprang to her side. "You're hurt. Here, let me help you."

Kate leaned against Claire and hobbled to the wall. "I think I sprained my ankle."

"Is there someone I can call to take you to the clinic? Or I can take you if you tell me where to go."

"I'm sure it will be fine if I can rest it." Kate glanced around. "Where's a chair when you need it?" She attempted a smile, but it turned into more of a grimace.

Claire reached for a paper towel and wet it under the water, then handed it to Kate. "Press hard to stop the blood. I don't think this needs stitches, but your ankle is really swelling."

"I don't have insurance, so I'd rather just rest it and see how it does. Could you help me to the dining room? I don't think I can make it to my car just yet."

"Of course. I wouldn't mind coffee and a snack. It's a couple of hours until dinner." Claire handed her a dry paper towel. "I'm here with my family, but most of them are out on a whale-watching charter so I'd love some company."

"Thank you for reaching out to a-a stranger." Kate tossed the soiled paper towel in the trash, then followed her out of the bathroom and toward the delicious aroma of lobster bisque.

Should she tell Claire? She desperately wanted to. Even if their father had rejected her, maybe Claire would welcome the thought of a sister. Everything in Kate longed for a sister like Claire, one who seemed to care about other people. It felt as though they were two lonely people looking for some kind of connection. Or was it Kate's wishful thinking?

Claire asked for outside seating, and the hostess led them across the dining room and out the French doors to a pink-granite-paved terrace. The scent of potted honey-suckle and roses curled around them as they settled at a glass-topped table. Kate took a seat where she could watch the door. If their father came to find Claire, she had no idea how she would explain being with her half sister.

But surely he wouldn't be back for hours. She'd have time to get to know this new sibling. At least she prayed nothing would derail it, not now that she'd finally found Claire.

NINETEEN

Luke drove the sleepy streets of Summer Harbor on Tuesday afternoon. The ferry to Folly Shoals launched from here. Like his own hometown, charming cottages stair-stepped up the hills overlooking the crescent-shaped harbor, and with his window down, he could smell the lobster roll stands out on the wharf.

There was an outfitter on the outskirts of town he'd forgotten about yesterday, and it wouldn't hurt to stop and show the picture folded up in his pocket. He parked on the side of the clapboard structure and got out. A sea breeze lifted his hair and carried the tang of sea salt as he went around to the storefront. He pushed open the wooden screen door and went inside.

A few tourists carrying cameras around their necks browsed the aisles of tents and propane grills. The peninsula was part of Acadia National Park, and rusticators would be descending all summer. A baby sleeping in his father's arms made Luke smile. An unfamiliar longing struck him as he watched the little one sucking his thumb. He'd likely never have a child to hold, not with caring for his father. He turned away and went to the desk.

Approaching the clerk, he pulled out the picture of Claire's attacker and passed it over the scarred wooden counter. "This fellow look familiar at all?"

The clerk, a young woman with a harried expression, reeked of tobacco. She barely glanced at it before shaking her head. "Never saw him before."

"Look again. He's local, I'm sure."

She redid her ponytail with brusqueness. "Look, don't be a dubber. Unless you're a cop, you need to leave me alone to take care of my customers. I don't want to get fired." Looking past him, she gestured to the person behind him. "Next."

He stepped out of the way and glanced through the window. Isabelle worked across the street. She hadn't given them much of a description of Jenny's secret boyfriend, but maybe this picture would jog her memory. He dodged tourists and exited the shop to hurry across the street to a clapboard building painted blue and white. Through the window, he saw Isabelle pecking away at a keyboard.

He stepped inside and approached her desk. "Isabelle, you have a minute?"

Jenny's best friend looked a little less upset today than she did on Sunday. Dressed in a yellow dress, her brown hair was a riot of curls around her face. Luke passed the picture over, and as she studied it, a frown began to form between her eyes.

She handed it back. "I think this is the guy Jenny was seeing. Like I said, I don't know his name, but she showed me a selfie of the two of them on her phone. I'd swear it's the same guy."

His pulse sped up. Finally, some kind of lead. "You have any idea where he lived? He can't be local to Folly Shoals or someone there would know who he is, and I've been hitting dead ends."

"They often met at Bar Harbor so maybe he lived on the other side and it was the central place. Jenny never said. She didn't want to meet him in town in case Andy caught them."

"Was it only that she didn't want Andy to know about this guy, or could he have been married too?"

Isabelle chewed her lower lip. "I think that's what started the trouble between the two of them. He always took her to some little hole-in-the-wall where they wouldn't be noticed. You know, like a dimly lit bar or something. She began to push him a little and ask if he was ashamed of her or something." She held out her hand. "Let me see that picture again."

Luke pulled it back out. "Would you say it's him for sure? Do you see any differences at all?"

She carried it over to the big plate-glass window and studied it. "This looks like a painting."

"It is. Claire painted it. It's the man who attacked her."

Her mouth twisted. "You're still helping that woman."

Luke tapped the picture. "I think this guy killed Jenny, and Claire is his next target."

Isabelle's eyes narrowed before she shrugged and looked back at the picture. "Jenny's boyfriend looks older than the guy in this painting. There's more gray in his eyebrows and hair. And his skin is more weathered." She handed it back. "But the resemblance is there."

"Thanks. Now I just need to put a name with the face. Thanks. I'll leave you to your work."

Back in the bright sunlight, he squinted

and pulled out his sunglasses. Maybe he should head down toward Bar Harbor and beyond. Maybe he'd find some information in Blue Hill. It was worth a try.

He rounded the corner and stopped in his tracks when he saw his truck sitting on its rims. Even from here he could see the slashes in the tires. Coincidence or a warning?

Kate savored the comforting taste of buttery lobster bisque on her tongue and smiled across the table at Claire. Her half sister. She had a sister. It was almost too much to take in. And they were out of the sight of prying eyes. Even if their father came in, he wouldn't look out here. She peeked at the door just to make sure. All clear. They had the entire patio to themselves.

Kate took a sip of her iced tea, then put it back on the table. "So tell me about yourself, Claire. Do you have any siblings?"

Claire shook her head. "I'm an only child, unfortunately. I used to pretend I had a sister, but Mom and Dad never obliged by providing me with one. How about you?"

Oh how Kate wanted to let the truth just spill off her tongue. She swallowed and shook her head. "Just Mom and me."

"Your father's dead?"

Kate twirled a long red strand of hair. Why on earth had she ever dyed her hair this color? It looked atrocious. "He never married my mom, and after a while, he just quit coming around."

Claire winced. "I'm sorry. That had to have been hard."

"I got used to it. My mom and I have blueberry barrens about fifteen miles out of town." Kate dropped the linen napkin and bent to retrieve it. "Where did you grow up?"

"North Carolina. But we moved to the Boston area when I was in my teens. I love the energy of the city, and I bought my own place on the Atlantic five years ago when I got out of college."

Claire said it so nonchalantly, as if it were such a common thing to have your own multimillion-dollar house in your late twenties. Kate couldn't imagine such complacence. "Wow, you must have gotten some kind of high-powered job right out of school to afford a house out there."

Claire's face went pink, and she reached for her iced tea. "Well, I guess it's more accurate to say Dad bought it and deeded it over to me. I work for the family company, Cramer Aviation. I'm CFO now, but I'll take it over when my father retires. Mom wants him to retire next year, but I can't see him sitting around doing nothing."

A stab of envy lodged in Kate's chest. Claire's life was all planned out while Kate had no idea what she even wanted out of life. With her health, she'd been afraid to dream. "It's safe to say your parents doted on you."

"It's not as appealing as it might sound. They have a lot of expectations. I've gone along with it most of my life, but I'm not sure it's what I want to do anymore."

"What would you do if there were no expectations?"

"That's funny. A new friend just asked me the same thing." Claire's eyes went dreamy. "I don't know. Anything except be cooped up in a high-rise office where every day is planned around meetings and making sure the company exceeds its financial goals."

Kate tried to imagine Claire's regimented days and shuddered. Though she didn't make that much money on the blueberries, she was out in the sunshine and fresh air, and every day was different from the one before it. She glanced toward the door when a shadow fell into the courtyard. Her next breath froze in her chest when she saw their father standing there. A slight widening of his eyes was the only reaction he gave to seeing her there with Claire.

Claire waved and called to her father. "Dad, there's someone I want you to meet."

His face went white, then a forced smile crept into his face and he came toward them. "I expected to find you in your suite, Claire. You begged off going with Ric on the boat until tomorrow because you said you were tired."

Her smile faltered. "This is Kate Mason. She lives in the area and runs some blueberry barrens with her mom. Isn't that the most interesting thing you've ever heard? I just like saying it. It sounds so different and exotic."

"Pleased to meet you, Mr. Dellamare." Kate kept her voice pitched low and pleasant, though it took every bit of strength not to leap up and blurt out the truth to sweet Claire.

Her half sister didn't deserve having such a liar for a father. Kate could only imagine the hurt in Claire's face when she found out how many lies he'd told her over the years. And what about Mrs. Dellamare? Her pain would be even greater when the truth came out. Kate didn't want to hurt anyone. She just wanted her family to know she existed and to see if they could love one another. Was that so wrong? She could easily love Claire, and she believed Claire could feel the same way if their father didn't interfere.

But the way his nostrils flared indicated he wanted nothing more than to see the back of her. She narrowed her eyes and glared back. "Claire and I just met today. She's a lovely girl. You've done an excellent job raising her." She lifted a brow so he knew she was thinking, *But you didn't do much about raising me.*

"Thank you, I'm very proud of Claire." His eyes were flat above his smile.

Kate blinked at the sting in her eyes, but she forced back the moisture gathering. He hadn't had any part in her life, and she wouldn't allow him to make her feel shame. "Why don't you join us?"

Her father didn't sit. "Your mother wasn't feeling well so we had the boat drop us off. She wants to talk to you. Go on up and I'll take care of the bill."

Claire sprang to her feet, then paused and sat back down. "Tell her I'll be up as soon as I finish lunch."

He nodded. "Don't be too long. I want to tell you about a conversation I had with Ric." He smiled down at Kate as if he wished her anywhere but with his daughter, then walked away.

Claire waved off a honeybee. "I suppose I'd better go soon. We're in the middle of important merger discussions."

"And I imagine you're concerned about your mother. Does she have a chronic illness?"

Claire picked up her iced tea. "Only if you call being unable to cope with life an illness." She shook her head. "I don't know why I'm telling you all this. You're very easy to talk to."

Kate picked up her spoon for another bite of bisque. Her admiration for her half sister grew as she listened to the description of Claire's goal to bring about a merger with another company. With every word, she found she wanted to be Claire's confidant all the time.

TWENTY

Luke stepped into the hotel lobby at eleven on Wednesday morning. He made his way through the throng of guests waiting for an early check-in and across the oak floors to the elevators. He punched the Up button to go to Claire's suite. She was waiting for him, though she'd told him she only had half an hour before she needed to leave for a business lunch. He stepped off the elevator on the fifth floor. The thick carpet muffled his steps, but she still opened the door when he approached.

She drew him inside quickly and shut the door. He sent a grin her way. "Afraid your parents will see a strange man entering your room?"

Her laugh held a touch of unease. "It's truer than you know. Dad already thinks you're interested in me for my money."

He laughed. "Any man who thinks about money when he's with you is an idiot. And we Maine guys take pride in getting what we want the hard way — by working for it." Especially today, with her bronzed arms bare in that killer sundress that hugged every curve. The bright-blue color played up her eyes, and she'd curled a strand or two of hair out of her updo. Those curls just begged to be touched.

Pink tinged her cheeks, and her gaze lingered on his face. "You always know how to say the right thing. I think you're a ladies' man, Luke Rocco."

He'd be *her* man any day. The realization caught him off guard, and he bit back the words he wanted to say. "My sister would laugh you right out of the room. I get tongue-tied around beautiful women."

This time her laugh was genuine, and she took his arm. "Let's sit on the balcony. I need strength for the day." She led him out into the crisp air. She sank onto the lounger on the big balcony with her cell phone in her lap. "What'd you find out yesterday?"

Perching on the edge of the deck chair, he told her about running into Isabelle. "Some-one has to have seen them together. Some-one in the county knows who this guy is. We just have to show that picture to enough people and we'll have him."

"I hope so. I want this over."

He decided not to tell her about his slashed tires. It might not have been anything but coincidence.

She flipped on her phone. "I need to go. I want to wrap up the merger this afternoon. Wish me luck. I didn't get very far yesterday. Ric's father kept throwing up objections. I'll have Ric and Francisca to myself today, and maybe I can land this merger. Then I can concentrate on our investigation."

He took her hand and laced his fingers with hers. "Why don't you blow off this lunch and come with me instead? We'll go down to the wharf and eat lobster with so much butter it'll smear on our faces. We'll have sea salt taffy and fudge until we get a sugar high, then we can go out on the boat and watch the moon come up."

She squeezed his hand. "You make it really hard on a girl to resist. All my favorite things."

"How about we do it tonight, then, when you've got the merger in the bag?"

"I'd like that, Luke. I'll order dinner, and we'll have it on your boat."

His pulse blipped at her warm expression, and he put the brakes on his thoughts. She wouldn't stay in this place, and he would have to take charge of the cranberry farm.

■ ■ ■ ■

Gulls swooped and squawked over Claire's head as she reached the bottom of the pink-granite steps that led from the hotel grounds to the slabs of rocks lining the water. Steam rose from the heaps of kelp drying in the sun, and she breathed in the smell of the sea. Several boats, their white hulls gleaming in the sun, bobbed just offshore at their moorings. One of them was Ric's, probably the large sailboat with a mast that seemed to stretch to the fluffy clouds overhead.

Francisca had gotten to the bottom first, and she turned to smile at Claire. "You doing okay?" She wore khaki slacks and a red top that showed off her figure and her tan. A matching khaki jacket was slung around her shoulders.

"Much better. I think I might actually live." Claire pointed at the big sailboat. "Is that Ric's pride and joy?"

Francisca turned to look and nodded. "Looks like he's already there." She waved, and the figure on the deck waved back. "Yes, that's him."

Claire watched him lower an inflatable rowboat over the side. "Guess we'd better get out on the dock. He's coming for us."

She tipped up her chin and pressed her lips together. Her father was counting on her to seal this merger today. The large plane contract would be hard to fulfill without the power of Ric's company. She followed Francisca down the weathered boards to the end of the dock as the skiff reached them.

Ric looked every inch the preppy seaman in his white shorts and navy shirt. The white cap on his head contrasted with his dark hair in a way she was sure he'd carefully planned right down to his bare feet. Everything neat and perfectly ordered.

His smile broadened when he held out his hand to help her aboard. "Ahoy, *señorita*!"

She tucked her satchel under one arm, then grabbed his hand and stepped down into the boat. The thought of spending the day on the water enticed her. Talking business and enjoying the sea and sun made for a promising combination.

Francisca's text message alert went off, and she stopped to check it. "Uh-oh, I will not be able to go with you guys. Bridget is sick, and Papa wants me to come."

Ric frowned. "I got a text from him too, but I thought it was his way of trying to derail our merger talk. You think I should go too? Maybe it is not a ploy."

Francisca shook her head. "You know how dramatic she gets. She has probably convinced him she is dying. You two go hammer out the merger, and I shall sign it as well. Papa will come around."

Claire wanted to do a fist pump at Francisca's stamp of approval, but she sedately took a seat in the bow. "Call if you need us."

"I will. See you at dinner. And be careful where you stop to eat. I heard some staff talking, and there can be huge tidal differences. Not as much here as up in the Bay of Fundy, but still quite significant." Francisca set off down the dock.

"We are not going clear to the Bay of Fundy." Ric settled on the seat and picked up the oars. They cut through the blue water and propelled the boat to the steel ladder on the big sailboat. He attached the dingy, then held out his hand for Claire. "You first."

He held her hand and stood too close for her comfort. She gave him a quick smile and pulled her hand out of his grasp, then scaled the ladder. Standing on the deck, she looked around. His boat was gorgeous. She guessed it had at least two cabins below deck, and every surface gleamed. The canvas sails flapped a bit as they waited to be hoisted, something she was eager to do. Constant work had kept her out of a sailboat for several years. The rocking of the boat under her bare feet lifted her spirits. Maybe she should get her own boat. She could well afford it.

They spent the next few minutes working in tandem to prepare to set sail. Looking into the blue sky as the white sails unfurled above her gave her such peace. She'd never been able to figure out why the sea spoke to her so. She was never happier than when she was near the water. Could she have lived on the water in the missing year?

Fifteen minutes later the boat sailed past the little orca's enclosure. She cupped her eyes and made out a splash as the little guy flipped his fluke. He swam as close as his pen allowed. Did he recognize her?

Ric squinted toward the pen. "What is that?"

"It's a small orca. A friend found him near death and is rehabilitating him. The little guy is doing well. I think he'll be able to go home in another week."

"Home? You know where he lives?"

She shook her head. "We have to try to find his matriline and take him to it." She saw the confusion on his face. "His matriline is his immediate family, mother, father,

228

siblings. There will be a bigger group, a pod, that he's part of. Orcas stay in their family unit all their lives. It's pretty amazing, really." She warmed to the subject. "And if they lose a family member, they mourn for years just like humans. They will also welcome in solo members of another pod."

Ric smiled. "You could lecture at a university on orcas." He turned his attention back to the wheel and guided the boat into deeper water away from the island. "I thought we would set sail up the northeast coast toward Jasper Beach. Then we will stop for lunch on the way back."

"I can't wait." Claire watched the jutting coastline slide by. She tried to bring up the merger several times, but Ric always stopped her and said it could wait until after lunch. It was a perfect day for a sail. The sails filled with wind and glided over the calm sea. They passed Great Wass Island, and she dug out some binoculars. "I see puffins!" She'd been dying to see some of the colorful birds that had been brought back from the edge of extinction.

She handed the binoculars to Ric and let him see the birds too. He was in a grand mood as well, which gave her hope that they'd finish the merger today.

He pointed out a stretch of beach on

another island. "Let's eat there."

The cove he pointed out ended in a crescent of sand that gave way to thick trees. She didn't like how deserted it appeared. "It doesn't look like you can even get to that beach except by boat."

"You can't. My map calls it Dead Man's Cove. A little gruesome, but the concierge told me it was a pretty spot that would be perfect for a picnic."

As the beach grew nearer, Claire went over what she intended to say. She had to get his signature on the dotted line.

TWENTY-ONE

The warm sand baked the soles of Claire's bare feet. Ric — or more likely the waitstaff — had thought of everything for the picnic, right down to the red-and-white checkered tablecloth she spread out on the flat rock. The basket contained thick roast beef sandwiches, potato salad, coleslaw, apple chips, and blueberry pie.

"I didn't get much breakfast, and I'm ready for lunch." She sat across the table-cloth from Ric and dug into the food with gusto.

The roast beef was tender, and the horse-radish had a pleasant bite on her tongue. She eyed Ric, who was staring at her with an intense gaze that made her squirm. She left the last bite of the blueberry pie on her plate. "I'm done. What a great lunch, though. Blueberry pie is my favorite."

"I tried to pick things I knew you would like." He took her plate and ate the last of her pie, his gaze on her face the whole time.

She found his expression a little creepy. It was way too proprietorial, like a shark looking at dinner. She curled her fingers into the warm sand to ground herself and took strength from it. She needed to get this over with so she could relax. She reached for her satchel. "Did you review those figures I gave you the other night?"

"I did." He reached over and twirled a lock of her hair around his finger. "You are most beautiful today, my dear." His voice was husky. "I have been looking forward to this time alone."

"Um, Ric. I really want to hammer out an agreement between our companies. Were you in favor of the dollar amount?"

His hand left her hair and stroked down her arm in a long, sensuous stroke. "Your skin is so soft." Leaning over, he pressed his lips to her neck.

His hot breath wafted over her face and neck. She froze as she evaluated her options. He'd brought her out here for something very different than talking about the merger. If she rebuffed his advances, would he walk away from the deal?

As his lips moved closer to her face, she suppressed a shudder. Putting her hand on his chest, she twisted her face away. "Don't,

Ric. This is business."

"One can mix business and pleasure. It's the best kind of merger." His thick voice was muffled by another attempt to pull her closer.

She scrambled back away from him on the tablecloth. "I'm not interested in that kind of merger, Ric."

He made another grab at her arm, but she managed to get to her feet. She snatched up her satchel and held it across her chest. "Let's talk business, please."

He got up and planted his feet wide. His nostrils flared as he looked her over. "I find I am not much interested in discussing the business merger with a woman as cold as you."

His stance with his arms crossed over his chest told her all she needed to know. "Then I suggest we get back." She didn't wait for an answer but bent over to put everything away.

When she heard his steps retreating, she breathed a sigh. Let him go pout awhile on the boat. They weren't far from the hotel dock, an hour or so by boat. He'd get over his snit and be willing to discuss business when he realized she wasn't about to sleep with him to broker a deal.

The sputter of the engine caught her by

233

surprise. She jerked around and saw the boat, sails down, moving out to sea.

She ran to the edge of the water and waved her hands. "Hey!"

He glanced at her briefly, and she recoiled at the venom in his face before he turned his back and steered the boat out to open ocean. The picnic basket slid from her slack hand. He couldn't just leave her here. She waved her hand and shouted again, but he never turned back around. After a few minutes, the boat was just a speck in the distance.

She turned back around and looked at her situation. The trees began twenty feet from the water's edge and grew thicker as the land began to soar up a slope. Was it possible to walk out of here to a road? She had a compass on her phone, but the hike wouldn't be pleasant. At least she had her cell phone. Luke had a boat, though she cringed at the idea of telling him what had happened. He'd be ready to take Ric out.

Sighing, she reached into her purse for her phone and looked at it. No bars. She turned around and stared at the forest. She had no choice but to try to walk out, at least until she got a cell phone signal.

The hotel lobby was quiet when Luke

stepped in. Only one woman, dressed in a navy skirt and white blouse, manned the reception desk. No one was at the concierge desk when he passed either, and the scent of lemon wax hung in the air.

Luke approached the front desk to ask the receptionist to ring Claire's room. When there was no answer, he thanked the clerk and turned toward the restaurant. Maybe he could find someone in her family to see if they'd heard from her. He'd told her he'd call at four so they could make plans for dinner, and she hadn't answered any of the four times he'd tried. It was five now, well past time when he should have spoken with her. He couldn't quell his unease.

He stepped into the wide hall, and the elevator doors opened. He'd still been in the lobby when Claire left with a woman earlier, and he saw the same woman coming out of the elevator with a man who looked so much like her they had to be siblings. She wore a brightly colored sundress, and her dark hair was twisted atop her head. The man wore such an arrogant expression that Luke wanted to punch him. He looked dressed for dinner in light-gray slacks and a navy jacket.

"Excuse me." The man tried to step around him.

Luke blocked his move. "Ric Castillo?"

"That's right. And you are?"

"Luke Rocco, a friend of Claire's. I've been trying to get ahold of her for over an hour. Do you know where she is?"

"Check her room."

The woman glanced up at Ric. "She didn't answer when I knocked either. When did you see her last?"

Ric's jaw jutted out. "Stay out of this, Francisca."

He tried to go around Luke again, but Luke stepped into his path again. "You know where she is, don't you?"

Ric pulled his cell phone from the pocket of his slacks. "I will call hotel security if you don't move out of my way."

The woman frowned. "I want to know where she is too, Ric. You've been odd ever since you got back this afternoon." Suspicion glimmered in her eyes. "You made a pass at her and she turned you down, I suspect. Is that why you have been simmering with rage? What did you do to her?"

"I did not do anything to her," Ric snapped. "She was fine the last time I saw her."

Luke narrowed his eyes at Ric. "And where was that?"

"On the beach at Dead Man's Cove. She

seemed to prefer it to my company."

The woman's mouth gaped, and she punched him in the arm. "Ric Castillo, I cannot believe this, even of you! What kind of man leaves a woman stranded on a beach?" She looked at Luke. "Would she be about back to the hotel by now if she walked?"

Luke curled his fingers into his palm and wished he could smash in Ric's smug face. "There's no way she can walk back to a highway. The high tide will wash out the little strip of land connecting that part of the land from the mainland in a couple of hours. I need to get to her. What time did you leave her?"

Ric glared back at him without answering. Luke glanced at the woman. "Any ideas since the silent caveman isn't talking?"

"I saw my brother at about two without her." She cast a troubled glance at the man. "Seriously, Ric, what were you thinking?"

Ric's hands curled into fists. "This is none of your business, Francisca."

"It most certainly is. This merger would be good for Castillo Aviation, and you may have ruined everything with your raging libido. Do you have to make a pass at anyone in a skirt?"

"Be quiet. You're making me look foolish," he hissed.

His sister put her hands on her hips and lifted a derisive brow. "You do not need any help looking foolish. You can do that all by yourself."

Luke stepped between them. "You can argue later. What stretch of the beach did you leave her on? There are two sides to the cove."

Ric shrugged. "I took the boat in by a funny-looking tree with big, gnarled branches."

"I know it." He had never wanted to hit someone so badly in his life. The man seemed not to understand what he'd done. "I think you'd better pack up and get off this island. I wouldn't want to be in your shoes when Claire gets back. She's not one to take this, you know."

"I can handle Claire Dellamare," he said with a curl of his lip.

Francisca gave her brother such a hard shove he reeled back and his arm struck the wall. He straightened and rubbed his arm, but she punched him again. "You should leave now, Ric. Claire will go straight to her dad. How do you think he will react? And you will be lucky if our father does not toss you out on your ear for such behavior. Never have I been so ashamed of you. And that is saying something." She shoved him again. "Go. Now." She pointed at the elevator, and Ric shrugged, then hit the Up button with a defiant stab.

The elevator doors opened, and Ric stepped inside, then turned. "She deserved it," he spat out.

Luke started toward him but the doors closed. He stood with his hands clenched into fists. "You've got some brother, Miss Castillo."

"Call me Francisca. I am ashamed of the Castillo name about now." Her bewildered expression cleared and she held out her hand. "I am pleased to know you, Luke. Go bring Claire home so I can apologize, even if my brother will not."

"I'll do that." Luke hurried for the doors. As he ran for his boat, he prayed she'd have the sense not to try to go through the woods. She could easily get caught by the tide.

TWENTY-TWO

The brambles caught at Claire's legs and left long bloody scratches on her skin as she fought her way through the shadowy forest. Gnats attacked her face and eyes, and she batted at them before checking her cell phone again. Still no signal. Maybe at the next rock she could get one bar. The more she'd trekked in this wilderness, the more she was ready to do battle with Ric when she saw him. Even his father would be livid.

Her ribs ached, and she wanted nothing more than a glass of iced tea. She'd been forging her way through the brush for several hours, and she had no idea how far she was from the highway. Probably hours yet in this kind of terrain. Early tendrils of fog hung in wisps through the tops of the evergreens. She broke through the tree line and stopped in her tracks. The tide was quickly washing out the path she'd intended to take. Would she have to wait until low tide to reach civilization?

A wave made her retreat farther back in the trees. Now what? The water came closer and began to push her toward a hillside. She couldn't go back the way she came. She felt out of breath, but she was going to have to climb that hillside.

A wave washed over her foot, and she scrambled up the hill. Her chest burned with the exertion, but she gritted her teeth and put one foot in front of the other until she finally stood on the top. From this vantage point, she could see the forest marching along the rocky coastline. A shiver went down her spine at how isolated she was out here. The ocean lapped at the stones. If only she had a boat or some way to travel by water.

Luke had surely missed her by now. She squinted at the sun glaring in her face and saw a boat heading toward the cove. Had Ric come back for her? She could only imagine Francisca's reaction when she found out her brother had abandoned her on a deserted beach. Claire eyed the rock face. Could she climb down to the beach from here since the way she'd come was cut off by water now? The slope wasn't that bad, and there were plenty of tree roots for hand and foot holds. If she were in tiptop shape, she wouldn't hesitate, but the dull pain radiating through her ribs gave her pause. She sidled closer to the edge and looked closer.

She peered up at a dark hole about fifteen feet below her in the rock face. The thought of a cave made her shudder at what might be inside. Bats and spiders, most likely. She squinted and thought she saw something brightly colored. A scrap of material or clothing? The bright-red material enticed her forward.

It seemed an easy climb down. She could rest on the cave ledge, then get down the rest of the way. She grabbed hold of a heavy root and shook it. It seemed sturdy enough. She kicked off her flip-flops and slid her toes down to rest on an even stouter clump of roots. Bit by bit, she crept down the slope with the wind buffeting her until she was three feet above the cave.

There was a ledge outside the opening. Holding her breath, she kicked off from the face of the rock and let go. Her feet landed on the soft dirt, and she fell to her hands and knees facing the cave opening. As she hit, she caught a whiff of something rank and decaying. The wind whipped around her in a nearly deafening whistle. Wrinkling her nose, she grabbed her cell phone and turned on the flashlight app, then shone it into the opening. Her gaze traveled over the heap that seemed to be a pile of clothing until the light landed on tangled blond hair.

A squeak escaped her mouth and she backpedaled. One foot reached for the next step and found nothing but air. She pinwheeled forward and grabbed at a rock in time to avoid plunging over the edge. Her heart thumped against her sore ribs in a painful staccato. She sat up and felt the world tip as her head spun. She quickly bent her neck and drooped her face forward until the spinning stopped, but she couldn't erase the vision of the body she'd just seen. There was no mistaking death in the greenish-gray cast of the woman's skin.

Could it be Jenny? She thought she recognized that blond hair. Shuddering, she lifted her head and inched toward the opening. She had to know for sure. Her hand shook as she aimed the light into the opening again. This time there was no doubt of the corpse's identity. Jenny Bennett, the hotel's front desk clerk.

Claire turned off the light and checked her phone. Still no bars. She turned and looked down at the beach. The boat was closer now, near enough to make out that it wasn't Ric returning for her, but Luke's older and sturdier boat. Of course. Who else would rescue her except Luke? She couldn't wait to learn how he'd found her. Maybe he'd forced the truth out of Ric. The thought made her smile.

It didn't matter how he'd found her. Nothing mattered except that the one person she most wanted to see had come when she needed him. But she had to get down from here. The next part of the trek looked more dangerous. Maybe she should stay here until she got Luke's attention. He might have a rope or a climbing apparatus that would help. She watched him drop anchor a few feet offshore, then jump over the side and wade to shore.

He cupped his hands and shouted her name, though she could barely hear him with the wind whistling around the cave opening. She waved and shouted, but he didn't seem to hear. She looked around for something to attract his attention and saw a large rock. It was all she could do to push it over the side. It rolled and thudded down the side until it landed at the bottom.

When he turned to see what had caused the rock to fall, she waved and screamed as loudly as she could. Luke shaded his eyes with his hand and looked her way. She jumped up and down, waving her arms.

He waved back and walked to the bottom of the cliff, then cupped his hands. "Claire, are you all right?" His voice faded as the wind whipped his words away.

She pointed at the cave and shouted back down to him. "I found Jenny."

His face changed as he caught her words. "Dead?"

She nodded. "I'm not sure how to get down. Do you have a rope?"

"I'm coming up." He jogged back to the boat and returned with a rope slung over his shoulder.

She couldn't wait to get away from the way Jenny's dead eyes seemed to look accusingly her way. Shuddering, she crossed her arms over her chest and watched him inch his way up the rock face. As he neared, she crouched over the edge, then he hauled himself up to stand beside her.

Without thought, she practically fell into his arms. He held her close, so close she could smell his skin, salty with perspiration. The sensation of his heart thudding under her ear and his comforting embrace around her made her want to burrow closer. Why did he affect her this way? The firm and sure way he held her drained the jitters out of her. She clung to him until she gathered her composure and stepped back with her arms to her side.

His expression held such a flicker of tenderness that it gave a hitch to her next breath. She turned back toward the cave to break the invisible connection between them. "Someone had to have hidden her body there, but what a chore to drag it up here."

He looked back out over the sea. "I'm going to secure the body for Beau, and then I'll get you down from here."

Luke shone his small flashlight into the darkness of the cave. The stench made him hold his breath. When he saw Jenny's body, his gut clenched and he fought nausea. Claire hovered close to his side and clutched his arm with cold fingers.

He focused the light on Jenny. "The body appears intact. I don't think she was in the water. The fish would have gotten to her by now. Someone put her here." Flipping off his light, he pulled Claire out of the close, fetid cave. She huddled next to him, and he put his arm around her, pulling her against his side. "Are you okay?"

She nodded. "Ric told you where I was?"

He curled his free hand into a fist. "Only with persuasion. His sister cornered him too. She'd been trying to call you, and he told her you were in your suite. She knocked, but you didn't answer so she was suspicious. I bet he's already headed out of town. I suspect your dad will be outraged at his behavior."

She took his fisted hand in hers. "Thanks for rescuing me, Luke. I should have known you'd find me. You're my hero."

She could have died out here. Hugging her, he looked down the rock face. "You're not home free yet, honey. We have to get down now."

"We could climb back to the top and walk down."

"That would take hours, and we'd miss our romantic dinner."

Her dimples came and went. "I think we're already going to miss it. We'll be lucky to get to the beach by sundown at eight."

"You have a point." He released her to reach down and grasp the rope he'd brought up, then looked around for a place to tie it on. A sturdy tree root seemed the best choice, but he didn't entirely trust it. Looping it through, he tested its strength. "I think this will do. You think you can climb down or do you want me to lower you?"

She hesitated. "Normally I'd say I could climb down, but I'm pretty wiped out and my ribs are hurting. I can try, though."

He shook his head. "Better to let me just lower you, then. I'm going to make a harness. I may only be able to get you about five feet above the sand, but you shouldn't get hurt by jumping from there."

Knotting the rope, he fashioned a harness. "When you're ready to let go, just tug on this end and it will pull free. Got it?"

"Got it." She leaned over and brushed her lips across his cheek. "Let's go."

He touched the warm spot where her lips had been, then dropped his hand back to his side. Her time here was drifting away too fast. Once she unraveled the mystery surrounding her disappearance, she'd go back to her life in Boston, and he'd move on with his role at the cranberry farm.

"Step in here." He helped her don the harness. "Okay, now sit on the edge of the ledge and dangle your feet over. I'll start lowering you."

As she slipped into place, he wrapped the rope around his waist and planted his feet. She looked back up at him. "I'm a little scared."

"I won't let anything happen to you."

"I know." She inhaled and scooted closer to the edge. "I'm ready."

The rope grew taut as he lowered her over the edge. The rough hemp bit into his torso as he took her weight. The rope rasped against his hands as he fed it through. He moved quickly to make sure the tree root held. When the length had played out, he leaned over the edge and gazed down. Her feet still looked about six feet above the sand.

"That's all I got," he called down.

She looked up, her face a pale moon in the fading light. "I'm still pretty high. Can you get me a little closer?"

He checked the length at the tree root. If he untied it, he might get her a little lower, but he ran the risk of not being able to hang on to the rope. If she fell when she wasn't expecting it, she might get hurt. It would be safer to instruct her how to fall.

He peered back over the edge. "I want you to let out the harness, then fold into a ball and roll as you hit the sand. It's not as far as it seems."

Would she do it? She seemed to be assessing the distance, then she gave him a thumbs-up and reached for the harness. Pulling her knees to her chest, she tugged the harness, and the knot came loose. She plummeted to the ground, then rolled onto the sand. He held his breath until she got up, brushing herself off.

"I'm okay! Come on down." She went to

the bottom of the rope.

"Coming over now." Before he grabbed the rope, he stepped into the cave and snapped a picture of Jenny's body on his phone. Then he went to the edge of the ledge and grabbed the rope. It was short work to rappel down, something he often had to do in his job.

He dropped the last couple of feet and rolled when he hit the sand. She was at his side in an instant. "You made it."

Gesturing at the sky, he smiled at her. "I think I have some beef jerky onboard. It's not quite what I had it mind, but at least we can look at the moon coming up."

TWENTY-THREE

The hotel bustled with late dinner guests as Claire and Luke crossed the lobby to the elevator. By the time she reached her suite, every muscle in her body ached from the exertion of the day. She glanced at the door to her parents' suite. "I should let them know I'm back and everything is all right." She'd reassured her mother on the phone, but knowing Mom, she'd want to see her with her own two eyes. Yawning, she inserted her key card into its slot. "I'll do it later, though. I need chocolate."

"I thought coffee cured everything." Luke grinned and pushed open the door after the green light came on. "Let me check out your room."

She reached past him and flipped on the light. "Just don't touch my chocolate or I'll have to hurt you."

"If it doesn't have peanut butter in it, I'm not interested."

"It's dark chocolate mint."

"Even worse." He went through the suite, checking under the bed and in the closet and bathroom before examining the balcony. "All clear."

The bed had been turned back, and she snatched up the Andes mint with glee. "Ah, my savior." She unwrapped the green foil and popped the sweet delight into her mouth. She closed her eyes. "Ah, blessed energy. Jerky just doesn't do it."

He stepped to her side and put his arm around her shoulders. "You mock my home-made jerky? It even had cranberries in it."

She gave him a cheeky grin. "I admit it was the best jerky I've ever had, but nothing beats chocolate."

"As long as you're happy, I'm happy." His lips were smiling, but his gaze searched hers.

The smile died on her lips. "Don't look at me like that. I'm fine."

"A jerk just left you to rot on an abandoned beach. That's got to take its toll."

Her eyes burned. "Well, when you put it like that . . ."

"Sorry. It just burns me that someone would treat you like that. Would treat anyone like that. Castillo should be shot. Drawn and quartered. Boiled in oil."

"Spoken like a true pirate." The chocolate

was gone, melted into the last of a sweet coating on her tongue. And she was so tired. "I have a feeling he's long gone. Otherwise I'd get the oil ready."

He dropped his arm from her shoulders. "Ah, that's my wench."

She'd like to be his wench. The warmth of his embrace seeped into her cold skin. All she wanted to do was pull on pajamas and fall into bed, but they both turned at a knock on the door. Her grandmother called her name, and Claire rushed to open it.

"Claire, I've been so worried."

She bent to hug her grandmother. "I'm okay, Grandma." Her perfume was a comforting scent.

"No thanks to that ruffian."

"Luke and I were discussing boiling him in oil." Claire straightened and managed a smile. Her grandmother would be on her side no matter what.

Grandma pulled a hanky from the pocket of her skirt and rubbed her eyes. "Thank you for rescuing her, young man. Maybe you're not the ladies' man I thought you were. You have backbone."

"More than you know, Grandma. He scaled a cliff and then lowered me down it with brute strength."

She hesitated and decided not to tell her

grandmother about finding Jenny's body. Luke had texted the picture to the sheriff, and they had stopped to give a statement on the way back to the hotel. No sense in worrying Grandma more.

Her grandmother reached over and squeezed Luke's upper arm. "My Claire needs a strong man to look out for her. I think you'll do."

Claire's face went hot. "Grandma!"

Luke chuckled. "I like a woman who speaks her mind." He brushed a kiss over her grandmother's powdered cheek. "I'll do my best to take good care of Claire." Turning toward the door, he touched Claire's shoulder as he passed. "See you tomorrow."

"Thanks, Luke. Rest well." Her tongue felt like it was tripping over itself. The door shut behind him.

"I take back everything I said about that young man. I think he's a good guy, Claire." Her grandmother wagged her finger in Claire's face. "I see the way you look at him, young lady. You've got stars in your eyes like I did when I met your grandpa. Don't rush things, though. You have all the time in the world."

Claire gestured to the sofa. "Have a seat, Grandma, and I'll get you some tea." With her grandmother in this good of a mood, maybe she could get her to talk.

"I can't stay long. Timothy won't go to bed until I get back, and he had a yawn as big as the Grand Canyon when I left." She moved to the white sofa and settled on the overstuffed cushion. "I don't like the things that have been happening to you. I think you should go home now that the merger talk is over. Hire a bodyguard. Keep your head down until they find that man."

"I'm not certain the merger is dead. I want to talk to Francisca." Claire wasn't about to give up that easily.

Luke hadn't often been in the sheriff's office. In fact, he wasn't sure he'd ever been in this fifteen-foot-square room that smelled of the sheriff's ever-present Altoids. The room was painted an unremarkable beige. A few pictures of Sheriff Colton's boys hung on the wall by the equally beige file cabinets. His hands in his pockets, Luke studied the picture of the smiling Little League team the year they won the state pennant title. Colton's wife was gone now, carried off by emphysema ten years ago, and the pictures were a sad reminder of a happier time. Those little boys were Luke's age and gone, too, from the fishing village where they grew up.

The Colton boys were living out their dreams. Jack was a high-powered lawyer in Seattle, and Ben owned a Cadillac dealership in Dallas. And here Luke was, back in the remote community he'd been all too eager to escape. He'd sworn never to come back here and live close to the father he always feared. All he'd ever wanted was to be a Coastie. He loved his job in the law enforcement division. Could he give that up to run Rocco Cranberries and deal with his father every day? The thought choked off his oxygen, and he went to the open window and took a few deep breaths of grass-scented air.

The door opened behind him, and the sheriff entered. A crumb of bread was stuck to his mustache, and it took all Luke's concentration not to reach over and flick it away.

He glanced at Luke and nodded. "Thanks for coming down right away, Luke. I didn't want to talk about this in front of your dad. He's already so frail." He pointed to the chair on the opposite side of his desk. "Have a seat. This won't take long."

Luke perched on the edge of the chair. Was that suspicion on Danny's face? Ever since Luke had first begun to worry that Pop might be guilty of . . . something, he'd

256

been looking for confirmation in the sheriff, who knew Pop better than just about anyone else.

He made himself rest his hands on his knees and forced a calm but interested expression. "Is something wrong, Danny?"

He steepled his hands together. "What's your take on Claire Dellamare?"

So this wasn't about his father. "I like her, and I respect her, which is even more important. Why? What's this all about?"

"I find it odd that she claimed Jenny was shoved off a cliff, then days later just *happens* to be the one to find her out at Dead Man's Cove. And we have that letter from Jenny. I'd like you to see if she will tell you about her relationship with Jenny. I'm not getting anything from Deputy Waters. He claims he never heard Jenny mention Ms. Dellamare, but there has to be some connection we're not seeing."

"Come on, Danny. She just got to town a few minutes before she saw Jenny's murder. She hardly had time to kill Jenny and then get the body off to the cove. You talked to her right there on the beach yourself. It would have taken hours to haul Jenny's body out to the cove, then lift it to the cave and hide it — if she were even strong enough."

Danny swiped at his mustache, dislodging the crumb. "I'm not saying she killed Jenny, but I think she might know who did and is protecting him. I wouldn't be surprised if she drew that painting to throw us off. I want you to draw her out and see if you can get anything out of her."

The man was as rigid as a post. Luke would have to tell him what Isabelle had said. "There's something you're unaware of." He launched into what they'd found out.

Danny popped three Altoid mints in succession, and his mouth grew more pinched. "So this should be right up your alley, Mr. Detective. I think your precious Claire is in this up to her pretty eyes. You can find out if you've got the guts to look."

"I'm not going to spy for you, Danny. Especially not when I don't believe Claire knows anything. She just happened to be in the wrong place at the wrong time."

"And she's somehow involved in your mother's death, Luke. Doesn't that matter to you?"

Luke stiffened at the derision in the sheriff's voice. "She was four years old when my mother died. Even if her crying was what lured my mother to her death, Claire was a child. She can hardly be blamed for what happened to Mom. Where is this coming from, Danny? I don't get it."

His fingers convulsed on the Altoid tin he held. "She seems my most likely suspect."

"What about Andy Waters? He was living with Jenny. Shouldn't you be looking at him pretty hard? The person closest to the victim is often involved. Maybe he found out she was cheating on him."

The sheriff exhaled so hard his mustache quivered. "Andy has an airtight alibi. He's devastated at Jenny's death. So it makes sense to look at Ms. Dellamare and anyone else close to the scene that day."

Luke stood and crossed his arms over his chest. "Want to look at me too? Meg and I were just around the curl of sand. Claire had been with us just before she was attacked. She'd only been gone fifteen minutes when Jenny was killed. So we were in the vicinity too. And there were hundreds of guests up at the inn. You checking them out?"

Danny rose too. "You should watch yourself, boy. Better men than you have been fooled by a pretty face. I think there's more to that woman than we know. And I aim to find out what part she plays in this."

Luke pressed his lips together and headed for the door. "You'll do it without my help, then, Danny. I want no part of persecuting Claire Dellamare." Danny's phone rang as Luke slammed the door behind him and stalked down the hall.

He'd just reached the door when Danny came running after him. "Luke, another body's been found on your property. We've got to get out there."

TWENTY-FOUR

Morning sunlight slanted through the kitchen window and illuminated dust motes dancing in the air. The aroma of coffee filled the air as Kate slathered her mother's blueberry jam onto her toast as she kept an eye on the driveway. Mom had asked her over for breakfast, and Kate braced herself for a scolding. So far her mother hadn't mentioned anything as she stood at the stove fixing omelets.

The growl of an engine erupted with the crunch of tires on gravel. A big black Cadillac rolled to a stop in the drive. She'd seen the rage in her father's eyes when he saw her sitting with his precious Claire, so she wasn't surprised by the sight of his long legs sliding out of the car.

Spatula in hand, her mother turned. Only now did Kate notice the pressed slacks and form-fitting top that revealed her mother's curvaceous figure. Her hair was usually up in a ponytail, but today it curled around her shoulders. The high-heeled espadrilles were the finishing touch. A girlish flush on her cheeks showed her excitement. And she wore makeup, something Kate hadn't seen her do in years.

Kate's stomach plunged. "He called, and you planned an ambush. Nice."

Her mother fluffed her short brown hair. "You have no one but yourself to blame, Kate. I told you to leave it alone." Her lips curved in a welcoming smile as his shoulders blocked out the sunshine streaming through the back door. She stepped to the door and threw it open. "Harry, it's been a long time. Join us for breakfast?"

His smile seemed forced to Kate, but her mother preened when he put his hand on her shoulder, then brushed past her into the house.

His presence dominated the room even more than his Giorgio Armani cologne overpowered the coffee aroma. Kate's hands shook as she rose to face him. "Hello, Harry."

"So it's Harry now? What about Dad?"

She eyed the smile that seemed to say all the right things. "I thought you didn't want to have anything to do with me."

"You caught me off guard, honey. And I

don't know how to break all this to my wife." He shot an uneasy glance at Kate's mother before looking back at Kate. "That doesn't mean you and I can't have a relationship. I'd like to get to know you better, get caught up. What's this about being sick?"

She managed to loosen her tight grip on the coffee handle and set it on the kitchen table. "I have aplastic anemia."

He reached out and ran one finger over the bruises on her arm. "Your disease caused these?"

She flinched and pulled her long sleeve down over them. "Yes, just a slight bump bruises me when it's acting up. I got it after a viral infection when I was eighteen."

"You need money? I can give you what you need, Kate."

"I need a stem-cell transplant. Mom isn't a good match. You might be, but Claire would have an even better chance."

His eyelids flickered. "I'll take some of that coffee, Mary."

"Of course." In her haste to get it, she nearly spilled her own cup.

Harry leaned forward. "Here's the thing, Kate. If you and I are going to have a relationship, it needs to be kept quiet. My wife would never understand. Claire wouldn't understand. Surely among all the people in this country, we can find a donor for you. I can be tested too. But let's leave Claire out of it, okay?"

He seemed so logical, so earnest. She should have known better than to expect him to be the dad she needed. All he cared about was hiding her away. His smiles and kind words were only meant to get her to stay quiet.

She ducked her head. "That's not why I wanted to meet her. She's my sister. How would you feel if you had a brother you never got to see? Claire deserves to know she has a half sister."

He licked his lips. "Give me some time, honey. When the time is right, I'll tell Claire."

His lie coiled in the room like a rattle-snake. Pressing her hand to her throbbing temple, she bit back the angry words on her tongue. "Why now? Why try to have a relationship with me now?"

"I shouldn't have cut you off, Kate. I'm sorry for that. But let's not upset Claire and Lisa over my shortcomings. This is between you and me, not them."

Kate's eyes stung at the way her mother moved beside him in a solidarity stance. She wouldn't cry, not in front of him. "What's your precious Claire been through? I bet it's nothing like what I've endured growing up fatherless and thrown away like some piece of trash. And when I got sick, you never even —" She looked away.

"I didn't know you were sick. You seem fine now, healthy and strong."

She opted not to answer that. He wouldn't care anyway. "You never even sent a birthday card. It was like I didn't exist."

He glanced at her mother again. "We thought it best for me to stay away."

Kate gasped and studied her mother who wasn't refuting his statement. "You agreed he shouldn't see me anymore? You wanted the money, and it didn't matter how it affected me, right?"

She was done with them both. Neither of them had given any thought to how this transaction might affect her. "It would serve you both right if I got in the car now and drove straight to the hotel to tell Claire the truth. I doubt she would be as approving of your neglect as you are."

He held out his hand toward her. "Please don't do that. I know I've been a lousy father, but there's no reason to ruin my wife's and daughter's lives because of it. Think about someone besides yourself."

She wanted to hit him. "I've done that all my life. You'd know that if you'd ever been around."

Was he right? Would knowing the truth hurt Claire? Kate didn't want to bring her pain, but she'd understood her half sister's longing for more family. Wouldn't the news come as a wonderful surprise?

Her mother touched his arm. "Let's all sit down and have some breakfast. We can discuss this as adults."

He shook off her touch. "I've said all I came to say. I can't change the past, Kate. Just stay away from Claire and Lisa."

His peremptory tone stiffened her spine again. "I'll give you forty-eight hours to tell Claire and your wife yourself. If you don't confess, I'll tell Claire the truth. I think she'll believe me."

She didn't tell either of them she feared the frequent weak spells she'd had lately meant she needed her sister's help more than ever. Tomorrow's appointment would tell her for sure.

The sun beat down in an unseasonably warm day, and vultures swooped in the blue sky over the woods where Luke stood watching the events unfold. Circles of sweat stained the shirts of the diggers bending to their task in the ditch. It had only been a week ago tonight since Luke had stood in this old field and looked down on his mother's remains. Who else had died here, or had they found more of his mother's bones?

His expression somber, Beau approached Luke. "Sorry to put you through this again."

"More of Mom's bones? At least we'll have them all for the memorial service."

Beau shuffled his boots in the freshly turned dirt. "Can't really tell yet. The coroner just got here, and we should know more soon."

Luke frowned at the way Beau seemed way more interested in checking out the dirt. Why wasn't he talking? "Looked like quite a few bones from what I could tell."

Beau didn't reply. He stood off from Luke a few feet with his hands thrust in his khaki slacks and his expression carefully blank. The coroner gestured for the sheriff to join her. Beau started forward too, and Luke found himself walking quickly through the weeds and scrubs toward the men clustered around the coroner, Genevieve Ross, who huddled protectively over the pile of bones.

Genevieve had been coroner for as long as Luke could remember. She had to be in her seventies by now, but she walked the rolling hills with as much grace as a thirty-year-old.

Beau turned and frowned. "You'd better stay back, Luke."

Luke folded his arms across his chest. "This is Rocco land, Beau. I'm staying unless you want to arrest me."

His old friend heaved a sigh. "Keep your mouth shut or the sheriff just might do that."

Luke craned his head over the top of Beau's shoulder and didn't answer. The scent of freshly upturned soil hung in the air. Genevieve was saying something, but he couldn't make out the words. He edged closer and let his gaze sweep over the scene. Her iron-gray hair hung down her back. Flecks of mud marred her navy slacks, and she used a latex-gloved hand to push her glasses up on her nose. She'd quit talking by the time Luke got close enough to hear.

"So you're saying these are definitely not the remains of Victoria Rocco?" the sheriff asked.

"That's right." Genevieve reached down and retrieved a long, thin bone. "This femur belongs to a child of three to five. The remains are clearly not those of an adult woman. There is long blond hair attached to the small skull as well, so I believe this is the body of a little girl."

Oh no. Luke took a step back at the

268

thought of a child being found here. A distressed murmur raced through the group assembled there. No one liked to think about a child lying undiscovered out here.

The bones looked pitiful in the dirt. Poor little thing. "How long has she been dead?" The words were out of Luke's mouth before he could hold them in.

Danny turned at the sound of Luke's voice. "I told you to stay back." His voice vibrated with displeasure.

Luke ignored him and stepped closer to Genevieve. "How long ago did she die? Can you tell how she died?"

"I'll need to run more tests when I get the remains back to the morgue, but it's been at least a couple of years since there's no flesh on the bones."

Luke couldn't recall a search for a missing child in recent memory. He only prayed they would figure out who the girl belonged to and give her family the same closure he'd felt yesterday when he'd heard the confirmation that they'd found his mother.

One of the deputies called out from ten feet away, "I found some clothing scraps." The man carried a paper bag to the coroner, and she took it with eagerness and reached inside. She brought out a scrap of pink fabric. "Looks like a bit of a dress with some lace."

Pink with lace. Where had he heard of a little girl wearing a lacy pink dress? Then it hit him. When Claire went missing, she'd been wearing a pink dress, but that had been twenty-five years ago. These remains were newer than that, weren't they?

He looked at the coroner. "What's the oldest they could be?"

She shrugged. "Could be decades. It's hard to say. Do you have an idea who it might be?"

Luke glanced from her to Danny. An awful suspicion began to take hold. "Anything else in there?"

"This was lying near the body." Genevieve held out a small locket in her latex-covered palm.

"Did you open it?"

"Not yet." She scowled over it. "I'll need to pry it open back in the lab, but there are initials engraved on the back: *CD.*"

Claire Dellamare. What had happened the night Claire went missing? Had there been some other little girl who disappeared too? And if so, how had she gotten Claire's locket? Maybe the two little girls had been together.

Danny's brow furrowed, then his expres-

270

sion finally cleared. "I think we shouldn't say anything about this until we find out more about what happened, Luke. Agreed?"

Luke's chest squeezed. "Agreed."

If Claire had been upset about her missing year before, how was she going to feel when she found out another little girl had been missing that night too? And she hadn't made it home like Claire. Was there a monster preying on children in these peaceful fields?

TWENTY-FIVE

Friday afternoon Claire hurried across the pink-granite rocks toward where Luke waited for her. The puffs of clouds floating lazily across the blue sky eased the tension from her as she waded into the cold water of the orca's pen with a pail of fish in her hand. She slapped the water to call him, and he zipped quickly over to nudge her hand before doing flips in the water as if to coax Claire to feed him. She laughed and tossed him his lunch.

Luke moved her way down the pier, then sat on the side and dangled his legs over the edge. "How'd the talk go with Francisca?"

"She is in favor of the merger, and she's going to talk to her family. I'm not sure she can convince them, though."

"You don't sound upset about it."

The cold water numbed her legs. "I'm not. We'll manage one way or the other."

The fish were gone in minutes, and she

rinsed her hands in the cold salt water. "I'm all out of food, little man."

Luke jumped over the side of the pier into the water and smacked his hand in the water, then shot a splash her way. "I don't think he believes you."

The shock of cold water made her laugh harder. She splashed him back, then tried to run as he approached threateningly. She was giggling so hard that her right foot slipped on a wet rock and her head went under. The next thing she knew, a wave grabbed her and tossed her to the bottom. A hand grabbed the back of her blouse and yanked her up. She came up gasping for air and found herself clasped tightly against Luke's broad chest. He made no sudden move to release her.

She looked at her fists, tightly bunched in his wet shirt. She really should let him go, but she couldn't seem to force her fingers to release their grip. His hands, the fingers splayed to cover the most area possible, spanned her waist and held her securely. The scent of his skin mingled with that of the sea, a very enticing aroma. Her gaze went to his mouth, and she wished she dared to run her finger along the outline of those firm lips. Her pulse had never raced like this in her life, had it?

His brown eyes darkened to nearly black, and his grip on her waist tightened as he drew her just a bit closer. His head started down, and her eyes drifted shut as she turned her face up to welcome the kiss she knew was coming.

His lips brushed hers, and she inhaled the masculine scent of his skin. The kiss deepened, and she curled her fists into his shirt.

"Uh, Luke," a male voice said behind her.

His hands released her so quickly she nearly fell back into the waves foaming around her knees. She whipped around to see the sheriff and Luke's deputy friend standing just out of reach of the waves rolling onto the sand. The sheriff's eyes narrowed as he looked her over, and her face flamed. He'd seen them kissing.

His gaze was cold, and she could have sworn she saw deep suspicion and distrust. She'd liked the sheriff until now, so his manner made her stumble as she exited the water and reached for the towel she'd left on the sand.

"We'd like to speak with you, Ms. Dellamare." A steel undertone layered his formal request.

She wiped off her face and hair. "Of course. Is it about Jenny?" The cool breeze touched her chilled skin, and she shivered, then draped the towel around her shoulders.

Luke's warm fingers pressed into the flesh at her elbow, and she took comfort from his touch of courage. Something was very wrong, and she gripped her hands together as she waited for Sheriff Colton to tell her why his hazel eyes were so cold and why his manner was so stiff.

She sidled a step closer to Luke. "What's wrong, Sheriff?"

He glanced at Luke. "Did you tell her what we found yesterday?"

Luke knew about this? Claire slanted a glance up at Luke who was shaking his head. "Luke? What's he talking about?"

"I didn't know much, Danny, so of course I didn't say anything. I assume you're here because you know more." Luke heaved a sigh and ran his hand through his damp hair. His fingers tightened on her arm, and his eyes held compassion. "There was another body found on my land yesterday."

Another body? She took a step back. "Oh no. Do you know who it is?"

"I'll have to let Danny explain himself because I'm not sure," Luke said.

The sheriff shuffled closer, his black shoes just inches from the water. "I thought I'd have to wait on DNA results for the body, but we got an immediate match on dental records. I couldn't believe it, so I rechecked it myself and spoke to the dentist where we obtained the records. There's no doubt on the child's identity. The locket helped too. I'm going to run DNA, just because it involves Dellamare, but I'm sure."

"Child?" Claire leaned against Luke, and his hand left her elbow and went to her waist as he pulled her closer into his side. "Locket?"

The sheriff nodded. "A four-year-old child, to be precise, Ms. Dellamare. We also found scraps of a lacy pink dress. The little girl had blond hair."

A child the same age she'd been when she wandered off. Was there some kind of serial killer out there? And even if there was, why were the sheriff and his deputy staring at her like she might change into an alien at any moment? Nothing about this situation seemed to concern her, and certainly it shouldn't have lodged such suspicion in their eyes. Surely they didn't think *she'd* killed the child?

Her mind raced in a thousand directions and landed nowhere that made sense. "Who is the child?"

"The locket held a picture of Mr. and Mrs. Dellamare. It was engraved on the back with the letters *CD*. The little girl has been identified as Claire Dellamare. She just had a dental appointment before her birthday when she chipped a tooth."

Claire held up her hand. "Wait, that can't be true. I'm Claire Dellamare. There can't be two of us." What did this mean? She couldn't process it.

"Precisely, Ms. Whoever-You-Are. I can't call you Claire Dellamare because we have no idea who you are or who told the Dellamares that you were Claire." The sheriff leaned closer, and his minty breath washed over her face. "I'll tell you what I think. I believe Jenny figured this out, and you killed her to stop her from spilling the beans."

Luke's fingers tightened around her waist. "Come on, Danny! Whatever happened, Claire had nothing to do with it. Can't you see how shocked she is at this news? Heck, I'm shocked. I mean, I knew you'd found a child, but I assumed some other little girl was missing at the same time."

"She's a good actress." The sheriff clenched his fists. "I'm going to be digging into this, and I'll find out who she's been in contact with from here. Because this didn't happen by itself with no intervention."

The roaring in her ears increased to a deafening sound that blocked out all reason and thought. *Not Claire Dellamare.*

Luke touched her arm. "Claire?"

Leaning into Luke's strength, she managed to hold up her head and face the sheriff's derision. "I think we'd better talk to my parents."

The familiar smell of doctor's office antiseptic and new carpet enveloped Kate like a forgotten memory. She flipped through a *Cosmopolitan* but didn't really see the words fluttering by. Her mother was engrossed in a conversation with a bald little boy of about two who had brought his tractor to show off.

Kate watched them a moment. Had her mother ever shown her that much attention as a child? If so, she didn't remember it. Her childhood had been spent in the blueberry barrens, and her uncle Paul had been more of a parent than her mother. But since she'd gotten sick, her mom had changed.

Kate shot to her feet when the nurse called her name and hurried across the brown carpet to follow the white-clad uniform to the first door on the right. Her mother followed them and went to her spot in an upholstered chair in the corner. Kate settled on the examination table. The white paper crinkled as she shifted to submit to a blood pressure check.

The nurse raised her brow. "Up a little, Kate. One fifty over ninety."

Kate managed a smile. "White-coat syndrome."

Seascapes decorated the brown tweed walls, and she concentrated on the impossibly white sails of a large ship. From the rocks and landscape, she recognized the location as Acadia, one of her favorite places. She avoided looking at her mother. They both feared what the doctor would say. The lurid bruises on Kate's arms and shins told a grim story.

The door opened, and Dr. Bain stepped inside. A tall, handsome man in his fifties, he wore a kind manner like a favorite shirt. "Ah, my favorite patient. How are you doing today, Kate?" His voice was a pleasant rumble.

"Okay."

He stepped to her side and tilted her chin up, looking her in the eyes. "Lots of fatigue?"

She nodded. "And bruises." She showed him her legs and arms. "The news is bad, isn't it?"

He settled on the stainless steel stool at his small desk and flipped open her chart. "Hmm." Flipping through several pages, he read each one, then closed the chart. "This latest drug isn't working."

Kate's stomach clenched, though she'd been expecting it. The telltale fatigue. "I could have told you that without all the tests. Now what?"

He glanced at her mother. "How are you holding up, Mary?"

Kate's mother looked down at the floor. "It's hard watching your daughter struggle. But she's going to be all right. We just have to change drugs."

The doctor sighed, a heavy sound that tightened Kate's gut and made her sit up straighter. "What is it? Worse than we expected?"

He rolled his pen between his fingers. "I just don't know what to do next, Kate. We've been through all the normal treatments. I've never seen aplastic anemia so resistant to treatment right out of the gate. I'd like to try a stem-cell transplant, but we haven't found a good donor."

She already knew a transplant offered the hope of an actual cure, but her antigens were rare or something. She didn't totally understand it. "What about my uncle? Mom wasn't a match, but we never did test Uncle Paul."

"Have him come in and we can check him, but your mom is so far off I think it's unlikely your uncle would work."

Her mother gripped her hands together in her lap. "Can't we just try my cells? Maybe they would work."

"No, Mary, I'm sorry. We can't put Kate through that when success is so doubtful. I think for now we'll have to rely on blood transfusion. And pray for the right donor."

I am going to die. Kate struggled to draw in a breath. She had to stay positive and keep the fear at bay. "The more transfusions I have, the less likely it is that a transplant will work, right?"

"Yes." His large hand dropped onto her shoulder, and he squeezed.

She accepted the reassuring touch. "What if I don't find a donor? How long will the transfusions last? How many can I have before we have to give up the idea of a stem-cell transplant?"

"We can put the first one off a few days, but you'll need one very soon. Then you may not need another for weeks, and with any luck, we can find a donor before you have too many transfusions." He looked down at the floor. "But let's check you again in a couple of days, and if the levels drop even a little more, we'll do a transfusion."

The pressure in her chest intensified. "You don't think this is going to work, do you?"

The doctor held her gaze. "I'm going to fight right alongside you, Kate. I want you to hold on to your faith and fight with everything in you. Will you promise me that?"

She nodded, too choked up to answer him verbally. Her gaze sought out her mom's face, and she found resignation there.

Her mother gave a slight nod. "I think we'd better talk to Harry again."

TWENTY-SIX

Not Claire Dellamare.

"I'm not Claire." The constriction grew in her chest as the sheriff and his deputy stared at her. "Who am I, Luke?"

His fingers pressed her arm. "We don't know much yet, honey. Let's wait for the results of the DNA tests to come back. Maybe the sheriff is wrong about the dental records. After all, you were a child, so there might have been very similar X-rays for another child."

The sheriff loomed over her. "You're grasping at straws." Perspiration dotted his forehead, and he swiped at it, his hand shaking.

Why was he so upset when he'd basically told her that her entire life was a lie? Then she saw the reason for his agitation. Her father's raised voice was enough to scare the little orca right back out to sea. His pants were covered in sand, and his hair stood up on end as though he'd raked his hand through it.

He pointed his finger at the sheriff. "I got your ridiculous message. You can't possibly think I wouldn't know my own daughter! And you think my wife was in on the collusion? Next I suppose you'll say we murdered the real Claire and put someone else in her place. I'm calling my lawyer. I won't stand for this!"

Claire hadn't thought through the implications. Her father was right. If there was one thing she was certain of, it was that her mother would defend her to the death. She might have her own ideas about how Claire's life ought to go, but it was only because she loved her so much. If someone had brought another child to her and insisted she was Claire, her mother would have seen through that in a heartbeat.

The sheriff had to be wrong. The dental records were wrong.

Luke still held her, and she wished she could put her face against his chest and ignore the world. Unfortunately, she would have to bring calm to this chaos.

She brushed the sand from her legs, then pushed her hair out of her face, realizing her hair was nearly dry. Over Luke's shoulder, she saw Francisca was here too. Mom sat on a large rock off to one side of the melee. Her hands covered her face, and her shoulders shook with the ferocity of her sobs. Francisca stood beside her with her hand on Mom's shoulder. Claire caught Francisca's worried gaze and smiled to let her know things would be all right.

"I need to reassure my mom."

Luke glanced toward the two women. "I'll try to calm your dad. He's about to strangle the sheriff."

"I just might join him." She pressed her lips together and walked across the rocks.

Francisca's hair was still damp as if she'd been called while in the shower, and she wore black workout shorts and a tank. Her anxious gaze lingered on Claire's face. "You're very pale, Claire. I think you'd better sit down."

"Claire?" Her mother dropped her hands and wobbled to her feet. She grasped Claire by the shoulders and pulled her tight against her chest. "Oh, Claire, it's awful what they're saying! Just terrible. The sheriff seems to think we might have killed that poor little girl in the field and had you take her place. Where could he get such an insane idea?"

Claire closed her eyes and inhaled the aroma of her mother's Hermès perfume and coconut body wash. The scent made her wish she could be a little girl and climb into her mother's lap for a good cry. Her back stiffened and she pulled back gently. Nothing could be gained by avoiding this.

"I need to ask you about the day I was returned to you, Mom. I want to be sure in my own head what happened. How did you know it was me? I'd been gone a year. Children change so fast."

Her mother's fingers tightened on Claire's shoulders as though she was going to clutch at her again, then her shoulders sagged and her arms dropped back to the sides of her slim-fitting black sundress. "You'd changed, of course. Grown a bit taller, and you had a Maine accent." Her smile broke out. "It was quite cute, to tell you the truth, but I had to hire a speech therapist to get your accent back to normal."

Claire's mom was a master at changing the subject to avoid a topic that made her uncomfortable, but Claire couldn't afford to let her get off on a tangent. "About my appearance. Was there anything at all that gave you pause? Anything that suggested I might not be your daughter?"

Her mother picked at a nail and didn't look at her. The wind teased wisps of blond hair loose from her French twist. "Nothing important. I knew as soon as I saw your big blue eyes."

Claire glanced at Francisca, who had straightened and widened her eyes. "What did you see that you thought was unimportant?"

Her mother finally looked up with an almost guilty expression. She swiped the hair from her eyes and bit her lip. "It was so minor that it's ludicrous to bring it up now, Claire." She eased back onto the rock and clasped her hands together on her knee. "I really should calm your father down so we can get back to the hotel for dinner."

Claire knelt on the warm sand in front of her mother. "You're not going anywhere until you tell me, Mom. I have to know."

"Oh, for heaven's sake, Claire, you'd think it was a matter of life and death." A tinkling laugh came from her pale lips. "Fine, I'll tell you. Your father said things like that can change and grow over, and of course he was right. You had a scar on your right knee from falling off your trike when you were two. It was gone. But scars fade, of course, and you were so young that it made sense. One good thing was that you never had another asthma attack either. I think the cold air healed your lungs in that missing year."

Did scars like that fade? Francisca's face reflected the same doubt that Claire felt rising in her chest.

Moonlight filtered through the open window of her suite, and it was nearly as bright as twilight. Claire knew she ought to get up and close the drapes, but every muscle in her body ached. She moved her bare legs along the soft cotton sheets and buried her face in the sweet-smelling down pillow. She'd dozed off when she first went to bed, but the questions prodded her awake just after one, and her lids refused to stay shut.

She rolled to her stomach and punched her pillow. Prayer would help. She just needed to let go of this burden. While she didn't know for sure who her earthly father was, she knew who her heavenly Father was. That should be enough, shouldn't it?

Lord, calm me. Take this fear and uncertainty away.

Her eyes drifted shut, and she deliberately slowed her breathing. In and out, in and out. Her limbs relaxed, and she smiled at the sense of peace that began to claim her. She let herself remember Luke's smile, the way it flashed in his tanned face. His thick black hair always drew her attention and made her want to put her hands in it. She hadn't dared so far, but she was going to do it as soon as she had the courage.

He made her feel safe and treasured, and when she was in trouble, he always seemed to appear. Was that by God's design? This was the first time she'd ever felt such a strong connection to a man. When he looked at her, she felt as though he could see right inside, to the deepest secrets she never told anyone. Did he feel that way about her at all? He seemed to seek her out, but was it mere attraction or something deeper?

When the first thump came, she thought she'd knocked a pillow from the bed. Then she heard it again and opened her eyes. Before she could throw the covers off the bed, she saw movement from the corner of her eye — a man in black moving fast toward her. She didn't even get out a scream before a soft pillow came down on her face.

She fought against the hard hands holding her down. Struggling to draw in a breath, she found his wrists and tore at them to no avail. Spots danced in her vision, and she struggled to breathe past the suffocating softness pressed against her face. She had to get him off or she would die. She renewed her attack on his arms, digging her newly gelled nails into his skin.

He growled, and the pressure released slightly. Kicking off the covers, she brought her feet up and kicked him hard in the chest. He reeled back, and the pressure on her face eased. With the pillow off her nose, she coughed and drew in a sweet breath of air. She rolled to the opposite side of the bed and landed on the carpeted floor where she leaped to her feet and grabbed the lamp from the table.

The black ski mask he wore creeped her out. She shrieked a battle cry at the top of her lungs and brought the lamp crashing down on his head. He crumpled to his knees, and she raced for the door. She wrenched it open and tore down the hall toward the elevator. Screams ripped from her throat as she ran, pausing long enough to bang on other suite doors as she went.

She reached the elevator and punched the Down button, then turned to face her attacker. No one was there. He must be escaping. Did she dare go back to the room to try to identify him? She took a step back toward her room as her father rushed from his suite across the hall.

His blond hair askew and in his favorite blue pajamas, he hurried toward her. "What's wrong, Claire? I heard you scream."

"Someone was in my suite and tried to smother me. Call the sheriff." Though Sheriff Colton was the last person she wanted to see now. Her vision dimmed, and she leaned her head against the wall. "I feel a little woozy. Just give me a minute."

Her mother, still dragging her filmy white robe on over the matching nightgown, rushed from their suite and took Claire's hand. "Honey, are you all right? Harry, call the doctor. She's as cold as ice."

The silky feel of the white negligee encompassed her as her mother hugged her tight. "I'll be all right. I just need air." Claire dragged in several long breaths until her vision cleared. "Let me up, Mom. I need to see if he's still in there."

One by one, doors opened all down the hall as guests peeked out. Two security men dressed in blue uniforms dashed up the exit stairs. They were both young and beefy, and seeing their bulk and determined expressions, Claire felt safe enough to briskly step toward her door.

"Let me, Ms. D-Dellamare." The tallest security guard sent a sidelong glance her way, and she knew the news of her identity had raced through the town.

She lagged back to let him enter before

her. The lights flipped on, and she peeked through the doorway into her suite. At first nothing looked disturbed except for the pillow and lamp on the floor, then she saw her easel overturned. "My picture of Jenny's attacker — it's gone!" She stepped closer and saw her sketchpad was gone as well. He'd been here for several reasons, but who was he?

And would he be back to finish the job?

TWENTY-SEVEN

The sun pushed back the shadows as Kate drove her Volkswagen off the ferry and found a spot in the hotel parking lot. Her hands trembled as she punched the lock button and shut the driver's door. How did she even begin to tell Claire who she was? Yes, they'd had a pleasant though distant lunch, but how would a young woman of Claire's background react to such a wild statement by a complete stranger?

At least Kate had managed to wash out some of the atrocious red dye from her hair, though it still gleamed like copper in the light of the sun. The aroma of bacon and maple syrup drifted out the windows of the restaurant as she marched toward the hotel's front door. Did she call up to Claire's room and ask her to come down, or should she call her father and give him one more chance?

She brushed by several people checking

out and went to sit on the sofa by the fireplace while she considered her options. Stretching out her jean-clad legs, she people-watched for a few minutes while she gathered her courage. It was about nine, so maybe Claire hadn't had breakfast yet. All she had to do was pick up the house phone on the table beside her and ask to be connected to Claire's room, then invite her to come down for breakfast. If it was so simple, though, why did her hands go moist? She wiped her palms on her jeans and picked up the phone.

She stared out the window and listened with half an ear to people talk about the grisly find of a child's bones in a nearby cranberry field.

Claire's voice came over the earpiece. "Hello?" Her voice was flat, as though she was depressed.

"Claire? It's Kate. I wondered if maybe you'd want to have breakfast this morning?" A long pause stretched out, and she gripped the phone receiver so tightly her fingers went white. "Claire?"

"Sorry, Kate, it's just been a bad morning. I'm supposed to meet my parents for breakfast. You're welcome to join us."

Kate bit her lip. Did she have the courage to do this? "Of course. I'll get a table. See you in a few minutes." She replaced the receiver and stood. By the time she got a table, Claire and her parents would be down.

"Kate, what are you doing here?"

The familiar male voice made her whirl to face her father as the entry door closed. The scent of fresh air still lingered on him. Dressed in linen shorts and a casual blue shirt that opened at the neck to reveal a patchy bit of white hair, he stood with his feet apart and his hands on his hips.

She straightened and met his gaze with a defiant stare. "Exactly what I told you I was going to do. I'm going to tell Claire who I am. I think she will be happy to know she has a sister. Half sister," she amended when his gaze slid to the side and his face went white. Kate turned to look too.

Claire stood staring at the two of them. She glanced from her father to Kate. "What did you say?" Her blue eyes were shadowed and sad, and she looked pale, as though she hadn't slept well. She wore a pale-pink sundress that showed off her toned arms.

Her father shot Kate a warning glare. "Nothing much. Kate said you're having breakfast."

Claire stepped closer, her high-heeled white sandals slapping against the wood floor. "Dad, don't lie to me. Not anymore. I heard Kate say we were half sisters quite clearly. Is it true? I can't take any more deception." Her voice was low and choked.

Kate eyed Claire's white face. "What's wrong? Has something happened?"

Claire pushed her hair behind her ears. "Apparently I'm not a Dellamare. At least according to some dental records."

"I-I don't understand." Kate glanced from Claire to their father. "Look at us, Claire. We look so much alike." She flipped the ends of her garish hair. "This is dyed. I only did it to hide our resemblance for a while. Your father had an affair with my mother, and I'm the result. I bet if you put our baby pictures side by side, you wouldn't be able to tell us apart. We have the same big blue eyes. And look at the shape of my nose and lips. Isn't it like looking in a mirror?"

Claire's lips flattened and she shook her head. "You are mistaken, Kate. Is that why you cozied up to me in the bathroom? You thought you could get money from Dad with this claim? I'm sorry to burst your bubble, but becoming my friend isn't going to get you anything. He may be your father, but he's not mine. I'm probably going to be out on the street soon."

Harry reached toward her. "Don't be

ridiculous, Claire. Of course you're my daughter. This is all going to be sorted out soon. I think we should just go home to Boston and let law enforcement figure out their mistake."

He didn't look at Kate once during his plea. She couldn't take being ignored, not any longer. She plunged her hand into her pocket, brought out her trump card, and held it out. "I have proof, Claire. Here is a picture of me with Harry when I was five. Let's have a little chat with your wife. She might have some questions too. Here she comes."

Claire's chest tightened as she watched her mother approach. Dark circles shadowed Mom's eyes as though she hadn't slept well, but her blond bob was smooth and neat, and the clear turquoise of her top brightened her complexion. The hum of conversation around the hotel lobby made everything seem so normal, and yet it wasn't.

Claire had managed to hold herself together by clinging to the thought that the dental identification might be wrong, but Kate's defiant proclamation brought her to the edge of her control.

Kate stood off to one side. She twisted a lock of hair around one finger and bit her lip. What had she hoped to gain by coming here? Claire knew her father, and he didn't take kindly to being pushed. He could be all smiles while he was guiding his adversary to a cliff.

Claire stepped out to intercept her mother. The hotel lobby wasn't the right place to have a discussion like this. "Hey, Mom, let's get some breakfast." She took her mother's arm and tried to steer her back toward the clink of silverware and the scent of bacon in the breakfast area.

Her mother looked over Claire's shoulder to where Kate stood. "What's going on here?"

"Nothing." Dad smiled at Kate. "Just meeting as planned for breakfast."

Kate clenched her hands together and burst into noisy sobs. "I'm not going away. If you don't tell her, I will."

"Tell me what?" Mom's brows winged up, and she took a step back.

Claire stood frozen as she waited for some sign of what her dad would do. Her mother was one of the most possessive wives she knew, and she would erupt at this news. If it was even true, and Claire wasn't convinced Kate had told the truth. For all she knew, this was some kind of elaborate scheme to get money.

She released her mother's arm, then turned toward Kate. "Let's go talk this out. We don't need to go into this in front of the entire hotel."

Kate shook her head. "I'm not going anywhere. It's time there were no more secrets. Besides, I'm *sick*. I need help from my biological family."

Life-threatening sick? Claire took in the other woman's sallowness and the way her hands shook. Could she need an organ transplant or just money? Staring at her, Claire saw truth blazing out of Kate's blue eyes. However ludicrous the story seemed, Kate believed it wholeheartedly.

Claire's mother began to shred the tissue in her hands. "What does that have to do with us? Who are you?"

"This is Kate Mason." Claire went to Kate's side and took her arm. Heat radiated off Kate's skin, and up close, Claire could see how sick she was. "I'll listen to what you have to say, Kate. You can tell me about it over breakfast, and I'll help if I can."

Kate shook off Claire's grip. "I'm not going anywhere." She faced Claire's mother. "Your husband is my biological father."

When her mother swayed at the news, Claire leaped to catch her. Her mom glared at her husband. "Oh, Harry!" Her voice shook. She looked again at Kate. "You're Mary Mason's daughter, aren't you?"

Kate straightened. "You've met my mother?"

"She was my first housekeeper when we were newlyweds. She left to care for her sick brother." She went to the sofa by the fireplace and practically fell back onto it. "Or so I was told." Leaning forward, she put her face in her hands and moaned. "I can't believe this." She looked up and shot her husband a glare.

Claire sat beside her and put her arm around her mother's shoulders, but she shook off the embrace. Claire staggered when her mother pushed her, but Kate caught her arm and steadied her. Her mother had never acted so out of control before. Claire didn't know how to calm her. Maybe only Dad could.

Her mother lifted her head and glared at her husband, who took a step toward her. "When I confronted you about Mary, you made me think I was crazy, jealous for no reason. And all this time . . ." Her face went red, then white. "She was from this area, so you set her up here and continued to see her, didn't you? I remember the frequent visits you used to make. And you just had to have Claire's birthday party here. Everything that's happened is because you couldn't keep your pants zipped. How could you, Harry?"

The last sentence was a wail that made the hotel employees and guests turn and look toward the small group clustered in front of the fireplace. Claire's mother grabbed a metal basket of decorative balls placed on the table fronting the sofa, then seized the top one, a heavy ceramic red one, and threw it at her husband. It struck him in the chest and bounced to the polished hardwood floor.

He stood blinking stupidly at his wife until another round missile zoomed toward him. He ducked the blue ball. "Lisa, stop it. You're causing a scene."

A security officer headed their way, and the other guests gawked and whispered. Claire's mother didn't seem to notice as she continued to pelt her husband. The noise the balls made when they struck the hardwood floors reverberated around the lobby's tall ceilings. Tears streamed down her face, and her mouth contorted in a silent scream.

Ducking and zigzagging, Claire's dad managed to cross the ten feet separating them. When he reached his wife, she threw the empty basket at his head. His eyes wide and disbelieving, he touched his forehead and looked at his bloody fingers.

"I hate you," she panted. She rushed past the gaping guests and hotel employees.

Claire started to go after her, but her father put his hand on her arm. "Let me." He didn't look at her or Kate as he caught up with his wife near the elevator.

Claire closed her eyes and sighed. Everything was broken in a million pieces.

TWENTY-EIGHT

As soon as he entered the hotel, Luke turned toward the raised voices and picked up on the agitation in Claire's voice immediately. He quickly stepped past the bellman's desk. Everyone in the lobby craned their necks toward the two women near the fireplace. He was sure causing a scene was the last thing Claire would want, so whatever had happened had to be extreme.

Claire and the other young woman both had their hands balled into fists at their sides as they watched Harry Dellamare lead his wife into the elevator. The woman with Claire looked out of place with her faded jeans and tennis shoes under the gleaming crystal chandelier. Her dull hair was poorly dyed.

Claire bent down to retrieve a silver basket on the floor and put it on the table. She turned and saw him, and her gaze latched on to him as if he were her lifeline. "Luke."

She looked so beautiful and fresh in her pink sundress that he never would have guessed there was a problem if not for the circles under her eyes. She held out her hand, and he moved to take it. Her fingers were cold and shaking. "What's wrong?"

He knew she'd be upset from the revelations last night, but from her demeanor, he suspected something else had happened. Maybe the DNA had come back with incontrovertible truth. She drew closer as if to take strength from his presence. No one seemed to be eager to answer his question. The other young woman was biting her lip and shifting from foot to foot, but her defiant expression never changed. She couldn't seem to look away from Claire either.

He pressed Claire's hand with as much comfort as he could muster and waited for someone to answer him. "Do you need to sit down? You're pale."

She nodded, and dodging decorative balls, he led her to the tan sofa by the fireplace. The other woman hadn't moved from her spot. If she kept twisting that lock of hair, she was going to pull it right out of her head. She slowly followed and sank onto a chair opposite the sofa.

"Tell me," he said once Claire was seated. She licked her lips. "So much has happened that I don't know where to begin. Someone broke into my room last night and tried to smother me."

"What? Did he hurt you?" What if he'd come here this morning to flashing lights and a coroner carrying her out? "Did they catch him?"

She shook her head. "But he took the painting I did of the man I saw kill Jenny. And my notes of everything I remembered."

"Did you call the sheriff?"

"Yes, he's come and gone. Then there was this news about Kate this morning."

"What news?"

She didn't answer Luke, but the shaking in her hands eased as she looked across at Kate. "You're really a Dellamare, Kate, not me. That's going to take awhile for me to absorb."

What was Claire talking about? Luke took a moment to study Kate. She didn't look well with her sallow skin and the dark circles under her eyes. "I don't understand."

"This is Kate Mason. Kate is D-Dad's daughter. A secret family we knew nothing about. She informed us all this morning." Claire gestured at the balls around the room. "Mom threw stuff at him when she found out." Claire bit down on her trembling lower lip.

Kate finally quit twisting her hair. Her hands dropped to her lap. "I'm sorry, but I was desperate." She tipped her chin up. "And I think maybe you're all playing me. You just don't want to help me."

Claire straightened and pulled her hand away from Luke's. "What did you mean you're sick? If you need a kidney or something, I'm not going to be a match. I have no idea who I am, but it's clear I'm not a Dellamare." She bent down and picked up two decorative balls on the floor around her feet. They clattered as she put them back in the silver basket on the table.

Kate choked back a sob. "You *are* my sister. I don't know what kind of game you're all playing, but it's cruel. All I ever wanted was to be part of your life. How do you think it made me feel to know Mom and I had to be hidden away like something to be ashamed of?"

She leaned closer and jabbed an unpolished finger in their direction. "But I have news for you. I'm not trash under your feet. I'm smart, and I have a lot of common sense. I'm not going to hide in the shadows and pretend I'm not real. Not for you or anyone else."

Kate turned and stalked toward the door as Luke put it all together. He jumped up and went after her, catching her by the arm just inside the big glass doors. "Please, I don't think Claire wants you to go. This is all so overwhelming for you both. Stay and talk. Tell her what you need."

Kate shook off his hand and bolted through the door. He watched her jog across the street and get into a Volkswagen.

He rejoined Claire on the sofa. "I can track Kate down and see what I can find out about her."

"I accused her of trying to meet me to get money out of Dad. I feel badly about that now. I think she really does believe we're sisters."

"You don't believe it?"

Her blue eyes were woebegone. "I'm not a Dellamare, Luke. I don't know who I am."

He picked up her hand and cradled it in both of his palms. "Someone knows who you are, Claire. And we'll find out."

She pulled her hand away and stood. "I think my grandmother knows more than she's saying. And I'm going to find out what it is." Looking down at him, she laid her palm against his cheek. "I need to do this alone."

He nodded. "I'll be here when you're done."

He wanted to believe the change in her

circumstances might mean something could develop between them, but she was likely to run from this place and never look back.

Her grandparents' suite was much like Claire's own with black leather furniture on a plush cream rug. She practically fell into the room when Grandma opened the door. She had been here long enough that the place held the scent of her Tabu perfume and the scent of raspberry tea.

"Why, child, you're as white as a sheet. Did that man come back?" Her grandmother still wore her pale-blue negligee and fitted slippers. "Sit down." She guided Claire to the sofa.

Claire collapsed as the strength ran out of her legs. She leaned forward and buried her face in her hands. She choked back sobs. Her chest felt tight, as though she couldn't get any air.

Her grandmother thrust a cool glass in her hand. "Here, drink some water."

Claire obeyed, and the cool water eased some of the panic clamoring to get out. She raised her gaze to her grandmother's face and found sad knowledge in those wise eyes. "You knew about Dad's other family, didn't you?"

Her grandmother nodded. "He told you?"

Claire set the glass down on the coffee table next to the sofa. "Kate told me."

"Your sister."

Grandmother doesn't know. She shook her head. "Kate thought I was, but she hadn't heard the news."

"What news?" Her grandmother's voice trembled.

"I'm not Claire Dellamare. A little girl's bones were found on Luke's property, near where they found his mother's remains. There was a locket with the initials *CD* found with the bones. And there were scraps of a pink lace dress. Dental records confirm the remains as those of Claire Dellamare." She jumped to her feet. "Who am I, Grandma? I don't know."

She rushed toward the door to the balcony. Air, she had to have air. And the ocean breeze on her skin would calm her. Fighting the door, she relaxed when her grandmother's wrinkled hand clutched her arm.

"Sit down, honey. Be calm. Nothing will change my love for you. You're safe here. Wanted." Her grandmother's voice grew husky.

Claire turned to her grandmother. "Why didn't you tell me? Why did you let me find out this way?"

Tears flooded those wise eyes. "I promised

your father I wouldn't. He's still my son-in-law, though he's been a rascal, and I wanted to protect Lisa. I'm sorry, Claire. I should have told you."

"And Kate. That poor girl is sick and thought finding her family would help her." Claire finally succeeded in unlocking the door. "But how could she find help when all we have holding us together are lies?"

As she fled down the carpeted hall, her grandmother called after her, but she didn't stop. She had to find Luke and get out on the water. Maybe there she could hear God's voice and find peace.

TWENTY-NINE

The salt-laden sea breeze in her face, Claire could almost forget the events of the last twenty-four hours. Almost. Her nerves still jittered as if she were waiting for the next blow to fall. She leaned on the railing at the bow of Luke's boat and lifted her face to the blue sky overhead. "Thanks for bringing me out. I couldn't take one more thing today, and I needed the ocean."

Luke cut the engine. "I think you're a mermaid."

The sudden stillness let her hear the call of the terns swooping out along the edge of a small island with their distinctive *kip* and *kee'ar* sounds. The boat bobbed in the waves as its forward momentum slowed. She watched a particularly aggressive tern scoop up a wriggling fish and carry it back to its nest. The rhythm of life on the sea. Eat or be eaten. Right now she felt like that fish, squirming and flailing to escape a certain fate. In this case, she feared her fate was to never know who she was.

Could it all be a mistake? She clung to that hope, but uncertainty bobbed like flotsam in her gut.

Luke tossed the anchor overboard, then joined her at the bow. "You're very pensive. It's a lot to take in."

She closed her eyes and inhaled the scent of the sea. "I want to forget all about it for now. That's why I asked you to bring me out on the water. Out here, I'm myself. Whoever that is." When she opened her eyes, she found him staring at her with a tender expression that made her look away.

"God has given you everything you need to weather this storm."

She managed a nod. "My head knows you're right, but my heart still trembles like a baby bird fallen from the nest." The birds still swooped and cawed. "So I keep thinking about how God says not a sparrow falls that he does not know about. This didn't come as a surprise to him. What's that psalm? 'He knit me together in my mother's womb.' Whoever that mother may turn out to be."

The pain of even considering she might have another mother took her breath away. How would she cope with that if it happened? She shook her head, then looked out over the waves churning foam as they spent themselves on the rocky shoreline of the little island. "Do you think we can find any orca pods out here?"

"I've seen one or two hanging around this island." He reached down to grab an odd-looking contraption and tossed it over the side, then tied the other end of the rope to the railing.

"What's that?"

"A hydrophone. I can listen to the sounds under water, and we might pick up some matriline dialect if they're down there. Our little orca is about ready to rejoin his family."

"I wish it were that easy for me." The cold metal railing bit into her palms, and she forced herself to ease her grip. "If I could find out who had me for that year, it might answer all our questions. It might even tell me who I am."

"You don't doubt the results of the dental ID anymore? I think you should be at least a little skeptical until we get the DNA back. You and Kate resemble one another so I think it's likely you're Claire Dellamare. I don't know whose bones we discovered, but I don't think you should jump to any assumptions."

"Blue eyes and dimples are hardly unique. She just saw what she wanted to see. I did some research online and found out that dental records have been used for two hundred years. It's pretty foolproof." The warmth from his body seeped against her side, and she wished she had the courage to turn and throw herself into his arms. If he kissed her, maybe she could forget all she was dealing with. She held herself erect and in control. A Dellamare never lost control.

She stopped her thoughts before they could go any further. She probably wasn't a Dellamare anyway. And maybe loss of control wasn't such a bad thing. It might help her learn something about herself.

She inhaled and turned to face him. She searched his gaze. Those dark, dark eyes held her transfixed. Why did he have to be so handsome? He looked like a male model on the cover of a pirate romance novel, all rippling muscles and strong jaw. It wasn't just his startling good looks that drew her, but something much deeper. When she looked into his eyes, she felt like a piece of herself was looking back. It unnerved her.

Her fingers were buried in the soft cotton of his shirt, and she'd moved closer. He didn't smile, and a muscle in his jaw jumped as he reached for her with a groan and pulled her close enough to bury his face in her hair. The fragrance of his spicy cologne enticed her to bury her face in his shirt, to press her lips against the skin at the warm base of his throat. His pulse jumped in that soft spot, and she let her lips linger there.

She should say something and pull back, but she couldn't do it. He was silent, too, and she was lost in a place where time didn't exist, where all that mattered was the touch of his hand at her waist and the sound of his ragged breathing in her ear.

His fingers touched her chin and tipped up her head. His gaze seemed to ask permission, and she gave it with a tremulous smile. He bent his head, and his lips brushed hers. She inhaled the sweet scent of his breath and reached up to lay her hand across the rough stubble of his cheek. She should close her eyes, but she wanted to savor the taste of him as she looked into the seascape she loved so much. He was as much a part of the ocean as she was.

He deepened the kiss, and she wrapped her arms around his neck. His firm lips coaxed a response from her, and she let down her guard, kissing him back with everything in her. All the pent-up loneliness, all the betrayal and hurt. His kiss soothed it all.

He pulled away and cupped her face in his hands. "I've known you only a week, but it feels like forever." He must have seen the fear in her eyes because he rubbed his thumb across her cheek. "I will never hurt you, honey. Never."

His lips came down on hers again, and she closed her eyes this time, tasting him fully, wanting him like she'd never wanted anything before in her life.

How she could come to care like this so quickly, she didn't know. But she never wanted him to let go of her.

Luke sat with his arm settled around Claire as they leaned against the back of the bench seat on the starboard side of his boat. They'd gone back to Folly Shoals to get the little orca, and they'd brought him back to join his family.

A pod of orcas played about ten feet away, and from their vocabulary, he was certain this was his little orca's pod. "There they are." Reaching over the side of the boat, he cut the net around the little one. The calf lay motionless for a moment. Luke dropped the hydrophone over the side, and whistles and clicks began to sputter through the speakers. "They're calling him!"

Dorsal fins swam nearer, and the calf

flipped his fluke. He leaped in the water, then his small fin joined three others about twenty feet off the starboard side of the boat.

Claire leaned over the railing. "They're reunited!"

He draped his arm around her. "They didn't forget him. I knew they wouldn't. I can only imagine how his mother feels about now."

The turquoise of the sea reflected the blue bowl overhead, and kelp floated just offshore the island. He couldn't remember the last time he felt this content. The mainland was out of sight, and so were their problems for now.

Claire leaned over the side of the boat and slapped the water. The little orca swam to her but quickly went back to its pod. She smiled. "It's the way it should be. He'll soon forget all about us and the way we called him."

He smiled down at Claire, and his pulse did a little flip in his chest. "Let's stay out here awhile and forget everything back on land. You're a mermaid today."

She looked like a mermaid today too. Her light-brown hair, whipped by the wind, hung in a shiny tangle down her shoulders. In white shorts and a blue top that emphasized her gorgeous eyes, she looked tanned and beautiful. He'd smelled coconut oil when he kissed her, and he could have buried his face in her neck all day.

Her teasing smile came. "And you're Poseidon. We just have to find you a trident."

"Would you believe I have one at home? My sister got it for me when I joined the Coast Guard. It's hanging on the wall back home in Portland."

She straightened a bit. "Are you going back? You weren't sure the last time we talked about it."

"I don't think I have a choice. It's almost time for me to reenlist or get out. I'm not sure I'll be happy with a world as narrow as Folly Shoals. I love the difference I can make in the Coast Guard." He shrugged. "Though I haven't e-mailed my boss yet. I guess I keep hoping for a miracle."

She passed her hand over her forehead. "At least you have options. I'm not sure what's going to happen to me." Her blue eyes were filled with anguish. "If I'm not Claire Dellamare, who am I, Luke?" Her fingers trembled in his. Her eyes were luminous with tears.

Her hand was soft and trusting in his, and he squeezed it.

The pathos in her voice tore at his heart.

"Claire Dellamare is just a name, honey. You're still you. You love the sea, and you will fight for the downtrodden, even if it's just a little lost orca. You're smart and beautiful and kind. You don't let anything deter you when you're on a quest, and you're gentle with your parents even when they drive you crazy. Because they are still your parents, Claire. That relationship is the same even if you don't have their blood."

"I'm not so sure. My mom *threw* things at my dad. I'll be surprised if their marriage survives this."

He couldn't argue with that. With his thumb Luke caught the tear rolling down her cheek and rubbed it away. "A mermaid's tears are precious. Sea glass is said to be made of mermaid tears."

She fingered a sea glass pendant at her neck. "I collect sea glass, so maybe you're right."

He pressed his lips against her sweet-smelling hair. "Have you always had an affinity for the sea?"

She nodded under his lips. "Ever since I can remember. My parents have always rolled their eyes at how often I begged to go to the beach when I was little. Mom can't swim and Dad hates to get in the water. I'm like a fish. I bob to the top even when I try to kick my way to the bottom. I'm not sure I could drown even if I tried."

The passion in her voice made his own love of the sea seem tame. Maybe she really was a mermaid.

She sat up, away from the circle of his arm. "We should get back. I'd like to talk to Priscilla Loughenberry who works in the hotel. She was there when it all happened. Maybe she can tell me who else to talk to." Leaning her back against the railing, she turned to face him. The wind tossed her thick hair over her head. "I'll run up to my suite and change, then meet you in the lobby."

He rose and put his hands in the pockets of his shorts. "I don't think we have much time. We've got to resolve this. Someone thinks you can identify him or he wouldn't have broken into your suite and tried to smother you."

His gut clenched as the likely scene played out in his head. She'd been alone, defenseless. A monster walked the streets of Folly Shoals. Could it be someone he knew?

She nodded. "He'll be back, Luke. I know it. I'm going to try to recreate the picture I painted of his face."

"I still have my copy. I can get posters printed, and we can put them up all over the coast, even over to Summer Harbor and Bar Harbor. Someone will recognize him."

His confidence felt hollow, though, and he could feel the grains of sand falling through the hourglass.

THIRTY

A low cloud of gray hovered over the horizon, and the sea breeze hinted of rain as it stirred the white sheers on either side of the glass doors. Tendrils of fog swirled through the evergreen branches in the distance. Claire stuck a few pins in her wind-tossed hair, then headed down to meet Luke. She opened the door and came face-to-face with her mother, who held a tissue to her nose and peered back through red-rimmed, puffy eyes. Dad stood right behind her, and he was white as well. "Mom, Dad."

Her mother dabbed her eyes. "We need to talk to you, honey."

She stood aside for them to enter. "Of course."

Uncertain how to comfort her mother, Claire stood with her hands awkwardly at her side. "Are you all right, Mom?"

Her mother shook her head, and fresh tears rolled down her cheeks. Claire had never seen her mother in such a state. Her eyes were nearly swollen shut, and she'd cried off every bit of makeup. Dad looked more controlled, but he shifted from foot to foot.

Her mother went to perch on the side of the unmade bed. "You tell her, Harry. I can't."

Her father wandered over to the desk and flipped through the black binder of hotel information as if he couldn't look her in the face. Claire barely breathed as she waited for him to speak. She glanced back at her mother who was crying again. Claire shivered at her expression of desolation.

Her father turned to face her. He tugged at the neck of his button-down navy shirt. "Everything Kate said is true, Claire. She's my daughter. I haven't seen her or her mother in at least seventeen years. I'm sorry." He glanced at his wife. "The affair was a terrible mistake. After all we went through, I knew Lisa was the woman I truly loved."

That was it? But looking at her father's face, she knew another blow was about to be delivered, and she fisted her hands.

Her mother twisted the tissue in her hands. "Tell her the rest."

Dread curled through Claire's midsection.

"What's Mom talking about?"

He passed his hand over his hair and exhaled. "It's about when we found you." He glanced at his wife as if he hoped she'd stop him, but she kept her head down and didn't look at him. "After Claire wandered off, your mom had a nervous breakdown."

He hadn't said *you*. Claire grabbed the back of the armchair for support.

"The doctor admitted Lisa to a mental hospital for observation after she took a bottle of pills. I was desperate to find Claire, so I came back here on the anniversary of her disappearance. I knew I had to bring Claire home or I'd lose Lisa too."

Claire gave a slight nod. She wasn't their daughter. The evidence stared her in the face. *God, give me strength.*

"I found you in the woods. You were alone, and you looked so much like our Claire that I was sure I'd found you, even though you didn't recognize me. So I just . . . took you home with me. I never bothered to find out where you'd been. All I wanted to do was get to the hospital so Lisa could hold you."

She clearly understood what he wasn't telling her. "You didn't want to run the risk of someone proving I wasn't really Claire Dellamare so you kidnapped a lone little girl in the woods and took her out of state before anyone could object." The strength sagged out of her legs, and she sank onto the cushions of the chair.

"I guess that's the bald truth of it, honey."

Rage began to simmer in her belly, burning its way to her cheeks. "So what you told me about trying to find out where I'd been that year was a lie. Right?"

Red spotted his face, but he held her glance and nodded. "I couldn't lose you and your mother. I had to bring you back." He glanced at his wife. "She's forgiven me."

"I have forgiven him, honey, and you need to do the same." Her mother rose and knelt in front of where Claire sat still stunned in the chair. "This doesn't change how we feel about you, Claire. You're *our* daughter and no one else's. Someone else may have given birth to you, but no one loves you like we do."

Claire felt nothing as her mother's hands clung to her. Numbness encased her limbs. She couldn't think, couldn't get past the crushing news. She rose and brushed past her mother and went to gaze out the window onto the balcony. The sight of a few sailing ships, their white sails billowing in the wind, normally calmed her. But not today. Maybe nothing would calm her ever again. Her throat was too tight to force a syllable past it.

Stolen.

Harry Dellamare had stolen her from someone else as if he had the perfect right to claim anyone he wanted. As if his own wants superseded the grief he caused another family.

She whirled and faced him. "Where is my real family? I have to know."

He held out his palms in a gesture of entreaty. "I don't know, Claire. I just don't know. You'll always be our daughter. Please try to remember that. What happened doesn't change how much we love you."

Her eyes burned. She had to get out of here, away from his lying face. Running for the door, she ignored her mother — no, *Lisa's* cry. These weren't her parents. She had no idea who they were anymore.

Kate swiped angrily at her wet face as she pulled her Volkswagen behind her mother's car parked in front of her uncle's house. *Stop being such a baby.* What had she expected from her father and sister — open arms? And how stupid did they think she was? Only a blind person would swallow that story about Claire not being a Dellamare. She and Claire both had their father's blue eyes.

Maybe he'd confessed to her before Kate showed up, and they'd concocted that ridiculous story. When the car lurched to a stop, something pink rolled out from under the seat. Her old doll, Miss Edith. She'd evidently forgotten her the other day after cleaning her mom's closet. She picked up the doll, worn from so much love when she was little. For some reason, she tucked the doll under her arm for moral support.

Slamming the car door harder than necessary did little to relieve her agitation. Her legs were weak, and her head spun as she went up the steps to the house and banged open the door without knocking. She was going to need a transfusion soon. Her mother and uncle were right where she expected to find them — on the back deck drinking coffee.

Her uncle had constructed it last fall, and the cedar deck held everything important to a bachelor like him: huge grill, patio furniture, a pergola, a beer keg, and a mini fridge. The rosebushes used for landscaping had been Mom's idea, and their fragrance mingled with the scent of coffee wafting through the open kitchen window.

Her mother leaned back in a chaise with her feet up and her favorite red mug in her hand. Her hair was in its usual ponytail, and she wore white shorts and a pink tank top.

Her bare feet hit the floor as soon as she saw Kate. "What's wrong? Do you need to go to the doctor? You're very pale, and your color is off."

Kate dropped onto an upholstered chaise and laid the doll in her lap. "I'm pretty weak. I should probably go see the doctor tomorrow. But that's not the problem, Mom! You won't believe what my father is trying to pull now."

Frowning, Uncle Paul set his coffee mug on the side table. "Kate, you have got to stay away from him!" He must have just come back from lobstering because he still wore his floppy hat and his blue plaid long-sleeved fishing shirt.

She scowled at him. "Too late. I told him, his precious daughter, and his wife who I am. And you know what they said? They told me Claire isn't their daughter at all! They said a little girl's remains had been found and identified as Claire Dellamare. Do they think I'm stupid?"

All the color ran from her mother's face, and her mouth sagged. Her hand shook as she set her coffee down. "Kate, you didn't." She put her hand to her mouth. "I think

I'm going to be sick." She leaped up and ran to the edge of the deck where she bent over.

Kate's legs barely held her as she went to her mother's side and touched her as she retched. "I'm sorry, Mom."

Wiping her mouth, her mother sat back on her haunches. "Could you get the water bottle from my purse?"

Kate went to her mother's purse beside the chaise and dug out the bottle and a package of tissues. After uncapping the bottle, she spilled some water on a tissue, then knelt beside her mother again and handed the water to her. "Here. Are you all right?" She dabbed her mother's face with the damp tissue.

Her mother's green eyes narrowed. "Oh, Kate, you have no idea what you've just done." She looked at her brother. "Paul, what are we going to do?"

"Shut up, Mary." He rose and paced the deck boards. "Let me think."

Too weak to stand any longer, Kate went back to her chaise and sank down. Spots danced in her vision, and she leaned forward to put her head between her legs. The roaring in her ears prevented her from hearing the conversation between her mother and uncle. She didn't understand why they were so upset. There was no way her father could take away the blueberry barren. He might be rich, but he couldn't buck the law.

The strength began to seep back into her limbs, and her head quit spinning. She sat up and settled back on the chaise. No sudden movements or she'd be flat on the floor. Only her mother remained on the deck with her. An engine revved, then the sound of tires on pavement drifted around the house.

"Where's Uncle Paul going?"

Her mother perched on the deck railing. "He's gone to take care of some business."

Her color had come back, but she seemed unwilling to look at Kate and seemed more interested in watching the hummingbird feeder a few feet away. She leaned over and plucked a rose from the bush, then began to shred it.

"Mom? Are you all right?"

She still didn't look at Kate, and her voice shook. "You don't have any idea of the damage you've done. Your selfishness could very well destroy this family. I'm finding it hard to even talk to you right now, so I'm going to go home. Lock up when you leave."

Her selfishness? It was her mother's selfishness that had gotten all of them in this predicament.

Without a glance at Kate, her mother slid

off the railing, went down the steps to the yard, and continued around the side of the house. Moments later an engine started, and Kate saw her gun her car down the dirt road, a plume of dust spewing behind.

Her mother hadn't even stayed to make sure she got home safely. Kate wasn't sure she could drive home without passing out. She was sure Dr. Bain would have no choice but to give her a blood transfusion. She picked up her cell phone, then called the doctor's office to let them know she was heading in. She stood and her vision began to blacken again. There was no way she could drive. She called Shelley and asked for help, then sat down to wait with the doll clutched to her chest.

Once she was stronger, she intended to get to the bottom of what had just happened.

THIRTY-ONE

Birds chirped and splashed in the copper bath that led into the green, secluded garden, and Claire smelled the sweet aroma of blooming lilac bushes. She caught a glimpse of Luke sitting alone on a black iron bench and ran along the stone path toward him.

His eyes wide, he rose as she cried out his name. His arms opened, and she rushed into them. Her arms circled his waist and she buried her face in his shirt, smelling of fabric softener and laundry soap. His embrace was a haven she never wanted to leave. How did she deal with this? Where did she start looking for her family?

He kissed her head. "Your heart is fluttering like a bird. What's happened, honey?"

She forced herself to be still, to soak in his strength a moment, then raised her head. "My dad s-stole me, Luke. He found me in the woods and just . . . took me." She told him what her fa— no, Harry — had said. It was going to take awhile to get used to not thinking of them as her parents.

His dark eyes grew somber as he spoke. "The first thing we should do is check the records of any missing children from that time. It should be easy enough to find out who you are since you were kidnapped."

"You're right!" She slapped a hand to her forehead. "I was so upset that I didn't stop to think. Your friend Beau should be able to track down my family easily enough."

He nodded. "Here comes Priscilla. I'll make a call to Beau while you talk with her a minute. It may not really be necessary to question her now we know you were kidnapped."

She released her grip on his T-shirt and turned to wave at Priscilla Loughenberry. The food and beverage manager wore her turquoise uniform and a perky smile. A sparrow hopped closer, its bright eyes on a crumb by Claire's feet. She was just like that bird, hoping to scoop up some small bit of information.

As Priscilla drew nearer, Claire's smile faded. Wait a minute. Priscilla had told her *she* had found her in the hotel's garden. Yet Harry had told her he'd found her in the woods and had taken her home. And Priscilla had given her other kinds of details like her father crying. She'd never told him she'd spoken with Priscilla. Who was telling the truth? She'd been so upset by her father's admission that she hadn't compared the stories.

Claire motioned for Priscilla to have a seat beside her on the bench and struggled to maintain a friendly expression. "Thanks for agreeing to meet me again. I won't keep you long. I'm sure you're exhausted from working."

The wind tossed Priscilla's short salt-and-pepper hair, and she tucked it behind her ears. "It's no problem, Ms. Dellamare, though I don't know anything I can add to what I already told you."

"I apologize. I was upset when we spoke, so I'm a little murky on the details." She saw the other woman relax against the back of the bench. "I'd just like to go over it again. You said you were the one who found me in the garden, correct?"

Priscilla nodded and launched into the identical story she'd told the first time, right down to the note on her top. Claire watched her face as she spoke and saw no sign of deceit. The food manager held her gaze and spoke as if she'd told the story a thousand times. Could Harry have been lying? And if so, for what purpose?

Claire reached down and picked up the bread crumb the sparrow was still eying, then tossed it to him. "How quickly did my father arrive?"

"He flew in on his plane about three hours later. I kept you in the kitchen decorating cupcakes." Priscilla smiled at the memory. "You mentioned another name, but for the life of me, I can't remember it. We never did figure out who you were asking for. You had a bit of a lisp."

Another discrepancy that should have warned her mother. "My mother didn't come with my dad?"

Priscilla shook her head. "He told me she was ill, but seeing you would be enough to get her back on her feet. He was very appreciative of our help and tried to give me five thousand dollars. I turned it down, of course. I'd done what anyone else would have."

Claire could picture the scene. She'd often seen Harry throw money around like that. Though he demanded good service, he paid well to ensure it. If only she could remember. She closed her eyes and tried to summon up the taste of cupcake icing and sprinkles, but there was no sweet taste on her tongue.

Only the bitterness of betrayal.

The birds chirped overhead, and the wind rustled through the trees as Luke stood waiting on the phone to talk to Beau. He'd walked far enough away from the two women that he wouldn't disturb them, but he was getting tired of the elevator music. The hold time had already been five minutes, and he looked back at Claire to make sure she was doing all right. Her face turned away from him, she still sat on the bench with Priscilla.

Beau finally came on the line. "Sorry for the wait, Luke. What's up?"

Luke told him what Harry had said. "So could you check and see who reported a little girl missing about the same time?"

"What?" Beau's voice sharpened. "I'm sure no child was reported missing. I've been over and over those old files in the past week."

"You might not have noticed it since it wasn't really connected to Claire's safe return."

"Hold on."

There was a click, then classical music came back on. *Great.* He leaned against the rough bark of an oak tree and watched a porcupine lumber out from under a shrub.

The animal meandered across the path and disappeared into the woods again. Luke eyed Claire again and saw the tension in her outline. What was Priscilla telling her?

The music in his ear cut off, and Beau's voice came back on. "Luke, the sheriff wants to talk to you. Hang on."

Several clicks jittered across the line, then the sheriff spoke. "Beau tells me you think there's a little girl who went missing about the same time Claire was found. Well, whoever that woman is."

Luke tensed at the hostility in Danny's voice. "That's right."

"Bunch of baloney is what it is. Claire Dellamare is the only missing child we've had in these parts during my lifetime. Where'd you hear such a crazy story?"

"Harry told her he found her in the woods and just took her. If that's what happened, wouldn't her real parents have reported her missing?"

"I'd sure think so. Tell me exactly what Dellamare said."

"He told Claire as soon as he saw her, he knew she was his and that he just snatched her up and took her to Lisa, who had been committed to a mental hospital after a suicide attempt. Of course, now we know she never really was his daughter, so where is the outcry from the parents of a child literally kidnapped by him?"

"Luke, I'm telling you, I think there's way more to this story than we know and that the pretty woman masquerading as Claire is playing you for a fool. All these stories coming out." His voice was thick with disgust.

"Someone attacked her last night. What did you find when you got to the hotel?"

"Well, yes, something happened last night. I found no sign of a break-in, though. So if there had been an intruder, he had a passkey to the door."

"Claire was clearly traumatized. I saw her this morning, and she was still very upset."

"The hotel room had been torn up some." Danny's admission held reluctance. "But for all I know, Claire might have torn it up herself."

"The painting of her attacker was missing."

"So she said. Again, you seem to believe every word out of her pretty mouth."

"You've been listening to Andy, haven't you? He's got it in his head Claire had something to do with Jenny's death. Open your eyes, Danny, and investigate this for yourself. Don't let a grief-stricken deputy with an agenda keep you from having an open mind."

338

There was a long pause on the line. For a moment Luke thought Danny might have hung up on him. "Danny?"

"I'm here, Luke. I'll try to lower my suspicions of her if you'll raise them. Don't take everything she says at face value. Test it against what you know. You're a smart guy."

"Why are you so defensive about this? I expected you to be more open-minded."

Danny didn't answer at first. "Maybe I am defensive. It was my first big case all those years ago. I feel like maybe I missed something."

Luke pressed his lips together and bent to dislodge a burr from his shoelace. "And you're *sure* there's no child reported missing? You've checked neighboring counties?"

"Yep."

"What if someone had taken her from somewhere else and she got away? Could you run a check on the entire country?"

"Yeah, I can do that. It will take awhile to get results back, and I'm not sure what they will tell us. You're saying someone is taking little girls and turning them loose in our woods?"

Put like that, it was a stupid thought. "Okay, okay, sounds dumb, I know. But Claire had to have come from somewhere. I just don't understand why her parents didn't report her missing. It's like she was born at age five and just suddenly appeared."

"Maybe she was born under a cabbage plant." Danny guffawed at his joke.

Luke rolled his eyes but couldn't muster a laugh. "Thanks for checking, Danny. Let me know if you find anything. I'm going to post copies around town of Claire's painting and over in Bar Harbor. I put your office's number on the poster."

"Great. Now I have to deal with every slug that crawls out of the woodwork. Nice job." But the sheriff's voice held an interested edge.

"According to you, we shouldn't get a single call. I thought you'd want to field anything that came in yourself. Just in case you could pin it to Claire."

Danny laughed again. "You're wicked sharp, boy. I'll let you know if we get any leads. Not that I'm expecting to, mind you. Oh, and we're releasing your mom's remains. Where do you want them sent?"

Pressure built in Luke's chest at the thought of another argument with their dad. "Send them over to the funeral home. I'll make arrangements for a memorial and burial."

"Will do."

Luke ended the call and turned to look at Claire again. She sat on the bench alone, her shoulders slumped and her face in her hands. He started that way with his gut churning. Things hadn't gone well.

THIRTY-TWO

The equipment around Kate in the outpatient room beeped reassuringly. Though the room bore a coat of happy yellow, it did nothing to help her mood. She focused on a pair of seascape pictures and could almost smell the sea breeze instead of the pungent odor of alcohol and floor wax. Soon she could get out of this blue-and-white cotton gown and into real clothes.

Her arm ached a bit, but she ignored it and looked across the room at Shelley. "Thanks for coming so fast when I called."

Her red hair up in a messy ponytail, Shelley wore pink workout clothes and gray sneakers since she'd been at the gym when Kate called. "You sounded on death's door." Tipping her head, she studied Kate. "You've got more color now. The way you looked when I came to get you scared me to death. And you weren't making much sense." She put a cool hand on Kate's forehead. "Feeling better?"

"Much." Kate glanced at the IV cart. The last unit of blood was almost empty. Soon she could get dressed to go home. "Did you hear anything I told you? You know, before."

Shelley poured her a cup of ice water and adjusted the straw, then held it up to Kate's lips. "You said something about Claire not being Claire. I figured you were not quite with it."

Kate struggled to sit up better against the too-soft pillows. "It's true. I went to the hotel to tell her I was her sister and she came up with some kind of cock-and-bull story about not being Claire. And my father . . ." Bile rose in her throat at the thought of her conniving father.

Shelley zipped her jacket up and down and didn't look at her for a moment. "Didn't you read this morning's paper? Some bones were found out on a cranberry farm. One set belonged to a little girl, and the prelim identification seems to indicate they are Claire Dellamare's."

It felt as though an elephant stepped on Kate's chest. She sat up, then flopped back down when the room began to spin again. "I didn't see it. Wait, let me understand this. If the real Claire is dead, how did that happen? I mean, there she is, living with my dad and her mom. And we look alike!"

"Maybe we should talk about this later."

"I need to get to the bottom of this now!"

Shelley's shoes squeaked on the tile floor as she went back to her chair. "Well, at least you both have blue eyes. You might have seen a resemblance because you expected to see one, Kate. It's easy to do."

She opened her mouth to deny it, then closed it. Maybe Shelley was right, but she could have sworn when she saw Claire for the first time in the ladies' room that they were two peas in a pod. Expectations were funny things, though.

Shelley pulled a bottle of water from her purse. "And as far as how did the existing Claire take the place of the real one, I don't know. She seemed surprised by this news?"

"*Surprise* is a mild word for how traumatized she looked. She'd just found out, so she said." Kate went back through what she knew of the situation. "She was missing a year, then reunited with her parents. That's all I really know."

Shelley's brown eyes glimmered with interest. "Everyone was talking about it in the teacher's lounge today. I guess the sheriff got a letter from Jenny indicating Claire wasn't who she said she was. Some thought Jenny knew something about it and

344

was blackmailing Claire. They say Claire had Jenny killed."

"Claire wouldn't do that! Sheesh, Shelley, what a thought."

Her friend shrugged. "Just repeating the gossip. Someone had to know she wasn't really Claire Dellamare."

It was more than Kate could unravel in her weakened state. She glanced down to see Miss Edith tucked into her side. The doll's round blue eyes comforted her. Her pink dress could use a washing.

"You had a death grip on that thing when I picked you up, so I didn't fight you." Shelley uncapped her bottle of water and took a sip. "Why didn't your mother bring you here? You were kind of incoherent about that too."

Kate hadn't wanted to examine the pain of her mother's rejection. "She was mad at me. Uncle Paul too."

"Because you went to the hotel to confront your dad?"

Kate studied her hands with their short, stubby nails. "Yeah. I guess it was a stupid thing to do, but I'd given him an ultimatum. I didn't want him to think he could get away with treating me the way he'd always treated Mom. Uncle Paul was so mad he tore off in his car. Mom actually, well, she threw up."

Shelley slowly put the cap back on her water. "You're telling me your mom was so upset she vomited?"

Kate put her ugly hands under the sheet and nodded. "I didn't get why they were so upset. I thought Uncle Paul might hit me. And Mom said I had destroyed the family."

"What did she mean by that?"

"I know she thinks she'll lose the blueberry barrens, but you know I checked with the attorney, and that can't happen. There's no accounting for fear, though." Maybe she should call and make sure Mom was okay.

The door opened, and Dr. Bain poked his head inside. His genial smile seemed dimmer today, somehow guarded. He stepped into the room and closed the door behind him. "How's my favorite patient?"

"Much better."

He crossed his arms over his chest, his expression somber. "I should think so. Your counts were scary low. If you'd delayed getting in here even another twenty-four hours, I don't think you'd be walking out today." He pressed his lips together. "We really need to find a bone-marrow donor from your family. Is there anyone else you can send in to be tested?"

She exchanged a long glance with Shelley. Her father? It wasn't likely she could talk him into it. "What if I give you my father's number and you call him? Maybe he'd listen to a doctor."

"I'm game." Dr. Bain pulled out his cell phone. "What's the number? I'll go back to my office and call him."

Her father had lied. Claire waited until Priscilla's footsteps faded away into the hum of bees and the rumble of the mower on the other side of the hotel. She sat numbly as Luke came toward her. What did she do now? The more she dug, the worse the situation became.

Luke dropped onto the bench beside her and slipped his arm around her back. "How'd it go?"

There would be time to deal with this later. Right now she wanted to know her last name. "Okay. How about you?"

"Not so good." His voice dropped to a lower timbre.

She straightened and looked up at him. "What's happened?" His warm hand stroked her forearm, but she didn't want comfort now. Her need for answers overwhelmed everything else. "Tell me."

He pulled his arm away and leaned forward a bit to stare in her face directly. "No one reported you missing."

A bee hovered near her face, and she shooed it away, then stood to pace the walk. "That's not possible, Luke. What parent wouldn't report a missing five year old?"

He rose and thrust his hands in his pockets. A lock of dark hair fell across his forehead as he leaned down to pick up a stick and toss it into the woods. "Exactly what I said to Danny. He's checking nationwide in case the little girl got away from someone who had taken her in another state."

"You mean like some kind of pervert?" She hugged herself and shuddered. "Maybe that's why I can't remember anything at all about being lost or found. It was so horrible I blocked it out." A sour taste rose to her tongue, and she pushed away the lurid images she'd seen on TV over the years.

He stepped over and put his hands on her shoulders. "Don't try to second-guess what happened, Claire. Right now we just have to wait until we know more."

Heat flashed over her, and Claire pulled away, then went to perch on the edge of the water fountain. She held her hand under the cold water, then splashed some on her face until her heart quit trying to climb out of her chest. "I can't sit by and do nothing, Luke. That man might come back. I have to know who I am. Once I do, I'll know who he is. I'm sure of it."

Luke took a step her way, but his phone rang. He muttered under his breath and glanced at it before answering. "Danny, you find anything?" He turned his back and walked a few steps away.

She shook the water off her hand and followed him so she could hear. From his side of the conversation, she gathered that the news wasn't good.

Luke ended the call. "You heard? There is no little girl missing from that time period who is still unaccounted for."

She gestured toward the back of the hotel where a few guests lingered over coffee on the patio. "Priscilla says *she* found me with a note with the name *Claire Dellamare* pinned to my top and called my dad who flew in to get me. Yet Dad, I mean Harry, says he found me in the woods and took me. I think he's lying."

Luke nodded. "Beau read the full transcript of the day you were found. He mentioned a woman from the hotel called the office to report having found you. She'd already called your dad too. Why would Harry lie about that? He has to know we could check those details."

"I don't know. I think there's something

in how I was found that he doesn't want me to know."

"I'll be surprised if we can get the truth out of him."

She gasped as another idea hit her. "Luke, what if Harry somehow bought a replacement child? All he wanted was to pacify Mom. So maybe he paid someone to attach Claire's name on my dress and leave me by the hotel."

"Honey, you're grasping at straws."

It made a horrible kind of sense to her. Subterfuge was her father's second language. He always said he had to be gifted in it to be so successful at business. If she didn't pin him down now, he'd be very difficult to talk to. And what if last night's attacker came back? "Think those posters are ready? We can put them up in the area."

He nodded. "On my way out here to meet Priscilla, I asked the hotel to beef up security on your floor. They agreed to do that as well as issue you a new key card."

He was doing a better job of ensuring her safety than the man she called Dad. She gripped his hands. "I'm glad you're here with me. I wouldn't know what to do."

His warm fingers returned the pressure. "Oh yes you would. You're amazing, Claire. This trial will only make you stronger. I'm glad I'm here, too, but if I weren't, you'd find a way to get to the bottom of this."

Warmth spread along her spine at the confidence in his dark eyes. This was a bigger test of her mettle than she'd ever thought to face in her life, but she could do it. She *would* do it. Someone had to have seen her. Luke had been through a lot this week too. Finding his mother had to have been traumatic.

His mother's murder. Her fingers tightened on his, and she gazed up at him. "Wait a minute, Luke. We're forgetting your mother's murder in all this."

One brow winged up as he peered down at her. "I'm not tracking with you."

"We thought all along the real Claire's disappearance and your mother's murder were connected. What if I'm mixed up in it somewhere too?" She held up her hand when he frowned. "Oh, I don't mean I had anything to do with her death. But maybe finding who killed your mother will solve everything. I think we should go talk to your aunt again."

His hand enfolded hers as they walked back toward the hotel. "You don't sound frightened anymore."

She pulled a lilac bloom from a bush and sniffed it. "I'm not. I'm going to find out

351

what this is all about, and I'm going to
figure out where I belong."

THIRTY-THREE

The giant oak tree still held the swing Luke had played on as a child, and a new crop of children, his aunt's day care kids, squealed as they played in the side yard under the watchful eye of one of her workers. He parked in the drive behind his aunt's small blue car and glanced across the truck seat at Claire, who had her forehead pressed to the glass. She hadn't said much as they drove across town. Something was eating her, but she'd spill it when she was ready.

"Aunt Nan is expecting us. Ready?"

She lifted her head from the glass and reached for her door. "Okay." Her fingers curled around the door handle, then she stopped and looked across the gray seat at him. "I've been thinking about the possible scenarios here. I think he looked for a picture of a child that resembled Claire and paid for her to be left near the hotel for someone to find."

Though he'd pooh-poohed it the first time she brought it up, Luke absorbed her words, seeing it play out just as she said. "He'd have to know there was no hope of finding the real Claire."

Her blue eyes sparked with anger. "That's the conclusion I came to. Which means he knew the real Claire was dead. And how would he know that?"

He took a moment to think about it. The sun beat through the windows and heated the truck's interior. "He's got a lot of money, Claire. What if she was kidnapped and held for ransom and he knew the kidnappers killed her?"

"But why not reveal that to his wife?" She shook her head. "I think he's complicit in something and had to keep quiet about her death."

"Or else he killed her himself."

She looked out toward the children playing in the yard. "You mean he might have murdered his own child?"

"Maybe it was an accident, but he knew it would look bad. Or he knew his wife would never be able to live with him if she knew. So he let it appear she was still missing, hoping his wife would get over it."

Her hand went back to the door. "And when she ended up having a nervous breakdown, he knew he'd have to do something to bring her out of it."

"Maybe he did like you said and found a child who resembled Claire."

She opened her door. "Which means we still have no idea how to find my real family. If he paid money for me, my real parents aren't going to complain and they aren't likely to admit it either." She got out and slammed her door.

He exited the truck and jogged around to join her. The distant roar of a lawn mower and the scent of newly mown grass made the day seem so normal and ordinary when he knew her entire world had been shaken. A horn blew, and he waved at a friend as they walked across the yard to the porch where his aunt sat in a swing.

The steps looked a different color, and he caught the lingering scent of fresh paint. His aunt had a smudge of gray on her cheek. "Can we use these steps?"

Aunt Nan jumped up and put down her e-reader. "The steps are fine. I just finished the railing so don't touch that." She wore paint-splattered jeans and a pink sweatshirt.

"Taking a little break?"

His aunt nodded. "Abigail has it covered." Her gaze swept past him to Claire. "Have a seat. I have iced tea and cookies ready."

"Of course you do." He dropped his hand on her shoulder as he passed. "The porch looks nice. I like the gray."

"I was tired of plain old white." She gestured to the chairs on either side of a glass table that held glasses of iced tea and a plate of cookies. "I saw the newspaper this morning. I know why you're here."

He let Claire take the chair closest to the swing, then dropped into the other one and reached for a cookie. Peanut butter.

"Paper?" Claire's voice was husky.

Aunt Nan gave the swing a push with her pink-tipped bare toes. "And, Luke, the least you could have done was call me with the news that the real Claire's bones were found on your property."

He winced. "Sorry, Aunt Nan. It was in the paper? Danny said there would be no official announcement until the DNA came back."

"The reporter said she had a scoop. I would assume the sheriff is reaming out someone as we speak."

A child chasing a dog raced around the side of the house. The little boy's bright-red face held an ear-to-ear grin as he scooped up the puppy and carried it back to the side of the house.

Luke swiped the condensation from his

glass. Danny was likely livid. Who had spilled the news?

Claire picked up her glass. "Do you have a copy of the paper? I'd like to see it."

"Got it right here." His aunt reached beside her and pulled a newspaper from under her e-reader. "Front page."

Luke watched Claire as she took the paper gingerly. "I wonder if someone leaked it to embarrass your family. Maybe Andy Waters."

Aunt Nan tightened her ponytail. "Or Danny himself. You give the man too much credit, Luke. I wouldn't put something like this past him."

Claire passed the newspaper to him. "Why would he leak it?"

"He doesn't like you much, Claire. Maybe he wanted everyone to believe you're an imposter." The picture beside the headline was of a little girl with blond hair. Claire at age four. He scanned the article and found one surprise. "The article confirms that Priscilla is the one who found you."

"I noticed that." Her eyes were shadowed, and she ran her finger around the beaded moisture on her glass. "Nancy, do you know if your sister ever met my parents?"

"Whoa, where did that question come from?" Luke laid the paper aside. "Of course not."

"Actually she did, Luke." Nan curled her legs under her. "Vicky and I both met your parents, Claire. I was helping her make cranberry jam when your parents stopped by with you in the car. They bought some things. Does it matter?"

"You said your sister heard a child crying. How tight was money back then?"

"Tight," Nan admitted. "The cranberries were just starting to produce."

He saw where Claire was going and it was crazy. "You can't seriously think my mother had something to do with young Claire's disappearance."

"Right now I don't know what to think." The warmth she usually showed him seemed lost in the steely slant of her mouth and the hardness along her jaw. "They were found together. What if my dad paid your father to hold the real Claire for a while?"

Her suspicions rocked him back in his chair. The problem was, nothing was off the table because nothing was as it seemed. "I think I'd better talk to Pop."

"And I'll talk to Harry."

Of course her father was golfing. Where else would he be but schmoozing on the golf course while her whole world fell apart? The wind at her back, Claire marched along the path to the greens. It wouldn't be the ideal place for a confrontation, but this morning's revelations had taken place in front of a dozen guests and hotel employees. Luke had gone to talk to his dad while she talked to hers.

She spied her grandpa's hat first. With his plaid beret cocked at an angle and his matching knickers, he would have been at home on the greens in Scotland. Careful to avoid a spiderweb, she paused between two box hedges and watched them putt. Maybe Grandpa Timothy would tell her more than her father would.

Once her father sank his putt, she started forward. Her sandals sank into the soft grass, and her feet were wet by the time she reached their cart. "I need to talk to both of you a minute."

Her father frowned. "Can it wait, Claire? We still have nine more holes to play."

His terse tone tore at her heart. The last time she'd seen him he said he loved her, but there was no love in his cold blue eyes. "It can't wait." And to make doubly sure he knew she was serious, she moved in front of the cart. He'd continue only by running her over.

"Fine. What's wrong now?"

Her grandpa put his putter in the bag nestled in the back of the cart. "What isn't wrong, Harry? Have a little compassion for your daughter. She just found out you're not the man she thought you were."

Her dad's face went red, and he turned the key on the cart. "Get out of the way, Claire. Your mom has talked me to death. I can't discuss this anymore."

She stepped to the side of the cart, then reached in and turned off the key. She pocketed it, then folded her arms across her chest. "You lied to me, Dad. You didn't find me and rush me to see Mom. One of the workers here at the hotel found me and called you and the sheriff. It's all in the transcript."

Best not to mention she'd heard the first-person account from Priscilla herself. The last thing she wanted was to get the woman in trouble. The transcript was public record.

Grandpa put his big hand on her shoulder and squeezed reassuringly. "I'm sure there's some answer, Claire. Give your dad a chance to answer without sending him to the gallows before he explains."

Any other time she would have tucked herself under his arm and looked up at him with adoration. He was one of her favorite people in the world, but everything felt off now. Different. He wasn't her jokester grandpa, the one she could come to with any problem. She wasn't even blood.

"Did you know about any of this, Grandpa? The affair, Kate's birth, the fact that I'm not really Claire?"

His hand left her shoulder and went to rub his forehead. His fingers left a smear of dirt on his skin. "I knew some of it, honey. I know it's been a shock. We've kept quiet all these years to protect your mother."

"Are you trying to give Dad time to concoct an answer?"

Hurt flashed through his hazel eyes, and he shoved his hands in his pockets. "Just trying to bring some balance to the discussion."

Nothing would ever be the same again. Not between her and her grandparents, not between her and her parents. Even Francisca and the rest of the Castillo family would keep their distance when the truth came out. She caught her breath at the sheer magnitude of how her life was likely to change.

She curled her fingers into her palms. "You know what *really* doesn't make sense, Dad? If you'd just said you got the call I'd been found and rushed to get me, I would have accepted that. But you brought up something even weirder. You said I looked like Claire so you just took me home. That seems to indicate that you likely knew you were never going to find the real Claire. Did you kill her?"

The words were out before she could stop them. A cry escaped, and she put her hand to her mouth. Until she'd spilled that accusation, she hadn't realized where her suspicions had taken her. But it made a horrible kind of sense.

"Don't be ridiculous, Claire." Her grandfather folded his long legs into the passenger side of the cart. "Give your father the key and go calm yourself before we talk about it anymore. I'm surprised you'd say something so outrageous after all Harry has done for you."

A band tightened in Claire's midsection. Her grandpa believed it too. She'd seen it in a flash before he turned away. "What happened, Dad? I'm sure it was an accident. I don't believe you're capable of murder." She leaned forward and put her hand on the steering wheel. "Who am I? I have to know."

Her father stared straight ahead, his jutting chin betraying his stubborn refusal to look at her or to speak. His lips were pressed together so tightly, they'd lost all color. He got out and stepped up to his ball. His jaw-line was as hard as the granite boulders around the golf course as he whacked the ball. It veered off to his right, and he muttered an expletive under his breath before climbing back in the cart.

She put her hand on his shoulder, then removed it when he flinched at her touch. Numbly, she dug the key out of her pocket and leaned over to put it in the ignition. Without saying anything more, she stepped away from the cart.

Harry's cell phone rang and he pulled it out. "That same number again."

Frowning, he touched the screen. "Dellamare." He listened for a moment. "Look, I'm not coming down there now. I'm sure I'm not a match anyway. Parents usually aren't, and I've got enough on my plate with this. Thanks for calling, Doctor, but it's not possible." He ended the call.

"Kate's doctor?" Claire couldn't believe he'd been so abrupt.

Her father shrugged. "She's getting a blood transfusion at the clinic in Summer Harbor."

"And you're not even going to go? She's your daughter!" Claire looked to her grandfather for support.

"Claire is right, Harry. You should go

down there. You might be a match for her."

"It's not likely. She'll be fine, I'm sure." Her father started the cart and pulled away.

Claire stood with her mouth dangling open. If he wouldn't go, the least she could do was check on Kate. She took out her phone and called Luke, who was pulling up outside his father's house. He promised to meet her at the ferry in half an hour.

THIRTY-FOUR

The living room held the odor of the beef and cabbage cooking in the Crock-Pot. Meg put down her book when Luke entered. She held up her finger to her mouth and shushed him, but he shook his head and went to stand beside their father sleeping in the recliner. "I need to talk to him. It's important."

Pop's lids fluttered at the sound of Luke's voice booming in the living room. He snuffled, then finally opened his eyes. He reached for the red hanky in the pocket of his overalls and dabbed his mouth. "Luke. What time is it?"

"About four."

"Need water." Their father made a grab for the glass on his side table and missed.

Meg got up and took it to him, then held the straw up to his lips. "Drink, Pop."

He slurped up some water, then leaned back. "You look all spleeny about something. What's up?"

Luke glanced at his sister and shook his head. Looming over their father would get his back up so he went to sit on the sofa. "There have been some new developments."

Megan put down the glass and went back to the sofa. "We saw the newspaper. The second body we found on our property was the missing child, Claire Dellamare."

"That's only part of it." He stared hard at Dad. "Claire's father told her he found her in the woods. Obviously the child he took home wasn't his daughter, but then, who was that child he found in the woods? If he found another girl who'd somehow gotten lost in the woods, shouldn't someone have reported her missing?"

"Seems likely."

"That's what I thought. I had Danny check, and there's no child of that age who went missing in this area. So whoever had Claire before didn't report her missing. She wonders if her father paid for her. Maybe her parents were hard up, and he saw her resemblance to his daughter so he offered enough money that they couldn't pass up."

Megan's expression showed she was still suspicious. He clasped his fingers together over his knee. "Pop, you and Mom met the Dellamares."

"Did we now?" His father dabbed at his mouth with the hanky again.

"Aunt Nan told me they stopped by here and bought some cranberry jelly and other items. Do you remember?"

"Son, that was twenty-five years ago. I'm hardly likely to remember something from so long ago. If Nan says it's so, she might be right, but thousands of tourists have stopped here." He struggled to sit up straighter in the recliner. "You're saying Dellamare killed her?"

"I don't know anything much for sure. Pop, Mom's remains are at the funeral home now. We're having a memorial service on Tuesday."

Pop's eyes widened and he scowled. "Wicked stupid is what it is! Why put us all through that?"

"You don't have to come," Meg said.

"People will wag their tongues if I don't."

She rolled her eyes. "Since when do you care what people say?"

He chewed on his lip. "What time?"

"Two," Luke told him. "At the church." When was the last time Pop had come to church? Maybe Christmas ten years ago.

Pop grunted and fumbled for the TV remote. "I'll think about it."

Luke followed his sister into the kitchen.

"You think he knows more than he's telling?"

Meg went to the coffeepot and measured grounds into the filter. "He didn't act suspicious in any way. Nothing about meeting the Dellamares stood out to him. Um, Luke, I accepted the job. Have you heard from the Coast Guard about a transfer yet?"

"Not yet." He couldn't tell her he hadn't even asked. It appeared there would be no miracle for him. He would have to learn to deal with the cantankerous old man in the other room. He couldn't see Claire ever living in this old farmhouse either. "I need to meet Claire at the ferry so we can take my truck to Summer Harbor. We'll talk about it later."

Claire stood outside the hospital room with Luke by her side. A nurse wheeling a dinner cart clattered by reeking of chicken, and the place smelled like it had been newly waxed. The door stood slightly ajar, and the muted sound of the TV news filtered through the opening.

"I hope Kate's alone," she whispered to Luke. "Thanks for meeting me here. I was mortified when I heard how Dad talked to the doctor. None of this is her fault."

Luke put his hand on the door. "Want me

to go first?"

She shook her head. "I'm not that cowardly."

She touched the smooth metal door and gave it a push. Hooked up to monitors, Kate lay in the hospital gown with her hands crossed behind her head as she watched television in the pale-green room. With the beige curtains shut, shadows lined the space. Her lightly copper-colored hair was loose on the pillow.

Claire's shoes squeaked on the tile, and Kate glanced up. Her half smile vanished, and she punched the button to lift her head even more. "What are you doing here?"

"I came to see how you are." Claire crossed the floor to stand beside the bed.

Luke stepped to the window and opened the curtains. Sunlight flooded the room, and Kate squinted but didn't object. The sunlight streaming on her face showed more color than the last time Claire had seen her.

Claire poured her some fresh water and held out the cool glass. "You're looking better."

Her eyes wary, Kate took the glass and adjusted the straw to sip from it. "Thanks." She handed the cup back to Claire. "Harry isn't with you?"

Claire bit her lips at Kate's desolate

expression. "I'm sorry, Kate. I wish I really were a Dellamare. I would give you some bone marrow if I could. From what I gathered from my dad's side of the conversation, your doctor thinks you need that transplant as soon as possible."

"That's right. But there's always the hope that they'll find a match in the donor database."

Claire put the cup back on the stand. "You don't have to be a relative to give bone marrow? I could get tested."

Kate's lips smiled but her eyes didn't. "It would be a long shot if you're not a relative." She plucked at the crisp white sheets. "I'm not convinced about the identification of the child's bones. Can't you see the resemblance between us?" She tugged at her hair. "I wish I'd never dyed this."

"We have a similar look, but they say everyone has a double." Was Kate well enough to hear Claire's suspicions about how her father had searched for a lookalike? Maybe not just yet.

Claire turned at the slapping of flip-flops behind her. A woman about her mother's age came through the door. Her hair was caught up in a messy bun, and she wore denim capris and a white shirt that showed off toned arms. Her nails were short and bare, and she wore no makeup.

She froze when she saw Claire and couldn't seem to look away. Some dim memory made Claire inhale and freeze in place. She'd seen this woman before, but where? The details of the room fell away, and her ears filled with roaring. She closed her eyes and saw trees looming at her. She heard a little girl call out a name. Not Claire's name, but what was it? The memory was gone too quickly to snatch and hold it.

"Claire?" Luke touched her shoulder.

Her knees felt weak when she opened her eyes. "Sorry, I felt a little light-headed for a minute."

"Sit down." He guided her to one of the bedside chairs.

The woman jerked her gaze away and went to stand on the other side of the bed. "Kate, you scared me to death."

"Sorry, Mom."

Ah, Kate's mother. She'd worked for Claire's mother so surely they'd met when she was a baby. Vertigo hit again, and she realized they couldn't have met. Not when she wasn't really Claire Dellamare. Mary Mason had left the Dellamare employment before the real Claire's fourth birthday, well before she'd ever taken the real Claire's place. So why did Mary seem so familiar?

"Why didn't you call me? I would have brought you in."

"You left in such a hurry . . ." Kate held out her hand to Claire. "Mom, this is Claire. And her friend Luke."

He murmured a greeting as Claire rose and grasped Kate's mother's cold fingers. "Nice to meet you, Mary."

Mary winced when Claire spoke her name. "You too, Claire."

Claire couldn't look away from the warm green lights in Mary's eyes. The vertigo came again, and she finally managed to look away as she sank back onto the seat. She couldn't quite decipher the expression in the older woman's face. Curiosity or distaste? Longing or revulsion? Mary masked her emotions well.

Mary went to plump Kate's pillows. "When are you getting out of here?"

"I thought I was getting out soon, but the nurse just told me the doctor wants to keep me overnight. Would you mind getting me some toiletries and clean clothes?"

"I'll do that right now." Mary nodded at Claire and Luke, then rushed toward the door as if she couldn't wait to get away.

With Kate's mother out of the room, Claire could breathe again. She rose and grasped the bed's metal railing. "What do I need to do to see if I'm a good donor?"

"It's just a blood test."

"I'll do it too," Luke said. "Has the newspaper asked for the community to be tested? Surely there's a match somewhere close."

"That's very kind of you."

When Kate pushed down the sheets to reach for her cell phone, Claire saw a doll lying beside her. Her pulse quickened and began to hammer in her neck.

She picked it up. "Where did you get this? I have one just like it."

She'd always been told hers was one of a kind and handmade in Paris with human hair. The big blue eyes were much like hers and Kate's, and the mouth showed tiny white teeth. Claire's still sat on her dresser at home, but she hadn't really looked at it in years.

"It was a present from my dad after he went to Paris. For my fourth birthday."

"There's a mark on the foot — 1990 with a watermark that looks like a *B* with a circle around it." Claire upended the doll and removed one shoe to reveal the date and the watermark. She leaned over and showed it to Kate.

Her finger traced the watermark. "How'd you know that?"

"I have one just like it with the same

date." Claire reached for Luke's hand. Why would they both have the same dolls bought from the same manufacturer in the same year?

THIRTY-FIVE

The *beep, beep* of her IV was driving Kate crazy. She punched her call button to have the nurse come fix it, then sat up and swung her legs over the side of the bed. "What does this mean? I looked up the artist a few years ago. It's from some expensive shop in Paris."

She'd been totally shocked when Claire and Luke walked in. And even more shocked when they offered to get tested. But nothing rocked her like this. And from the way Claire's eyes fluttered and her color came and went, the other woman was just as flummoxed.

Kate reached for the doll again. "Your doll is identical in every way, right down to the date?"

Claire nodded and crossed her legs in the chair, then recrossed them the other direction. "I felt as though I'd met your mother too."

The nurse hurried in to check on the IV.

"Looks like you're done, honey. The doctor said I could disconnect your IV if you wanted me to, just to make you more comfortable."

"Please. And, Luke, can you cool it down in here? I'm about to burn up."

Though Kate wanted nothing more than to get to the bottom of this, she was eager to be untethered. Luke went to the window unit and fiddled with the temperature. Cooler air began to filter over Kate's hot cheeks.

"There you go." The nurse picked up the discarded items from the pic line and tossed them in the disposal container by the door. "Let your friends take you for a walk." Her white shoes squeaked away, and she closed the door behind her.

Kate looked up at the girl she'd come to think of as her half sister. A crazy, impossible idea began to take hold. Claire would likely vote to commit her if she actually said what she was thinking, but what did she have to lose at this point?

She pleated her gown at the knee with her fingers. "I had an imaginary friend once. Her name was Rachel."

Something shifted deep in Claire's eyes. "I've always liked that name. I think I had a friend named Rachel when I was little. I used to call myself Rachel when I was playing pretend. It drove my mom crazy."

"Do you remember anything about that friend?"

Claire frowned and uncrossed her legs again. "Why the questions? What does an imaginary friend have to do with this?"

"I have quite a few memories of my friend Rachel. I think she might have been real."

"You think Rachel is the little girl who was found?" Claire rose and paced the gray tile floor. "That makes no sense, Kate. She was identified by dental records, not DNA. At least not yet."

"No." Kate slipped out of bed onto the cool floor. The cold air from the AC unit blew down her spine. She dropped both hands onto Claire's shoulders. "Maybe *you're* Rachel."

Claire's eyes went wide, and Kate could see the fear shimmering in them. When she tried to twist out of her grip, Kate held on.

"Just think about it, Claire. See if you have any memories of playing with someone you loved. Let's go to Mom's house. You can take a look around my room and see if anything seems familiar."

Claire succeeded in twisting away. "This is crazy, Kate! A-Are you saying you think we might be *sisters*?" She shook her head.

"That's not possible."

"Explain the doll, then."

"I can't."

She grabbed Claire's arm and half dragged her to the bathroom where she snatched up two hand towels. She handed one to Claire, then wrapped her hair in the other one. "Put that around your hair."

In a trancelike state, Claire tucked her hair under the towel and turned to stare into the mirror with Kate. Two young women with similar noses and mouths looked back, but the biggest resemblance was their distinctive blue eyes. Surely Claire could see it now.

Luke's broad shoulders loomed in the doorway. "It's a pretty striking resemblance. It was hard to see past your red hair, Kate. What do you think, Claire?"

Claire reached up to touch the towel as it tried to slide. "I don't know. People resemble other people all the time." A dimple came in her cheek as she made a face in the mirror.

"See that dimple?" Kate put on a fake smile. "I have one just like it."

"There's one way to find out," Luke said. "Go down to the lab and get a DNA test run on both of you."

In the mirror, Claire's face reflected her doubt, but at least someone was taking Kate seriously. "And it would show if you're a good donor match for me too."

"I-I guess we don't have anything to lose." Claire pulled the towel off her head. It dislodged strands of her updo. "But why would Harry take me in place of Claire if I was your sister? And why would your mother allow it?"

Luke leaned against the doorjamb and crossed his arms over his chest. "That's what we have to find out. I say we go talk to your mother and see if she'll tell us the truth. If anyone knows it, she does."

Kate sat by the window of the truck, and Claire was in the middle with her arm squeezed against Luke's. At the sight of the blue shingle cottage, Claire pressed her hand to her stomach and closed her eyes. She had a brief recollection of two little girls playing on the wide porch and running through fields filled with flowers. Every nerve in her body vibrated with the awareness of this place, but she couldn't move.

Luke touched her hand, and she opened her eyes to see his worried face. "I'm all right. But, Luke, I've been here before." Her voice trembled.

"Let's take it one step at a time." He turned off the truck and opened his door.

"Kate might need help."

She nodded and slid out the driver's side door. Her legs didn't feel strong enough to support her, but she grew stronger and more determined as she went around to help Kate out of the passenger side. Kate waved away any help and clambered out of the truck with no problem.

Kate glanced toward the house. "You're pale. Are you all right?"

"I'm fine. Just shaken. This house used to be gray, didn't it?"

Kate's eyes widened. "Not for a long time. I've seen pictures of me on the steps when I was two, and it was gray then. I'm not sure when she painted it, but it's been blue for as long as I can remember. We can ask her."

Claire had never believed in time warps or other dimensions, but when she put her foot on the first stair step, she felt as though she were about to take a walk back through time. She stopped and looked to her right. "Was there a tree swing in that tree once?"

Kate gasped and nodded. "The rope broke when I was swinging in it the summer after I graduated from high school. Uncle Paul said he'd put up a new one, but he never did. You're remembering things, Claire. When I said I thought you were my sister, I didn't believe it myself, but I'm beginning to."

Claire shivered and rubbed at the goose bumps on her arms. "Maybe I just played here with you sometimes. It doesn't mean I'm your sister." She was suddenly eager to get it over with, to talk to Mary Mason and find out more. Either way, she had to know.

Her head high and her legs strong enough to leap fences now, she marched up the steps to the door. "Should you warn her we're out here?"

Kate moved past her to the door and opened it. "No, it's best we surprise her. Maybe she won't try to lie to us."

The muted sound of laughter from a sit-com filtered into the entry. The scent of a blueberry candle lingered in the air. Light flickered from the screen in the dimly lit living room. Her shoes clattering on wood floors, Claire got a vague impression of pale walls as she followed Kate. Luke took her hand, and she laced her cold fingers with his.

They paused in the doorway, and Claire took in the large, pleasant room. A flat-screen TV hung above a fireplace with painted brick. Mary stretched out on an overstuffed blue-and-white plaid sofa perpendicular to the TV. She appeared to be asleep. Several high-back chairs flanked the fireplace. Nothing in this room looked familiar, but the original furniture was likely long gone.

Kate stepped into the room. "Mom."

Mary rubbed her eyes and sat up. "Kate? What are you doing home? I thought they were keeping you overnight. I left your things at the front desk." Her slight gasp indicated she'd seen Claire and Luke standing behind her daughter. "Is something wrong?"

Kate gestured to the chairs. "Have a seat." She moved to sit beside her mother on the sofa. "We have some questions, Mom."

Claire settled into the comfortable chair to the right of the fireplace and glanced at Luke as he sat across from her. She rubbed her icy hands on her slacks. She was cold, so cold, and she trembled all the way through to her spine. She felt as though she were on a cliff about to plunge into a dark, unknown hole. If she found out she was really Rachel Mason, then what? It opened up an entirely new set of questions. Like why?

Mary's lowered lids shuttered the flash of fear in her eyes. "What about?"

"My imaginary friend, Rachel."

Mary's laugh held no real mirth, only

uncertainty. "Oh, for heaven's sake, Kate, I thought you'd forgotten about that long ago. You were a preschooler."

"Look at me, Mom." Kate leaned forward. "I was five when she went away, wasn't I? And I think Claire is really Rachel. Dad took her to replace Claire, didn't he?"

Eyes wide, Mary put her hand to her mouth. Only a gasp escaped, and she shook her head.

"Admit it, Mom. We're starting to put two and two together."

Claire clasped her hands together and leaned forward. "I had a blood test done so the DNA will tell us for sure. Denying it now won't gain you anything but a few days. I paid for a two-day turnaround. Please, tell us the truth. Am I Kate's sister? Are you my real mother?"

She choked over the last word. Did she even want to have a different mother? Lisa Dellamare loved her with everything in her. How did she even begin to come to grips with a world so changed? Did she even want to?

She studied the face of the older woman leaning against the back of the sofa so hard that it looked as if she might break it. Emotions warred on Mary's face: longing, fear, maybe even love. Claire read the truth in her face before Mary opened her mouth.

"I'm your daughter, aren't I?" she whispered.

Mary covered her face with her hands and burst into sobs. "I didn't want to do it, but he didn't leave me any choice."

Luke went to stand beside Claire. His hand came down on her shoulder. She shuddered as Mary's words struck home. Her eyes burned. She wouldn't cry. Wasn't this what she wanted — to know the truth?

"My father insisted?" Her voice was hoarse, and she sought out Kate and saw tears rolling down her face as well.

Claire had always somehow felt not whole and she'd begged her parents for a sibling. This was why. The two of them had been ripped apart. "Tell me what happened."

THIRTY-SIX

Had her mother really just confessed to giving Claire away? No, her name was Rachel. *Rachel.* It would take some getting used to. Maybe Kate should just call her Claire for now.

She watched as Luke grabbed a throw on the back of the chair and draped it around Claire, who was shivering with shock. He was a good man, and while he might not know it yet, he was more than halfway in love with her sister. The knowledge made Kate a little sad. She'd hoped to have her all to herself for a while.

Her mother rose from the sofa and went to look out the window. From here, she appeared to be shaking too. And no wonder. What could have driven her to allow Harry to take her child?

When Mary finally turned back to face them, her shoulders were squared. She licked her lips. "Of the twins, Rachel looked the most like Claire, so that's who he took."

Claire's lips parted and a gasp escaped. "Twins?"

Kate locked gazes with her. "We're twins?"

"Yes. And it's my fault Claire died so your father thought he was well within his rights to demand a replacement."

Kate's lips felt numb. "I don't understand. You murdered a *child*?"

Mary shook her head violently. She shivered and bent down to straighten a photograph of the two of them that had fallen over on the stand. "It was an accident, but she was still dead." She clasped her hands together in a gesture of entreaty. "I was jealous. There he was at the hotel with his *wife* and daughter. He didn't have time to take a half-hour boat ride to see me and my girls. He hadn't been to see us in a month. I went to the hotel and waited, hoping to catch a glimpse of him. Claire came out of the back when the children were playing hide-and-seek. In a spur-of-the-moment decision that I'll regret forever, I-I took her."

"Didn't she scream?" Luke asked.

"No. I told her that her mom had sent me to get her, that her dad had been in an accident. I hustled her to my car and drove off with her. I'd just thought to scare Harry a little, then I'd take her back." Mom ran

386

her hand through her blond hair and exhaled. "But I didn't know she had asthma."

Asthma. Kate wanted to cling to some kind of hope that her mother wasn't a murderer, but shouldn't she have known about the asthma? Maybe she'd secretly hoped the little girl would die.

Claire clutched the blue throw around her and stood. "Mom mentioned I used to have asthma, and she was glad I outgrew it."

Kate's mother seemed lost in a trance now with her gaze fixed on a spot above the fireplace. "I stopped a few miles from the hotel, and we got out. I was going to try to make sure she wasn't scared, but she ran off. I heard her crying and tried to find her. When I finally tracked her down, she was clutching at her neck trying to breathe. There was nothing I could do to save her." She reached to the lower shelf of the table stand and pulled out a tissue.

Nausea roiled in Kate's stomach as the scene played out in her head. That poor little girl. "Why didn't you take her to the hospital or call the sheriff?"

Her mother shrugged. "I had you girls to raise. What would happen to you if I ended up in jail? I-I called Paul, and he took care of burying her while I went to day care to get you girls. I'm so ashamed of it, but I can't change it."

"You called m-my father?" Claire asked.

Kate's mother shook her head. "I couldn't face him."

Her face flushed and perspiring, Claire shrugged off the throw. "But if Harry didn't know what you did, how did he get me?"

"He figured it out later. He kept looking for Claire, always looking. He wouldn't give up. He found someone who saw me near the hotel that night and confronted me. I was desperate to confess so it wasn't hard to pry the truth out of me. The guilt has eaten me up." She finally went back to the sofa, practically falling into its embrace. The blueberry candle had gone out, and she picked up the lighter. Her hand trembled as she held it over the wick and relit it.

Could she ever feel the same way about her mother after listening to this story? Kate took deep breaths to fight the nausea. What kind of person left a dead little girl un-claimed in the woods? It was heartless. The least she could have done was put her somewhere the body would be found.

Luke guided Claire back to her chair and stood over her protectively. "And your brother made all the arrangements with you to take possession of Rachel, didn't he?"

Mary nodded. "Harry didn't want to be

seen here until his little girl was found. He wanted to make sure no one figured out the truth."

"Why didn't he just turn you in once you confessed?" Luke asked.

"His wife." She spat the words and her mouth twisted. "She was in a bad way, and he feared finding Claire's body would totally destroy her. I sent him current pictures since he hadn't seen you both in a year, and he decided Rachel looked the closest to Claire. He promised me Rachel would lack for nothing and that he'd take care of me and you, Kate. But it didn't last. The few times he came back, it was clear he couldn't bear to even look at me. He finally stopped coming when you were ten or so." She looked down at her hands. "Not that I can blame him for that. I can't stand to look at myself in the mirror." She looked up at Kate with a pleading expression. "It was an accident. You forgive me, don't you?"

The cramps in her stomach hit again, and Kate bent over in pain. She wanted to run from this house and never look back.

Luke had Claire wait by the door while he checked out her suite. The pulled-back coverlet revealed crisp white sheets and a square of chocolate. The housekeeper had closed the curtains over the patio doors, but he checked to make sure no one lurked outside. After checking under the bed and in the marble bathroom, he motioned for her to come in.

"You look done in."

"I am." The door clicked shut behind her. She leaned against his chest, and he wrapped his arms around her. The clock at the bedside read ten, and she looked glassy-eyed with fatigue. It wasn't every day a person found out she'd been sent in as a pinch hitter for a half sister. He couldn't even imagine how she was feeling right now.

He buried his nose in her sweetly scented hair. She relaxed against him with a sigh. Nothing he could say would make it better, but holding her might. When she lifted her face up to his, her lids were half closed. Enticed by the invitation on her face, he bent his head and brushed his lips across hers.

She wound her arms around his neck, and he obeyed her silent urging for a tighter embrace. Her lips were soft and yielding, and he pulled her closer yet. He'd thought to offer a kiss of comfort, but the passion sparked between them in a rush of heat.

The *ping* of caution finally made him lift his head reluctantly. If he didn't let her go now, he wasn't sure he'd be able to. Her eyes were still closed, and he ran his fingers over her lids and down her cheeks, then stroked her lower lip with his thumb. "I could kiss you all night."

She opened her eyes and smiled up at him. "I could let you. I'm not crazy about being alone tonight, but it's too dangerous to let you stay." Pushing her heavy hair out of her face, she dropped her arms from around his neck. "All I can think about is that my real mother gave me away. It makes me feel like I was thrown out with the trash."

"The urge to survive is pretty strong. And I'm sure she thought you'd have a good life, honey. You did too. Love, a nice home, good schooling. You lacked for nothing."

"I didn't have my sister. My *twin* sister." She stepped away, then wandered over to the door out to the balcony.

He followed her out to cool night air. Lights from a couple of boats glimmered on the water, and more lights at the marina at Folly Shoals lit the darkness along the coast. When she shivered, he draped his arm around her and pulled her into his side. A couple on a lower balcony seemed to be having an argument, and their sharp tones mingled with the rumble of a car turning into the parking lot. Her hair tickled his chin, but he didn't mind as they stood there and looked out on the ocean.

She stiffened and looked up at him. "Luke, we haven't talked about your mother."

"What about her?"

"Your aunt said your mom heard a child crying. That means she heard the real Claire run away f-from Mary. She would have heard that just a few minutes before she died. What if she saw everything and Mary killed her?"

His fingers curled more tightly around her shoulder. "You're saying your mother killed her?"

"Don't call her my mother. She gave me away." She shook her head in a jerky motion. "She conveniently left that off, but someone murdered your mother, and Mary was right there trying to cover her tracks. I think we should go back and talk to her tomorrow. There's more she isn't saying." Covering her mouth, she yawned. "Sorry."

"I'm glad you're sleepy. I'm going to go and let you get some rest." He dropped a chaste kiss on her lips, then stepped back. He locked the balcony door behind them, then moved a table in front of it. "Just as an added precaution. There's a storm coming in tonight too."

"I sleep well in storms." She reached up and brushed a kiss across his cheek. "Will you go with me to Mary's tomorrow?"

"I'll pick you up at nine." Reluctantly, he unlocked the door to the suite and stepped into the hall. "Throw the dead bolt behind me."

"I will." She blew him a kiss.

He hurried down the thick carpeting to the elevator. He didn't want to believe Mary had murdered his mother, but he was beginning to think there were many layers to this story.

THIRTY-SEVEN

Claire sat on the steps leading down to the water from the hotel. Luke would have a fit if he knew she'd come out here after he left. She'd tried sitting on the balcony, but it wasn't close enough to the sea, her lovely, mesmerizing solace. The moonlight shimmered on the waves, and the sea breeze lifted the strands of her loose hair. A diesel truck lumbered along the access road spewing fumes that blotted out the scent of the ocean.

"Want to walk on the beach with me?" Her father stepped from the shadows by the box shrubs. He had changed into shorts, a rarity, and wore a casual T-shirt.

She rose so quickly that she lost her balance and nearly tumbled down the steep stairs, but he caught her arm. "Dad, what are you doing here?"

"I saw you from our balcony." He offered his arm. "I owe you an apology. Let's walk on the sand."

Could he see her anger, her disappointment? Probably not. The moon wasn't that bright, and the lights were only bright enough to cast dim illumination down the stairs. "Okay."

She barely rested her fingertips on his bare forearm, just enough to steady her down the steps. They didn't speak as they navigated the hillside down to the water. Away from the stench of vehicles she could breathe and think. How did she even begin to tell him all she knew? Luke might have warned her not to be alone with her dad, not after what her father had done, but he'd never given her a reason to fear him.

Her flip-flops slapped against the slabs of granite. Her father's gaze never left her, as if he was waiting for her to make the first move. When she started off toward the pier, he followed, still silent, almost morose.

"Claire."

She stopped and turned to look at him. "I know, Dad. I know my name is really Rachel, though it fits about as well as my toddler-size sneakers."

He reached out blindly for a nearby rock and sank onto it. "Mary told you."

"Yes, but Kate figured it out first. How could you, Dad? How could you let Mom raise me when you knew all along I wasn't hers?"

He swiped his hand over his brow. "Don't say that! You were hers just as much as Claire was. Have either of us ever given you reason to doubt our love?"

"Love built on a lie! What kind of love is that?"

"You can't possibly tell her the truth. It would break her heart."

"I can't live a lie, Dad! You can't ask that of me."

"I've never asked you for anything. All I've done is give, Claire." When she opened her mouth, he fixed her with a fierce glare. "You *are* Claire. A name doesn't change who you are. So what if you were first called Rachel? People change their names all the time. Who you are doesn't change, and your mother and I love you for all things you are — not for a name."

Pity clutched her chest when his eyes glimmered with moisture. He seemed older, beaten down in a way she'd never seen. Her eyes burned, and she longed to go to him and hug him. To tell him she'd do whatever he asked, but the cost was too great.

She took a step closer. "I think you should tell Mom."

"I can't." His shoulders slumped, and he

hung his head.

"She already knows I'm not Claire. She needs to know who I really am."

He jumped to his feet and shook his finger at her. "You think she won't turn her back on you if she knows? On me and our marriage? Do you want to send her back to that mental hospital? You're judging me, and you don't know what it was like back then for her, for me. You are still my daughter. I knew she could love you, and it would bring her out of that dark place where she lived. Surely you don't want her to go back there."

That stopped her. Could she risk sending her mother over the edge? "Of course I don't want to hurt her, but I'm not Claire. I'm Rachel." Something in her recoiled every time she said her real name. When would it begin to feel natural? Never?

He started back toward the steps. "Think it over, Claire. Don't ruin all our lives for some idea that truth is the only thing that ever matters. Truth can destroy, too, and if your mother dies, it's all on your head."

She watched the shadows swallow him up until the sound of his footfalls couldn't be separated from the roar of the waves. Part of her wanted to run after him and reassure him, but she couldn't. She didn't know how it would end.

The sound of the surf rolled around her in an embrace. Would her mother ever hold her again? And what about Grandma? Did she know about this?

"Very touching," said a male voice behind her.

Then the sound of the sea merged with a roaring in her ears, and her world went dark.

Kate barely closed her eyes all night. Every time she tried, she saw her mother's face and heard the way she tried to excuse her actions. She got out of bed and reached for her phone as the sun began to slant its beams across her pale oak floors. Claire didn't answer so she left a message, then Kate pulled on her jeans and a gray T-shirt. Who knew how long she had with her sister before she left town, and she wanted to make the most of every moment.

It was all she could do to occupy herself until nearly nine when she took the ferry from Summer Harbor over to the hotel and hurried to Claire's suite. The wide hall was empty when she knocked on the door. Though she tried several times, Claire never answered. She waited at least five minutes, then knocked again with the same result.

"No answer?" Luke spoke from behind her. "I was supposed to pick her up at nine."

He stepped past her and rapped on the door. "Claire?" He pounded on the door with his fist. "Claire, are you all right?"

Palpable tension rolled off Luke. The muscles in his arm flexed as he pounded again. "Something's wrong. I'm going to call security to let me in. Wait here." He jogged toward the elevator and entered it.

Could Claire be lying in there unconscious? Or worse?

A door on the other side of the hall opened, and her father stepped out. He almost did an about-face when he saw her. His lips flattened, and he quickly pulled the door shut behind him. "What are you doing here?" The strong scent of his cologne, obviously expensive, drifted toward her. The smell brought back memories that made her heart stutter.

"Claire isn't answering her door. Luke was here too, and they were supposed to meet at nine. He went to get security in case something is wrong. Do you happen to have a key card to her room?"

"Of course not."

The torment in his eyes made her turn away. "We'll just wait for Luke and security, then."

His feet shuffled on the dark-blue carpet. "Why did you have to meddle? You've ruined my life."

The wobble in his voice caught Kate off guard. She didn't want to feel pity for the man who had abandoned her, for the monster who had torn her twin sister from her, but compassion stirred anyway. "How do you think I feel knowing all you've done to destroy my family? Claire — Rachel — should have been by my side all my life, and we've lost twenty-five years together. She was my *twin*. You don't rip twins apart like that."

He made a dismissive motion with his right hand, and the heavy gold ring on his finger flashed in the light of the sconces on the walls. "She had a much better life."

"Even if that's true, what gave you the right to do it?"

His blue eyes, so like her own and Claire's, opened wide as if he couldn't believe she dared to talk back to him. He tugged at the collar of his Ralph Lauren shirt. "A father's right. I wanted what was best for her."

That hurt, but she managed not to wince. "Oh, and it didn't matter about me? If it was all about your care for your children, you would have taken us both. Mom said you checked us out to see which one looked most like Claire. You just wanted a substitute, and it didn't matter how it would affect her or me. Or Mom either, for that matter."

"You think I care if your mother suffered a little after what she did?"

"It was an accident!" How on earth was she even defending what her mother had done? Yet she couldn't stand by and let his platitudes be the last word.

His door opened and Lisa, dressed in white slacks and a red ruffled top, stood swaying in the doorway. Her face was nearly as washed out as her pants. Her tortured gaze went to Kate, then to her husband. "Harry." Tears ran down her cheeks. "I just *knew* there was something you weren't telling me." She rubbed her hands on the sides of her capris. "Claire is really this girl's twin? Still your daughter but s-she belongs to Mary." She spat Kate's mother's name like it was a bitter taste in her mouth.

His hand out, Harry took a step toward his wife. "Lisa, let me explain."

She held her hands out in front of her. "Don't touch me."

"Lisa, you are my everything. I did it all for you."

"You did it for yourself. Don't lie to me. I never want to see you again. Your things will be outside this door in half an hour. Hand over your key." She held out her hand, and he slowly reached into his shirt pocket for the key card. Her fingers closed around it. "You'll be hearing from my attorney." She slammed the door.

Thirty-Eight

The guard's hooded eyes said he'd been up all night, but his movements were quick and precise as he pulled out his key card.

"Open it," Luke said.

The gray-suited security guard slipped in his card and pushed open the door. "Ms. Dellamare?"

Luke pushed past him. "Claire?"

Kate and Harry followed, though they didn't look at one another. He'd sensed the tension between them the second he'd gotten back, but that was the least of his worries. They could work it out for themselves.

He glanced at the bed, still turned down for the night with the chocolate on the pillow, and he fisted his hands. "Her bed hasn't been slept in." Fear choked him. "I left her here at ten last night, and she locked the door behind me."

Arms hanging limply at his sides, Harry stood in the middle of the carpeted room.

"She went out later. I found her sitting on the steps looking out at the water. We went for a walk along the shore, and she told me she'd found out she was Kate's twin. W-We had words, and I came back to the hotel."

"You *left* her there alone? Where?"

"Near the sandbar."

He knew the tombolo area. "You knew she'd been attacked. How could you just walk away and leave her unprotected?"

The guard stepped between them with his hands up. "Everyone, calm down." He turned to Harry. "Do you want me to call the sheriff, Mr. Dellamare? It's clear she never came back last night."

"Yes, yes, call the sheriff. Tell him to spare no expense. I'm going to call in a private investigator too." He turned on his heel and rushed out of the room. "I must tell Lisa."

Good riddance to him and his expensive brown loafers and his hundred-dollar haircut. He seemed to think money and power were the answers to everything. He glanced around. "Do you see her cell phone anywhere?"

"I'll check the bathroom." Kate hurried through the door and returned a few moments later. "Not in there."

"Not anywhere in here either," the guard said.

She'd been missing close to twelve hours. And he knew in his gut that she wouldn't just walk away from the problems here. And she wouldn't leave what was developing between them without a word. The tenderness between them last night had kept him tossing and turning in his bed. This was the forever kind of thing.

"Do you have any security footage?" he asked the guard.

The guard turned toward the door. "This way." He led them to a service elevator that opened into the bowels of the hotel basement with fluorescent lighting that buzzed. A ten-by-ten room in the far corner held banks of equipment. The guard fiddled with the computer for a few moments, then the screen lit up.

They watched people coming and going outside. "There she is," Kate said. "She left with Harry."

"Let's check the outside camera." The guard maneuvered the mouse and pulled up the other footage. "There they are again."

They watched father and daughter walk toward the cliff steps and out of the camera's view.

Luke turned toward the door. "I'm going down to the water's edge." He and Kate ran for the elevator.

When they reached the ocean rocks, he saw only several male tourists dressed in loud shirts and sporting white legs beneath their shorts. He took off running for the tombolo. His legs pumped hard in the uneven sand, kicking up gritty particles that stung the back of his legs. The surf was high today, washing kelp and seaweed onto the sandy rocks before ebbing out to rage back with fresh fury. Had she been carried off by a rogue wave? No, she was ocean savvy. She'd know better than to turn her back to the sea.

He shaded his eyes and looked up and down the coastline. Was that a drag mark off the rocks and into the bushes? He pointed it out to Kate, and she ran ahead of him to push aside the brambles and dig through the thin soil.

When she turned with a pink-covered iPhone in her hand, his gut clenched. "That's Claire's."

"I know." Kate bit her lip and looked down. "And look here. I think she lay here awhile. The cell phone was in the deepest part of it. There are big footprints here too."

Luke knelt and examined the indentation in the sand. It could have been the depression where Claire lay for a while. Drag marks continued on for six feet, then the footprints went deeper as if someone had carried her out of here. He prayed that meant she wasn't dead, but there was no guarantee of that. Someone had killed Jenny very near here, then disposed of her body.

He stood and looked down the coastline to where the land curved into the Sunset Cove harbor. Sailboats and motorboats bobbed in their moorings. "I think I need to check the cave where we found Jenny's body."

Kate, her blue eyes wide and shadowed, clutched his arm. "You don't think . . . ?"

"Pray," he told her.

"I have been. Can I go with you?"

"I'd like you to check in with the sheriff and show him what we found. Give him the cell phone and let him check it for prints. I think it fell out of her pocket when she was dragged over here, but we can't be sure."

She nodded and pulled out her own phone. "What's your number?" When he rattled it off to her, she punched it into her phone. "I'll call you after I talk to the sheriff. If you get to the cave first, call me and let me know what you find."

He nodded and headed for his boat. A sick feeling lodged in the pit of his stomach, and he prayed God would keep Claire safe until he could find her. Lightning flickered in the dark sky. The promised storm was here.

Dribbles of water in her face made Claire gasp and crack her eyes open a slit. Her head pounded, especially a spot in the back. Nausea roiled when she touched the goose egg. She became aware of a rocking sensation that made her dizzy, too dizzy to want to open her eyes all the way. Gulls squawked and more raindrops hit her cheeks. The stench of gasoline added to her upset stomach.

She was in a boat.

She forced her eyes open, wincing as the daggers of light jabbed at her. Where was she? Her left hand touched what felt like a tarp, and a dull rumble under the boards indicated an engine powered the craft toward its destination. Her memory flooded back. She'd been down at the beach at night, and someone hit her on the head from behind. It was daylight now so she must have been unconscious for some hours.

Her hands and feet were free and unbound, but she'd been attacked. The sharp taste of fear lingered on her tongue along with a sickeningly sweet chemical taste. Ether? The bump on her head wouldn't have kept her unconscious so long.

Fighting dizziness, she struggled to a seated position, then got on her hands and knees before managing to stagger to her feet. She grasped the side of the boat to keep from falling back down to the deck. She searched her pocket for her cell phone, but it was missing. She had to get help somehow, but she couldn't think past the panic welling in her chest.

The vessel was a lobster trawler, with about a forty-foot beam. She was on the top deck, and the Bimini top wasn't up, which was why the cold rain continued to ping down on her. Looking out on the horizon, she saw no sign of land. Only the heaving sea.

Her gut clenched, and she grabbed the metal rail in a white-knuckled grip as she struggled not to vomit. They were heading due east. Toward Canada or open water? Was he meeting up with another boat out here, or did he intend to dispose of her body far from shore?

He is going to kill me. She had to find a weapon. No one could help her.

Clinging tightly to the rail, she descended the steps. She entered the back of the bridge. The man seated at the helm didn't turn, but she didn't have to see his face to recognize the neat ears and rough, dark hair.

It was the man she'd painted, the one she saw over and over in her nightmares.

Her tongue didn't want to work at first so she tried again and managed to choke out a few words, though she wanted to turn and run. "Who are you?"

He turned then, revealing a rather handsome face. His salt-and-pepper hair and his tanned, leathery skin made her guess his age at about fifty. His arms were ropy with muscles, so she'd have a hard time overpowering him and getting the boat turned around.

"You're awake." He rose and stretched. "I thought I had more time." His feet were bare, and he wore navy shorts and a white T-shirt.

She glanced around for a weapon but saw nothing. "Where are we?"

"About ten miles off from Folly Shoals." His face betrayed no emotion as he looked her over.

Something clicked in her head as she looked at him. The family resemblance was obvious in his eyes and the tilt of his mouth. "You're my mother's brother, Paul. The one who buried Claire."

He reached over to cut the engine. The sudden cessation of the throb under her feet was as loud as a bomb. "Very good. You were smart even at four." He took a step toward her.

Was that regret in his eyes? She backed up. "If you kill me, there's one more murder added to your list. I already redid the painting, and there are posters of it up all over the area. Someone will recognize you."

He balled his hands into fists. "I kept hoping you'd shut up and go away, but you kept poking and poking. I have no choice. My sister will give me an alibi for your disappearance, and I can talk my way out of just about anything."

"Jenny was going to turn you in, wasn't she? That's what the letter she sent the sheriff was about. She couldn't bring herself to report you directly but hoped implicating me would bring out the truth. So you killed her."

"There's no evidence tying me to Jenny. Especially with you gone."

Dizziness hit her hard, and she reached out a hand to steady herself. Images flashed through her consciousness, assaulting her like bricks. Horsey rides on his back, a sandbox he'd built for her and Kate, candy he'd bring to them.

And in an instant, she remembered it all.

The trees reached knobby hands for her. Rachel rubbed her eyes and tried not to cry.

411

Her daddy said only babies cried. But Uncle Paul promised to take her fishing. She loved going out on the boat with him. She'd gotten all ready, and then he'd said no, he was going to check his traps. When he walked off and left her and Kate with the babysitter, she'd followed, determined not to be left behind.

Now she wished she'd stayed with Kate. She wanted to be back home in her bedroom with the covers over her head, not here in these dark woods.

She heard someone cry out, a woman's voice. Maybe Mommy was looking for her. The twigs and leaves crunched under her feet as she headed in that direction. Something fluttered in the moonlight, and she stopped in a patch of white flowers her uncle called spurge to pick a scarf off a bush before continuing on toward the voice.

She stopped at the edge of a small clearing and watched a man struggle with a woman. In the moonlight, she saw a small girl about her own size lying on the ground with her eyes closed. Her gaze went to the adults. The man had his hands around the woman's neck, and he bent her backward until she fell to the ground.

Then he put his knee on her chest and continued to push his hands against her neck. The woman clawed at his hands, but his

412

hands went to her head, and he gave it a funny jerk. Then she didn't fight him anymore.

He rose and turned so she saw his face and the dead fox hanging on his belt. "Uncle Paul!"

Her first inclination was to run to him. Until she saw the rage and confusion on his face. She turned and plunged back into the forest, running faster and faster. Her ribs hurt, and she wanted to stop, but she had to find Mommy.

"Rachel, come back!"

Something in his voice made her run harder. She reached her tree with its secret hiding spot and stuck the scarf in it so she could climb the tree. Her foot slipped about halfway up, and she screamed as she tumbled toward the ground. Her head struck something hard, and everything went dark.

Claire blinked and realized he was only two feet from her. The anger on his face was just like that night. Not only had he killed Jenny, but he'd murdered Luke's mother. And Rachel had seen it all.

She turned and ran for the steps to the upper deck. Maybe she could find something to defend herself up there. Her foot hit the rung of the ladder and she began to climb, but she was slow, too slow, and his strong fingers closed around her ankle.

"I'm sorry, but it has to be this way, Rachel."

She kicked out and his hand fell away. She continued to scramble up the ladder, but she had little hope of evading him.

THIRTY-NINE

Kate sat in the sheriff's office waiting room in Machias with barely concealed impatience. A man in his thirties, eyes closed and reeking of beer, slept with his mouth open in a chair in the corner. Another man paced the floor waiting for his brother to be released from the overnight holding cell.

She rose and went to speak to the receptionist again. "Maybe I should just leave the cell phone with you. I want to be out looking for my sister." Her sister was missing, and no one seemed in a hurry.

The woman, a young thing in her twenties with a revealing top and dyed blond hair, looked up from the computer. "The sheriff said he'd be here in fifteen minutes."

"And it's been half an hour! I can't wait any longer." Kate slid the cell phone across the counter to her. "He can call me. I'm going to look for her."

As she wheeled toward the door, she saw

a bulletin board covered with wanted posters. A small one in the upper-right corner
leaped out at her, and she moved closer to
take a look. "Who's this?"

The woman rose and tugged her short
skirt down. "Claire Dellamare painted the
man she supposedly saw push Jenny Bennett
from the cliff."

A sick feeling lodged in the pit of Kate's
stomach. It was Uncle Paul. "Call the sheriff
and see where he is."

The woman rolled her eyes. "You're a
bossy little thing." She picked up the phone.

Kate paced the floor, avoiding the strides
of the man waiting with as much impatience
as she felt. The receptionist finally put the
phone down and approached her again.

"He's investigating a burglary at a gas sta-
tion and won't be here for another hour.
He says for you to wait for him."

"That's not going to happen. I'll be back
later." She ran for the door, ignoring the
shouts of the sheriff's lackey.

Maybe it was all a mistake. Claire might
be remembering seeing their uncle when
she was a little girl. It didn't mean he actually had her or that he'd done anything
wrong. Maybe she was overreacting. Kate
had to get the truth out of Mom. Out in the
sunshine, she jogged across the street to her

Volkswagen. She accelerated out of the parking lot toward her mother's house. As she drove, she dug out her cell phone and told it to call Luke.

It rang four times, then went to voice mail. "Luke, it's Kate. That guy Claire painted is our uncle Paul. I'm en route now to my mother's to see if she has any idea why Claire would have painted him. Call me when you get this." She tossed the phone into the passenger seat atop the litter of breakfast wrappers from a drive-thru.

Kate still couldn't believe her beloved uncle would do anything wrong. He'd been the steady figure all her life. There had to be an explanation.

When Kate's tires crunched in the gravel, her mother rose from working in the flower bed. As Kate got out of her vehicle, Mom pushed the hair out of her face with the back of her muddy hand. "Kate, what's wrong? You're way too pale. Do you need to go back to the doctor?"

"No, it's not that. Claire is missing."

Her mother swiped her hands down the sides of her jeans, leaving a trail of mud. "What does that mean? She ran off because of the shock?"

Kate kicked a pile of weeds out of her way. "Someone took her. I found her cell phone in the bushes, and Luke found drag marks in the sand. Her bed wasn't slept in."

Her mother fidgeted and looked away.

"You know something, Mom, don't you?" The next question wasn't something Kate even wanted to consider. "Does Uncle Paul have her?"

The sun struck her mother fully in the face, and her eyes dilated at the question before she looked down at the ground. Her mother turned toward the steps. "Of course not. Want some iced tea?"

Kate wanted to throw up. Every confirmation she needed was in her mother's evasiveness. She caught her mother's arm and pulled her around. "How can you just stand back and let Uncle Paul hurt her? She's your daughter too."

Her mother clenched her hands together. "She stopped being my daughter when Harry took her. If I thought otherwise I would have gone crazy. Anything that happens is your fault, Kate. You never should have gone to see your father. You put dangerous things in motion."

"Don't pin that on me. Someone attacked Claire before I ever went to see Dad. There's something more going on here than I understand, but I think you know exactly what it is. You have to tell me where he would have taken her."

Her mother crossed her arms over her chest. "Paul wouldn't hurt Claire. He loves you girls. He always has."

"He loved Rachel. I think he considers Claire tainted by Dad. And he's covering up something."

Her mother looked away, out over the fields of flowering blueberry bushes. "It's going to be a good blueberry year."

"Mom, stop it. You won't distract me. Claire drew a picture of the person she saw shove Jenny off the cliff. It was Uncle Paul. I know he was seeing someone on the sly. Was it Jenny?"

Her mother bent down and picked up her yard tools. "You'll have to talk to Paul yourself."

Kate took her mother by the shoulders. "Listen to me! He's going to kill Claire. Get your head out of the dirt and do something about it. You let Dad push you around, and now you're letting Uncle Paul do the same thing. Do you want Claire's blood on your hands too?"

Her mother looked away.

Kate wanted to shake her, but it wouldn't do any good. Her cell phone rang, and she glanced at it as she answered. "Luke, thank the Lord. Did you find her?"

"No. Nothing at the cave."

She closed her eyes, not sure whether to rejoice or be discouraged. At least Claire hadn't been killed and hidden in the cave. "Where are you?"

"At the marina at Summer Harbor. I thought I'd get you and we'd go back out to search."

"Look at slip fifteen. Is there a big lobster trawler there?"

After a pause, Luke said, "Nope, it's empty."

"Claire's on Uncle Paul's boat. I'll be right there." She ended the call and turned to her mother. "Where would he take her, Mom? What's his favorite area to fish?"

Her mother twisted her hands together. "Paul always looked out for us. What will become of me if he leaves me too?"

"Tell me where to look!"

Her mother took down her ponytail, then scooped it up again and corralled the loose ends. "His best lobstering is ten miles offshore out past Lobster Rock."

It wasn't much, but it was better than nothing. Kate ran for her car. Storm clouds hovered out over the water. If Claire was out there, she was facing a major storm.

The cold rain drenched Claire as soon as

she reached the upper deck, and she squinted through the downpour for some kind of weapon. She recognized the area. It was where she and Luke had freed the little orca. She remembered her boast to Luke about not being able to sink if she tried. Such a foolish comment. Seas like this would drown anyone.

Paul probably lived in fear that she would remember what happened to Luke's mother. And it had finally happened.

She flung open the storage compartments and reached inside. Surely he had a fillet knife or something stashed up here. Though the storm muffled his heavy tread on the stairs, she heard the thud as each foot hit a step, and her muscles tightened. She had to get away from him.

After finding nothing in any of the compartments, she flung herself over the edge of the railing and dangled over the lower deck. Her toes wouldn't quite reach any kind of foothold, and she found it hard to see through the driving rain. Her fingers lost their purchase on the rain-slicked railing, and she began to slip. She wouldn't be able to hold on to the wet metal much longer. Her flailing legs hit the side of the lower walls around the cabin, and she let go, sliding down the sides to land on the bottom deck.

Even with the poor visibility, he'd soon figure out she wasn't up there. The radio! She scurried into the bridge and grabbed it. "Mayday, mayday. This is Claire Dellamare, please help me. I'm being held prisoner aboard Paul Mason's boat. W-We're out in the middle of the ocean somewhere. Can you pinpoint my location? Mayday, mayday." She released the button and waited, but all she heard was static. "Mayday, mayday."

A hard hand jerked the radio away from her and shoved her onto her backside. She landed on the floor and saw stars when her head banged the side of the cabin. "They know it's you. Someone heard me."

He shook her so hard her hair flopped out of its pins. "Why did you have to come back? I don't want to hurt you, Rachel, you're blood. But you give me no choice."

"Why didn't you kill me when I saw you?"

His gaze flickered. "You didn't remember anything after you hit your head. I thought we were safe, me and Mary."

Ice encased her limbs. "Mary? What does she have to do with this? Does she know you intend to kill me?" She wrenched out of his grip and fell onto the heaving deck.

His lips flattened, then he reached toward

her and she crab-walked away from him. Rolling onto her stomach, she tried to regain her feet, but he grabbed her arm and yanked her to her feet, then shoved her out the door into the downpour again.

It was colder now, freezing, as the rain pummeled her. She shuddered, partly from the cold and partly from fear. Though she struggled, she couldn't break his grip on her arm. The rain obscured everything more than a foot in front of her face. "They'll catch you, and you'll go to prison for the rest of your life. If you let me go, I won't report you."

He marched her to the back of the boat by the ladder, and she glimpsed the monstrous waves before his fingers released her arm. A hard shove against her back sent her flying through the air off the back of the boat. The waves rose to meet her, and she crashed into the cold water. She came up spitting salt water. She went down sliding into a trough with the next wave twenty feet up the other side of it.

She wouldn't have to try to drown here. All she had to do was tire of her up-and-down ride through the troughs. That would be all too easy in this storm. She held her breath as the next wave crashed over her head. A murky green obscured her vision.

Her lungs burned with the need to breathe, and she fought her way back to the surface. She dog-paddled to meet the next wave as regret washed over her.

There would be no future with Luke. She would miss getting to know Kate better. Did her mother still love her? Claire was pretty sure she did. A mother's love didn't just evaporate, did it?

Her limbs grew numb with cold, and she thought she heard the *putt-putt* of Paul's boat heading away from her. She had no idea which way to even swim, but trying to keep up with him was a useless task with the roar of the storm filling her ears. Already her arms felt like heavy stones, and her calves were starting to cramp. Was this what drowning felt like?

A vision of her little orca floated in her head. She banged her hand on the water, but with this storm, he'd never hear her, even if the pod had stayed close by.

A wave broke over her head, and she inhaled water. It was cold going down but burned as well. *God, do you see me? Please make this easy. I'm scared.*

The verse in Isaiah she'd heard in church came to her. *"Even if the mountains heave up from their anchors, and the hills quiver and shake, I will not desert you."*

The struggle left her legs and arms. God had her. Though she might have regrets about the things she hadn't said or done, there was a better world waiting. She didn't have to fight this. Down, down she went into the green abyss. God would meet her here.

Her lungs burned with the need to breathe, but she couldn't make herself draw more water into her lungs. She would hold her breath as long as she could, and then she would step across the divide.

A nudge came at her leg, but it was too dark to see. A shark? Whatever it was began to lift her to the surface. She was in such a dreamy, half-conscious state that she couldn't muster the strength to look to see what was raising her to the surface.

Her head broke the waves, and she took in a big lungful of cold air. Something black and white flipped into the water beside her. The little orca! She recognized the long scar on his side. He came closer, nudging her again, until she managed to grasp his dorsal fin in her nearly lifeless hands. He propelled her through the water. Several times she lost her grip, and he came back to get her.

Something red floated on the horizon when the next wave lifted her. A buoy bonged to her right. She let go of the calf and struck out toward the buoy.

It seemed like forever before the rain began to patter to a stop, and her right knee hit something hard. She blinked. The buoy was just a few feet away. She grabbed the hard metal and climbed atop it, pulling herself closer until both arms wrapped around it.

The waves pummeled her, and it was all she could do to hang on.

FORTY

The huge rollers lifted Luke's boat to the skies before the bow slid down into each new trough. He didn't like the beating his boat was taking, but urgency drove him on. Kate stood out in the driving rain trying to spot her uncle's boat, but so far she'd seen nothing. The Coast Guard was on the lookout too.

The reason Paul had brought her out here didn't bear thinking about. How could her own uncle have wanted to kill her?

His radio crackled into life. "Luke Rocco, you copy?" It was one of his Coast Guard friends.

He snatched up the transmitter. "Rocco here, I copy."

"We have Mason in custody. No sign of Claire Dellamare onboard, though, and he denies any involvement with her."

"Have you examined the boat to see if there's any trace of her?"

"Affirmative. Nothing. But we picked up an SOS of a woman claiming to be Claire Dellamare. It was garbled, though. The boat captain who heard it thought she said she was on Mason's boat. So we're questioning Mason, and so far he's not budging in his story."

If she'd been there and wasn't now, Paul Mason had to have done something to her. Luke felt like he'd been kicked in the stomach. He signed off, then went to tell Kate the news. The rain was stopping, and the wind had begun to calm. The waves, while still very choppy, weren't the monsters they'd been when they first came out here.

Kate turned at his approach and crossed her arms over her stomach. "Tell me."

He told her what the Coast Guard said, and her stomach clenched. "I knew he had her."

"What could he have done with her? Is there somewhere out here he might have left her?"

Her blue eyes, so like Claire's, held only terror as she shook her head. "Only the open sea, I think. It depends on exactly where he was."

"I'm sure they're questioning him, but he's not going to tell them." He rubbed his head and tried to think. "Let's head toward

Lobster Rock and see if we spot her."

It was useless. If Paul had brought her out here, he'd dumped her overboard. While Claire was a strong swimmer, no one could survive cold rollers this size, especially without a wetsuit, and even that just delayed the inevitable hypothermia.

"We should go back, talk to Paul ourselves." He started to turn when he heard a giant splash from the starboard side. The little orca he'd rescued flipped out of the water again, then came up to the side of the boat. He acted agitated and was moving haphazardly.

Luke leaned over the side of the boat. "What's wrong, little guy?"

Kate joined him at the side of the boat. "He's acting strange."

"I think he's upset about something." He frowned and looked closer. The orca had something in its mouth. He patted the side of the boat to entice the killer whale closer. The orca's rostrum bumped the side of the boat, and Luke touched it, then ran his fingers down to the mouth with care. He didn't want to get bitten and dragged overboard. His fingers touched plastic, and the orca opened his mouth, releasing the item to him.

A flip-flop? He turned it over. Size seven.

Rhinestones decorated the pink shoe, so it belonged to a woman. "You ever see Claire wear something like this?"

Kate touched one of the stones. "Good quality. It might be hers." She watched the orca, still swimming erratically beside the boat. "Claire helped you with that orca, didn't she?"

"She loved him. She fed him a lot."

The hidden pain in Kate's eyes changed to hope. "What if this is hers and he's staying close to her?"

It was a long shot, but what other clue did they have? "Can you navigate the boat?"

"I've driven my grandpa's boat since I was ten. What are you going to do?"

He stepped to the bow. "I'm going to look in the waves for her. She might be out there."

His eyes burned with the wind in his face. All he could do was whisper, "Please, God," over and over. There were so many things he wanted to say to her. They had something special, something he didn't want to slip away. A tiny black spot grew on the horizon, and he heard a distant gonging as it rocked in the waves.

Luke reached into one of the compartments and drew out binoculars. Focusing them, he studied the formations and looked for any sign of life. Nothing moved, so he lowered them and looked for the orca swimming in circles. Luke brought the binoculars back up and trained them on the buoy. Was that a piece of driftwood on it? He adjusted the binoculars, and Claire's face leaped into focus.

"She's on the buoy!" He leaned out over the bow and resisted the urge to dive in. The boat would reach her before he could swim there. She hadn't moved yet, and he cupped his hands, shouting her name into the wind. She still didn't move.

Kate brought the boat in as close as possible, and Luke lowered the anchor, then jumped overboard. The shock of cold water nearly took his breath away, but he swam for the buoy as fast as he could. He climbed up next to Claire. When he touched her cheek, he winced at how cold she was. Was she alive? His pulse pounded in his ears as he pressed his fingers to her neck. For a long moment he felt nothing, then a gentle throb pulsed back against his fingers.

"Claire, can you hear me?"

She lifted her head and blinked. "Luke?"

He waved to Kate. "She's alive!" He pried her hands off the buoy. "Let's go, honey. I've got you."

He had to get her aboard and wrapped in

blankets.

She was cold, so cold. A voice called her name. Was it God? She tried to lift her head, but her neck wouldn't support it, and she let her cheek drop back against the buoy. Where was she?

"Claire!"

Luke's voice. She had to get up, let him know she was here before he passed by in his boat. Then warm hands touched her and scooped her up into strong arms. Luke's breath warmed her cold face, and he pressed his face into her neck. Something warm and wet trickled onto her skin, and she tried to focus her gaze but everything stayed blurry.

"Don't cry," she murmured. "I'm okay."

He gave a crooked grin. "Those aren't tears. It's the rain." His choked voice was hoarse, and he gathered her closer. "I thought I lost you, but you're going to be okay. You're on a buoy."

She managed to keep her eyes open and saw the last of the storm clouds billowing away in the blue sky. The sea still foamed around the buoy, but the waves were half the size they'd been. "The little orca. He saved me from drowning."

Luke lifted his head from its nest in her neck. "I saw him swimming out here or I never would have found you. They caught Paul Mason, but he claimed he hadn't seen you. The calf was swimming erratically and making sounds of distress. He had your flip-flop so I got out the binoculars and looked for you." He hugged her tighter. "Thank God."

She shuddered with the cold. "I'd have died."

"Let's get you to the boat and warmed up. I'll have to help you swim to the boat. I'm sorry you have to be back in the water, but it won't be for long."

She nodded and took a deep breath. The cold water closed over her head, and she struggled to the surface with Luke's hand on her arm. The shivering intensified, and she clung to him as he helped her dog-paddle to the boat. Kate's face peered anxiously over the side, and she climbed partway down the ladder to help. Claire grabbed her warm hand, and Luke boosted her behind, but even with both of them assisting her, she barely had the strength to get aboard. She collapsed onto the deck.

The boat swayed as Luke climbed up behind her. "Get a blanket!"

Kate darted to a storage compartment and yanked out a blue thermal blanket. Luke knelt by Claire and pulled her onto his lap.

Though his shirt was wet and cold, the heat of his skin under his clothing enticed her to nestle closer.

Kate dropped to her knees and wrapped them both in the blanket. "She's in hypothermia. We've got to get her to the hospital. Get her inside, out of the wind, and I'll turn us toward shore."

Claire barely felt Luke nod before lifting her and carrying her into the cabin. Her vision began to go in and out again. Was she still going to die? She clung to Luke with weak fists as he placed her on the padded bench.

"We've got to get her out of these wet clothes. Meg has some sweats in that compartment." He pointed. "I'll turn the boat around and you undress her and get her in dry clothes. I'll change too."

Claire was barely aware of hands tugging off her clothes, but the blessed relief of dry clothing made her sigh. Then Kate wrapped two dry blankets around her. "Luke, you come hold her now. I'll take the helm."

Kate's hands released her, then Luke cradled her on his lap again. He rested his chin on her wet hair and held her close. "I've got you. We'll be home soon."

She closed her eyes and let herself relax against his chest. His heart beat strongly under her ear, the rhythm soothing. *Safe, I am safe.* Then she stiffened and opened her eyes. "What about Kate's mother? M-My mother too, I guess. Did she know he was trying to kill me?"

"She knew he'd killed my mom, but they both had to keep quiet."

"I remembered. I saw it." Claire absorbed Luke's warmth. "How did you figure out he had me?"

"I saw his picture at the sheriff's office and went to Mom. She told me the truth, and we knew he had to have taken you. No one else would have." Kate turned back around to steer the boat.

Sickened by the revelations, Claire closed her eyes. There seemed no real place of home for her.

FORTY-ONE

The bed in her hotel suite felt like heaven. Claire snuggled under the duvet and sheet. At least she was finally warm. Moonlight streamed in through the open door into the room. By the time she'd been checked out at the hospital and had answered the sheriff's questions, night had fallen. Luke insisted she get right into bed, and she'd been happy to comply.

Luke flipped the metal bar on the door into the jamb. "I'm leaving this open. Your dad said they'd be over shortly. I guess your grandmother is driving everyone crazy." He grabbed the table at the desk and pulled it beside the bed.

Claire's heart squeezed. Grandma Emily wasn't really her grandmother since she was Mom's mother. "I think I know what Grandma meant by her strange comments about loving me from the first moment she saw me. I think she knew who I really was all along." She wasn't sure how things would change now, but there was no doubt her life would be very different.

Luke sat on the chair and reached for her hand. "I think things might not be the way you'd expect. You have a way of getting into a person's heart, Claire. I don't think they'll be willing to step aside for your real mother."

His thumb rubbed across her palm in a hypnotic movement that soothed her. "You always know the right thing to say, but I think you're wrong this time. Does your dad know my uncle killed your mom?"

Luke's eyes flickered. "He knows. He's wishing he'd listened to Mom's talk about the child crying."

"I bet he doesn't ever want to see me again. Megan too." The thought of Megan's sorrow hurt Claire's heart.

He raised her hand to his lips and kissed her palm. "You'd be wrong. You were a little girl. You're not to blame for any of it." He scooted over to sit on the bed beside her, then leaned over her and brushed his lips against hers. "I never want to be that scared again. When I saw you lying so still and pale on that buoy, I was sure you were dead."

"I gave up, just let the sea take me down. But our little orca had other plans. I'll need to take him some fish as a thank-you."

He twisted a lock of her hair around his finger. "I think your dad wants you to go home and put this all behind you. I hope you don't put me behind you. It's not that far from Boston to here."

She found it hard to think with the sensation of his hands in her hair. "You're definitely quitting the Coast Guard?"

He nodded. "I realized part of my resistance to coming home was pride, pure and simple. I'd always said I was going to get out into the world and make a difference. But I don't have to be working for the Coast Guard to do that. Folly Shoals is small and backward maybe, but that's not necessarily a bad thing. The world moves too fast now anyway."

She reached up and cupped his cheek. "I don't want to go to Boston."

His smile froze in place. "What are you thinking?"

"I don't know, really, not yet. I don't know what the future holds with my job at Cramer Aviation. The merger didn't happen, and right now I'm finding it hard to figure out what I want to do with my life. Planes are all I know. But blueberries are in my blood, and I'm a little intrigued to see what I might do in a different career."

Luke lifted a brow and grinned. "You ever thought about working in a cranberry bog?"

"You offering me a job?"

"Meg ran it. I'm not very good at that kind of thing. Give me a crime to solve, and I'm all over it, but it's going to take me awhile to get up to speed on anything else."

"I don't know anything about cranberries," she said, though her heart thumped at the thought of working with him. But could she leave everything she knew?

"Well, think about it."

Her grandmother stepped into the room and came to the other side of Claire's bed. She sat down and pulled Claire into an embrace. "Claire, don't ever scare me like that again."

Claire buried her face in her grandmother's neck and inhaled the sweet scent of her cologne. "I-I'm not Claire."

Her grandmother pulled back and cupped Claire's face. "Honey, I knew you weren't Claire the minute I laid eyes on you. I confronted Harry and he told me the truth. I always knew you were Rachel. But your appearance brought my daughter back from the dead. I couldn't tell her and see all her joy disappear again."

"I thought maybe you knew," Claire whispered.

"The differences were clear. No asthma, missing scars, the difference in the shape of your face. One tooth had a small chip in it where she fell against my coffee table. That was missing too. Lots of little things. Claire was always a little difficult right from the day she was born. But not you. You climbed on my lap as soon as Harry brought you home. You had me wrapped around your little finger from that moment. Timothy too. It doesn't take blood for love to flourish."

She drank in her grandmother's words. "I don't know what to call myself."

"I'd stick with Claire. It's what you know and how people know you. Take the trauma you've gone through and let it make you stronger and more compassionate." Grandma released her and slipped off the bed. "Your grandpa is clamoring to get in here. I'll let him know he can come in."

Everything was moving too fast for Claire to grasp it, but she caught the fact her grandma hadn't mentioned Lisa. "What about Mom? Does she hate me now? I'm the other woman's child."

"She's trying to reconcile her jealousy of Mary with her love for you. A small thing that really upset her is that your father bought three dolls when he was in Paris, one for each of his three daughters. And she never knew. But she'll come around. Give her a little time." Grandma leaned down and brushed a kiss over Claire's forehead. She slanted a glance at Luke. "Take care of her, young man."

"I will."

Her grandmother headed for the door, but Luke continued to look down at Claire. "You willing to see where we go from here, honey?"

She reached up and grasped his neck, pulling him down so she could kiss him. "I don't think you have any choice now. Not with Grandma on the warpath."

Organ music filled the rafters of the little church. The communion table had been removed to make room for the closed coffin. Luke sat on the front row with Claire on one side of him and Megan on the other. His sister had rooted through the attic to find a picture of their family in the happy days before their mother went missing. It rested atop the coffin.

His mouth was dry as he studied that picture. They looked so happy on the front porch of their home. He was looking up at his mom with an adoring expression. For just a moment, he thought he smelled the cranberry candles she used to burn.

His gaze lowered to the casket itself, a plain oak one topped with a flower arrangement that included cranberry blossoms. Finally they had closure. Their lives would have been so different if she'd lived. Claire's would have been different too. Would they even have met if circumstances had been different? It was hard to unravel the threads and know what might have been and what now was because of this tragedy. His grandmother had always told him God was in the habit of taking the awful things that happened in life and turning them into diamonds in our path.

Maybe she was right.

A murmur went through the church, and he turned to see Aunt Nan wheeling his father toward their pew. Pop had adamantly refused to come, and they'd left him at the house an hour ago. What had changed his mind?

He rose and went to help his aunt. "He call you?"

Aunt Nan nodded. "I was about to leave for the service, so I ran by to get him."

Pop's hands gripped the arms of his chair. "No need to talk about me like I'm not here. It's not a crime to change my mind." He sniffled and wiped at his face with the back of his hand.

Luke squeezed his dad's shoulder. "It's okay to grieve, Pop. It's been a long time coming."

His gaze transfixed on the casket, his dad nodded. "She deserved better than to be tossed into a field like a piece of trash."

Luke's eyes blurred, and he swallowed hard. "She did."

The grips of the wheelchair were still warm from his aunt's hands. Family was all about passing the baton, working together, dealing with the ugliness that existed even in people he loved, weathering the hard knocks of life by linking hands and stepping out in faith.

He pushed the chair beside the pew where Megan and Claire waited. *Rest in peace, Mom.* Maybe they all could now.

EPILOGUE

The last three weeks had passed in a whirl-wind. Kate lay snuggled in the bed of Claire's hotel room. She had been released from the hospital this morning, and Claire's grandmother had insisted on bringing her here so she could take care of her. Kate's small house had only one bedroom, and the hotel had been quick to bring in a rollaway bed for Claire to use.

Claire sat beside Mary, who was out on bail. She faced serious charges and would likely go to jail. Paul was still in jail awaiting trial for a double homicide and attempted murder. The relationship with Mary was still tenuous and guarded. Maybe it always would be. Neither of them could get very far past remembering that she'd so quickly agreed to give her up. Or that her jealousy had taken the life of a little girl. Though no one had confirmed it, Claire also suspected she knew Paul planned to dispose of her.

The door opened behind them, and the scent of corn chowder wafted into the room. Luke pushed the door shut with his foot and came to set the tray down. "Got your lunch. I ran into your grandmother. She's coming over shortly. How's Kate doing?"

Claire looked back at her sleeping sister. "Okay. She's still groggy. But the doctor thinks this will bring about a complete cure since we're twins, so it's all worth it."

The transplant had been a week ago, and Kate had been hospitalized until the transplant team was sure she was stable. Claire still easily tired after the surgery, but she barely felt a twinge in her hip where they'd taken the marrow.

They all turned at a knock on the door. "I'll get it," Luke said.

Her eyes red and swollen, Lisa peeked around the side of the door. "C-Can I come in?"

Claire's pulse jumped. "Of course."

Lisa faltered when she saw Mary, then tipped up her chin and entered the room. She stepped toward Kate, lying in the bed so still and pale.

Claire rose and stood with her arms awkwardly at her sides. This was the first time she'd seen the woman she called Mom in three weeks. Lisa had gone back to

Boston the day after Claire's rescue, and they hadn't spoken. Claire had picked up her phone several times to call but couldn't bring herself to do it. If Mom wanted to talk to her, she was open, but she wasn't the one who had turned away. Her heart clenched with love and pain. This woman had nurtured her in every possible way. It was impossible to turn off the love she felt for her mother in nearly every sense of the word.

What did she call her? *Mom* hovered on the edge of Claire's tongue. If she called her Lisa it might offend her, so she opted not to use any name. "I didn't know you were coming."

"Neither did I." Lisa's gaze lingered on Claire with stark hunger. "I-I've missed you, Claire."

Claire. She took so much hope from that one word. "I've missed you too." The words were barely a whisper, and she hadn't realized she'd moved until she was standing two feet away from the older woman. "Mom." She choked out the word.

Her mother's eyes flooded with tears. "Oh, honey, I'm so sorry."

She pulled Claire into a tight embrace, and Claire closed her eyes and breathed in that scent she'd missed so much. Tears

446

burned her eyes and soaked into the silk of her mother's blouse.

Her mother pulled away. "I realized that I was jealous, plain and simple, that you weren't mine in every way. Another woman gave you birth. So what? That's the case with adopted babies too. It doesn't mean I don't love you, though I admit I tried not to. But we're still a family. Your birth circumstances don't change that. We all know the truth now, and we have to grapple with it." She glanced at Mary. "I'm willing if you are."

Mary looked over at Kate, still sleeping. "I think it's best if we keep our distance, Lisa. I don't like you. I never did."

Lisa flinched but she didn't leave. "Fair enough. I don't like you either. There will never be friendship between us. But we share a daughter."

Mary shrugged. "I'd hoped you'd stay out of her life."

"And I hoped she wouldn't," Claire put in. "I love her."

Her mother's eyes flooded again. "I don't know what will happen with me and your dad. We're talking again, but that's about all I'm willing to do right now. We might go to counseling. I'm not sure I want to throw away thirty-five years of marriage." She made a face. "Though he'll likely have to serve some time. I doubt even his high-priced lawyer can get all the charges dropped."

Mary pressed her lips together and looked away. Claire could almost see her thoughts hovering in the air. *It was always a lie.* But was it? Her dad hadn't had a relationship with Mary in over twenty years. And he'd loved his wife enough to snatch Claire away from this woman, this birth mother of hers with the tight lips and smoldering anger.

Mary moved with jerky steps toward the door. "Call if Kate wants me. She knows my cell." She slammed the door behind her.

Claire exchanged a long glance with Luke. Mary hadn't had an easy life, and her future would likely include prison time.

Kate muttered at the noise and opened her eyes. She yawned, then tried to sit up. Claire sprang to plump her pillows. "How do you feel?"

"Pretty good, really." Kate glanced around the room. "Where's Mom?"

"She left for a while. I can call her."

Kate shook her head. "It's fine. I'd rather just be with you."

Claire's mother squeezed her hand. "I think I'll go let Mother know Kate is awake. She'll want to check on her. I'll be back in a little while." She exited much more quietly than Mary.

Claire moved to Kate's bedside and handed her a cup of water.

Kate took a sip. "I've been reliving everything, Claire. Our dad, mom, and Uncle Paul seemed so responsible and upstanding, but it was all a facade. Our half sister is dead because of all of them. It's hard to take in."

"And what does that make us? Are we a product of our environment or our genes? Either way, we're in trouble." The thoughts and worries had troubled Claire all these weeks as she'd prepared to give Kate the bone marrow she needed.

Kate set down her water and reached for Claire's hand. "It makes us wise enough to learn from their mistakes. You came to my rescue, and I came to yours. We aren't defined by their mistakes — only by ours, and we can use them to make us better people. That's how Mom messed up. She never took responsibility for her own actions. She always blamed other people. We won't do that, Claire."

Claire pressed her twin's warm hand. "If you ever see me do that, tell me, okay? And I'll make sure you don't either."

She glanced at Luke and drank in his

calm, steady presence. Her grandmother's words echoed in her head. *"God gives you what you need, not necessarily what you thought you wanted."*

If not for this situation, she wouldn't be the same person. She wouldn't have this prickly, two-edged family. But most of all she wouldn't have Luke. Though they were taking it slowly, they had a future together. And she'd found her place here on this rocky island with the wild wind and the even wilder landscape. Though her father insisted her role in the company hadn't changed, she'd taken a leave of absence to figure out what she wanted to do.

With Kate's hand clasped in her left, she reached over to clasp her other hand with Luke's. "God has given us what we needed in every way. Some families are born together, and some are forged in a different way. It's made us who we are, and I'm content with that."

DISCUSSION QUESTIONS

1. Reversing roles to care for a sick parent or grandparent can be challenging. Have you ever had to do that? How did you and your parent cope?
2. We live in such an age of consumerism, and it affects children. Our inclination is to give them everything like Claire's parents did. How do you keep your children grounded?
3. Working the land is almost a lost occupation. Do you ever wish you could go back to a simpler life and farm or do you shudder at the thought?
4. Why do you think Jenny implicated Claire in her letter? Why didn't she just go to the sheriff with what she knew?
5. Why do you think Sheriff Colton

was so determined to find Claire at fault? Do you ever make a snap decision and refuse to look at facts?

6. Claire always wished for siblings. What are some of the challenges of being an only child? Benefits?

7. Do you believe in love at first sight?

8. Do you have an unconventional family? My friend, Diann Hunt, was my sister in every way but blood. How did friends like that or an unusual family circumstance help shape you?

A LETTER FROM THE AUTHOR

Dear Reader,
What a fun ride it was to write this book imagining your gasps with every twist and turn! I wanted to explore family in this story. We all have a blood family as well as people who are such a strong part of our lives that they are like family. Some people become such a part of the fabric of our lives that we know only God could knit us together that strongly.

I firmly believe that every challenge we face in life can make us better people if we let it. We have to accept the things that come from God's hand and allow him to use them to mold and shape us. I can't say that I've been able to get to the place where I pray for trials, but at least I've come to see their value in my life. ☺ God gives us what we need to face every curve life throws our way. We just have to let the pressures push us in the right direction — to be more like Jesus.

This is a deeper, more complex story than I've ever attempted, and I hope I have done it justice. I'm eager to hear what you think! I'm so grateful for you, dear reader, and the joy you bring to my life every day. E-mail me anytime. I love to hear from you!

Love,
Colleen
colleen@colleencoble.com

ACKNOWLEDGMENTS

I had some great help on this book from some Maine friends. A special thanks to Rachael Farnsworth-Merritt, who gave me some great inside Mainer tips. And Christine Alexander, who owns Sugar Hill Farms with her husband, John, showed me all around the cranberry bogs. I was able to get a clear picture of where Luke's mother was found. Thanks so much, friends!

I'm so blessed to belong to the terrific Thomas Nelson dream team! I've been with my great fiction team for twelve years, and it's been such an inspiring time as I've learned more and more about the writing process from my terrific editor, Ami McConnell.

Our fiction publisher, Daisy Hutton, is a gale-force wind of fresh air. She thinks outside the box, and I love the way she empowers me and my team. Marketing director Katie Bond is always willing to listen to my harebrained ideas and has been completely supportive for years. Fabulous cover guru Kristen Ingebretson works hard to create the perfect cover — and does. You rock, Kristen! And, of course, I can't forget the other friends in my amazing fiction family: Amanda Bostic, Becky Monds, Jodi Hughes, Kerri Potts, Karli Jackson, Heather McCulloch, Becky Philpott, and Elizabeth Hudson. You are all such a big part of my life. I wish I could name all the great folks at Thomas Nelson who work on selling my books through different venues. I'm truly blessed!

Julee Schwarzburg is a dream editor to work with. She totally gets romantic suspense, and our partnership is pure joy. She brought some terrific ideas to the table with this book — as always!

My agent, Karen Solem, has helped shape my career in many ways, and that includes kicking an idea to the curb when necessary. And my critique partner, Denise Hunter, is the best sounding board ever. Thanks, friends!

I'm so grateful for my husband, Dave, who carts me around from city to city, washes towels, and chases down dinner without complaint. My kids — Dave, Kara (and now Donna and Mark) — and my grandsons,

James and Jorden Packer, love and support me in every way possible, and my little Alexa makes every day a joy. She's talking like a grown-up now, and having her spend the night is more fun than I can tell you.

Most important, I give my thanks to God, who has opened such amazing doors for me and makes the journey a golden one.

ABOUT THE AUTHOR

RITA finalist **Colleen Coble** is the author of several best-selling romantic suspense novels, including *Tidewater Inn,* and the Mercy Falls, Lonestar, and Rock Harbor series.